The KINGS TREASURIES
OF LITERATURE

GENERAL EDITOR
SIR A·T· QUILLER COUCH

NEW YORK E·P·DUTTON AND COMPANY

DANIEL DEFOE

NEW YORK E·P·DUTTON AND COMPAN

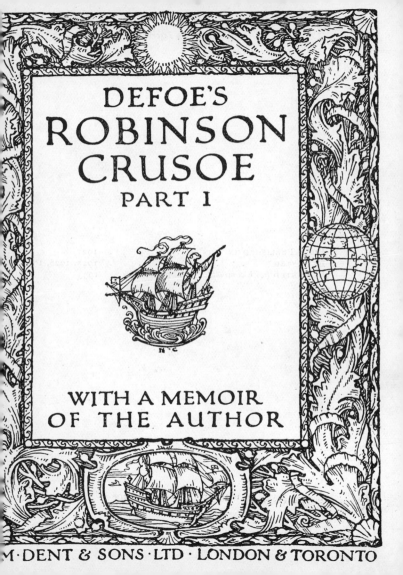

DEFOE'S
ROBINSON
CRUSOE
PART I

WITH A MEMOIR
OF THE AUTHOR

M·DENT & SONS·LTD·LONDON & TORONTO

First Published in this Edition . . 1921
Reprinted 1925, 1928, 1930
Reprinted (*with commentary and questions*) . 1933

PRINTED IN GREAT BRITAIN

CONTENTS

N.B.—The original book is not divided into chapters.

I AM monarch of all I survey,
  My right there is none to dispute,
From the centre all round to the sea,
  I am lord of the fowl and the brute.
O Solitude! where are the charms
  That sages have seen in your face?
Better dwell in the midst of alarms,
  Than reign in this horrible place.

*   *   *   *   *

But the sea-fowl is gone to her nest,
  The beast is laid down in his lair,
Even here is a season of rest,
  And I to my cabin repair.
There's mercy in every place,
  And mercy, encouraging thought!
Gives every affliction a grace,
  And reconciles man to his lot.

WILLIAM COWPER.

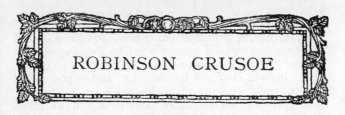

ROBINSON CRUSOE

CHAPTER I

EARLY LIFE

I was born in the year 1632, in the city of York, of a good family, though not of that country, my father being a foreigner of Bremen, who settled first at Hull. He got a good estate by merchandise, and leaving off his trade, lived afterward at York, from whence he had married my mother, whose relations were named Robinson, a very good family in that country, and from whom I was called Robinson Kreutznaer; but by the usual corruption of words in England we are now called, nay, we call ourselves, and write our name, Crusoe, and so my companions always called me.

Being the third son of the family, and not bred to any trade, my head began to be filled very early with rambling thoughts. My father, who was very ancient, had given me a competent share of learning, as far as house-education and a country free school generally goes, and designed me for the law; but I would be satisfied with nothing but going to sea; and my inclination to this led me so strongly against the will, nay, the commands, of my father, and against all the entreaties and persuasions of my mother and other friends, that there seemed to be something fatal in that propension of nature tending directly to the life of misery which was to befall me

7

My father, a wise and grave man, gave me serious and excellent council against what he foresaw was my design. He called me one morning into his chamber, where he was confined by the gout, and expostulated very warmly with me upon this subject.

He pressed me earnestly, and in the most affectionate manner, not to play the young man, not to precipitate myself into miseries which Nature and the station of life I was born in seemed to have provided against; that I was under no necessity of seeking my bread; that he would do well for me, and endeavour to enter me fairly into the middle station of life which he had been just recommending to me; and that if I was not very easy and happy in the world it must be my mere fate or fault that must hinder it, and that he should have nothing to answer for, having thus discharged his duty in warning me against measures which he knew would be to my hurt; in a word, that as he would do very kind things for me if I would stay and settle at home as he directed, so he would not have so much hand in my misfortunes, as to give me any encouragement to go away. And to close all, he told me I had my elder brother for an example, to whom he had used the same earnest persuasions to keep from going into the Low Country wars, but could not prevail, his young desires prompting him to run into the army, where he was killed; and though he said he would not cease to pray for me, yet he would venture to say to me, that if I did take this foolish step, God would not bless me, and I would have leisure hereafter to reflect upon having neglected his counsel when there might be none to assist in my recovery.

I was sincerely affected with this discourse, as

indeed who could be otherwise? and I resolved not
to think of going abroad any more, but to settle at
home according to my father's desire. But alas! a
few days wore it all off; and, in short, to prevent
any of my father's farther importunities, in a few
weeks after I resolved to run quite away from him.
However, I did not act so hastily neither as my first
heat of resolution prompted, but I took my mother,
at a time when I thought her a little pleasanter than
ordinary, and told her that my thoughts were so entirely bent upon seeing the world, that I should never
settle to anything with resolution enough to go through
with it, and my father had better give me his consent
than force me to go without it; that I was now
eighteen years old, which was too late to go apprentice
to a trade, or clerk to an attorney; that I was sure if
I did, I should never serve out my time, and I should
certainly run away from my master before my time
was out, and go to sea; and if she would speak to
my father to let me go but one voyage abroad, if I
came home again and did not like it, I would go no
more, and I would promise by a double diligence to
recover that time I had lost.

This put my mother into a great passion. She told
me, she knew it would be to no purpose to speak to
my father upon any such subject; that he knew too
well what was my interest to give his consent to anything so much for my hurt, and that she wondered
how I could think of any such thing after such a discourse as I had had with my father, and such kind
and tender expressions as she knew my father had
used to me; and that, in short, if I would ruin myself
there was no help for me; that I might depend I
should never have their consent to it; that for her

part, she would not have so much hand in my destruction, and I should never have it to say, that my mother was willing when my father was not.

Though my mother refused to move it to my father, yet, as I have heard afterwards, she reported all the discourse to him, and that my father, after showing a great concern at it, said to her with a sigh, " That boy might be happy if he would stay at home, but if he goes abroad he will be the miserablest wretch that was ever born: I can give no consent to it."

It was not till almost a year after this that I broke loose, though in the meantime I continued obstinately deaf to all proposals of settling to business, and frequently expostulating with my father and mother about their being so positively determined against what they knew my inclinations prompted me to. But being one day at Hull, where I went casually, and without any purpose of making an elopement that time; but I say, being there, and one of my companions being going by sea to London, in his father's ship, and prompting me to go with them, with the common allurement of seafaring men, viz., that it should cost me nothing for my passage, I consulted neither father or mother any more, nor so much as sent them word of it; but leaving them to hear of it as they might, without asking God's blessing, or my father's, without any consideration of circumstances or consequences, and in an ill hour, God knows, on the first of September, 1651, I went on board a ship bound for London. Never any young adventurer's misfortunes, I believe, began sooner, or continued longer than mine.

CHAPTER II

THE SHIPWRECK

After many varied adventures at sea, including two voyages to Guinea, Robinson settled down for four years as a planter in the Brazils, using San Salvador as his port. He prospered exceedingly, and made many friends among the planters and merchants, and often spoke to them about his trading on the coast of Guinea.

IT happened, being in company with some merchants and planters of my acquaintance, and talking of those things very earnestly, three of them came to me the next morning, and told me that they came to make a secret proposal to me. And after enjoining me secrecy, they told me that they had a mind to fit out a ship to go to Guinea; that they had all plantations as well as I, and were straitened for nothing so much as servants; that as it was a trade that could not be carried on because they could not publicly sell the negroes when they came home, so they desired to make but one voyage, to bring the negroes on shore privately, and divide them among their own plantations; and, in a word, the question was, whether I would go their supercargo in the ship, to manage the trading part upon the coast of Guinea; and they offered me that I should have my equal share of the negroes without providing any part of the stock.

This was a fair proposal, it must be confessed, had it been made to any one that had not had a settlement and plantation of his own to look after, which was in a fair way of coming to be very considerable, and with a good stock upon it. But for me, that was thus entered and established, and had nothing to do but go on as I had begun, for three or four years more, and to have sent for the other hundred pounds from England; and who, in that time, and with that little addition, could scarce have failed of being worth three or four thousand pounds sterling, and that increasing too—for me to think of such a voyage, was the most preposterous thing that ever man, in such circumstances, could be guilty of.

But I, that was born to be my own destroyer, could no more resist the offer than I could restrain my first rambling designs, when my father's good counsel was lost upon me. In a word, I told them I would go with all my heart, if they would undertake to look after my plantation in my absence, and would dispose of it to such as I should direct if I miscarried. This they all engaged to do, and entered into writings or covenants to do so; and I made a formal will, disposing of my plantation and effects, in case of my death; making the captain of the ship that had saved my life, as before, my universal heir, but obliging him to dispose of my effects as I had directed in my will; one half of the produce being to himself, and the other to be shipped to England.

In short, I took all possible caution to preserve my effects, and keep up my plantation. Had I used half as much prudence to have looked into my own interest, and have made a judgment of what I ought to have done and not to have done, I had certainly never gone away from so prosperous an undertaking, leaving all the probable views of a thriving circumstance, and gone upon a voyage to sea, attended with all its common hazards, to say nothing of the reasons I had to expect particular misfortunes to myself.

But I was hurried on, and obeyed blindly the dictates of my fancy rather than my reason. And accordingly, the ship being fitted out, and the cargo furnished, and all things done as by agreement by my partners in the voyage, I went on board in an evil hour, the [first] of [September 1659], being the same day eight year that I went from my father and mother at Hull, in order to act the rebel to their authority, and the fool to my own interest.

Our ship was about 120 tons burthen, carried six guns and fourteen men, besides the master, his boy, and myself. We had on board no large cargo of goods, except of such toys as were fit for our trade with the negroes—such as beads, bits of glass, shells, and odd trifles, especially little looking-glasses, knives, scissors, hatchets, and the like.

The same day I went on board we set sail, standing away to the northward upon our own coast, with design to stretch over for the African coast, when they came about ten or twelve degrees of northern latitude, which, it seems, was the manner of their course in those days. We passed the line in about twelve days' time, and were, by our last observation, in seven degrees twenty-two minutes northern latitude, when a violent tornado, or hurricane, took us quite out of our knowledge. It began from the south-east, came about to the north-west, and then settled into the north-east, from whence it blew in such a terrible manner, that for twelve days together we could do nothing but drive, and, scudding away before it, let it carry us wherever fate and the fury of the winds directed; and during these twelve days, I need not say that I expected every day to be swallowed up, nor, indeed, did any in the ship expect to save their lives.

In this distress we had, besides the terror of the storm, one of our men died of the calenture, and one man and the boy washed overboard. About the twelfth day, the weather abating a little, the master made an observation as well as he could, and found that he was gotten upon the coast of Guiana, or the north part of Brazil, beyond the river Amazon, toward that of the river Orinoco, commonly called the Great River, and began to consult with me what course we should take, for the ship was leaky and very much disabled, and he was going directly back to the coast of Brazil.

I was positively against that; and looking over the charts of the sea-coast of America with him, we concluded there was no inhabited country for us to have recourse to till we came within the circle of the Caribbee Islands, and therefore resolved to stand away for the Barbadoes, which by keeping off at sea, to avoid the indraft of the Bay or Gulf of Mexico, we might easily perform, as we hoped, in about fifteen days' sail; whereas we could not possibly make our voyage to the coast of Africa without some assistance, both to our ship and to ourselves.

With this design we changed our course, and steered away N.W. by W. in order to reach some of our English islands, where I hoped for relief; but our voyage was otherwise determined; for a second storm came upon us, which carried us away with the same impetuosity westward, and drove us so out of the very way of all human commerce, that had all our lives been saved, as to the sea, we were rather in danger of being devoured by savages than ever returning to our own country.

In this distress, the wind still blowing very hard, one of our men early in the morning cried out, " Land! "

and we had no sooner ran out of the cabin to look
out, in hopes of seeing whereabouts in the world we
were, but the ship struck upon a sand, and in a
moment, her motion being so stopped, the sea broke
over her in such a manner, that we expected we
should all have perished immediately; and we were
immediately driven into our close quarters, to shelter
us from the very foam and spray of the sea.

It is not easy for any one, who has not been in the
like condition, to describe or conceive the consternation of men in such circumstances. We knew nothing
where we were, or upon what land it was we were
driven, whether an island or the main, whether inhabited or not inhabited; and as the rage of the wind
was still great, though rather less than at first, we
could not so much as hope to have the ship hold
many minutes without breaking in pieces, unless the
winds, by a kind of miracle, should turn immediately
about. In a word, we sat looking one upon another,
and expecting death every moment, and every man
acting accordingly, as preparing for another world;
for there was little or nothing more for us to do in this.
That which was our present comfort, and all the
comfort we had, was that, contrary to our expectation, the ship did not break yet, and that the master
said the wind began to abate.

Now, though we thought that the wind did a little
abate, yet the ship having thus struck upon the sand,
and sticking too fast for us to expect her getting off,
we were in a dreadful condition indeed, and had
nothing to do but to think of saving our lives as well
as we could. We had a boat at our stern just before
the storm, but she was first staved by dashing against
the ship's rudder, and in the next place, she broke

away, and either sunk, or was driven off to sea, so
there was no hope from her; we had another boat
on board, but how to get her off into the sea was a
doubtful thing. However, there was no room to debate,
for we fancied the ship would break in pieces every
minute, and some told us she was actually broken
already.

In this distress, the mate of our vessel lays hold
of the boat, and with the help of the rest of the men
they got her slung over the ship's side; and getting
all into her, let go, and committed ourselves, being
eleven in number, to God's mercy, and the wild sea;
for though the storm was abated considerably, yet the
sea went dreadful high upon the shore.

And now our case was very dismal indeed, for we
all saw plainly that the sea went so high, that the
boat could not live, and that we should be inevitably
drowned. However, we committed our souls to God
in the most earnest manner; and the wind driving us
towards the shore, we hastened our destruction with
our own hands, pulling as well as we could towards
land.

What the shore was, whether rock or sand, whether
steep or shoal, we knew not; the only hope that could
rationally give us the least shadow of expectation was,
if we might happen into some bay or gulf, or the
mouth of some river, where by great chance we might
have run our boat in, or got under the lee of the land,
and perhaps made smooth water. But there was
nothing of this appeared; but as we made nearer and
nearer the shore, the land looked more frightful than
the sea.

After we had rowed, or rather driven, about a
league and a half, as we reckoned it, a raging wave,

mountain-like, came rolling astern of us, and plainly bade us expect the *coup de grâce*. In a word, it took us with such a fury, that it overset the boat at once; and separating us, as well from the boat as from one another, gave us not time hardly to say, " O God! " for we were all swallowed up in a moment.

Nothing can describe the confusion of thought which I felt when I sunk into the water; for though I swam very well, yet I could not deliver myself from the waves so as to draw breath, till that wave having driven me, or rather carried me, a vast way on towards the shore, and having spent itself, went back, and left me upon the land almost dry, but half dead with the water I took in. I had so much presence of mind, as well as breath left, that seeing myself nearer the mainland than I expected, I got upon my feet, and endeavoured to make on towards the land as fast as I could, before another wave should return and take me up again. But I soon found it was impossible to avoid it; for I saw the sea come after me as high as a great hill, and as furious as an enemy, which I had no means or strength to contend with. My business was to hold my breath, and raise myself upon the water, if I could; and so by swimming, to preserve my breathing, and pilot myself towards the shore, if possible; my greatest concern now being that the sea, as it would carry me a great way towards the shore when it came on, might not carry me back again with it when it gave back towards the sea.

The wave that came upon me again, buried me at once twenty or thirty feet deep in its own body, and I could feel myself carried with a mighty force and swiftness towards the shore a very great way; but I held my breath, and assisted myself to swim still forward with all my might. I was ready to burst with holding my breath, when, as I felt myself rising up, so, to my immediate relief, I found my head and hands shoot out above the surface of the water; and though it was not two seconds of time that I could keep myself so, yet it relieved me greatly, gave me breath and new courage. I was covered again with water a good while, but not so long but I held it out; and finding the water had spent itself, and began to return, I struck forward against the return of the waves, and felt ground again with my feet. I stood still a few moments to recover breath, and till the water went from me, and then took to my heels and ran with what strength I had farther towards the shore. But neither would this deliver me from the fury of the sea, which came pouring in after me again, and twice more I was lifted up by the waves and carried forwards as before, the shore being very flat.

The last time of these two had well near been fatal to me; for the sea, having hurried me along as before, landed me, or rather dashed me, against a piece of a rock, and that with such force, as it left me senseless, and indeed helpless, as to my own deliverance; for the blow taking my side and breast, beat the breath as it were quite of my body; and had it returned again immediately, I must have been strangled in the water. But I recovered a little before the return of the waves, and seeing I should be covered again with the water, I resolved to hold fast by a piece of the rock, and so to hold my breath, if possible, till the wave went back. Now as the waves were not so high as at first, being near land, I held my hold till the wave abated, and then fetched another run, which brought me so near the shore, that the next wave, though it

went over me, yet did not so swallow me up as to carry
me away, and the next run I took I got to the mainland, where, to my great comfort, I clambered up the
cliffs of the shore, and sat me down upon the grass,
free from danger, and quite out of the reach of the
water.

I was now landed, and safe on shore, and began to
look up and thank God that my life was saved in a
case wherein there was some minutes before scarce
any room to hope.

I walked about on the shore, lifting up my hands,
and my whole being, as I may say, wrapt up in the
contemplation of my deliverance making a thousand
gestures and motions which I cannot describe, reflecting
upon all my comrades that were drowned, and that
there should not be one soul saved but myself; for,
as for them, I never saw them afterwards, or any sign
of them, except three of their hats, one cap, and two
shoes that were not fellows.

I cast my eyes to the stranded vessel, when the
breach and froth of the sea being so big, I could
hardly see it, it lay so far off, and considered, Lord!
how was it possible I could get on shore?

After I had solaced my mind with the comfortable
part of my condition, I began to look round me to see
what kind of place I was in, and what was next to be
done, and I soon found my comforts abate, and that,
in a word, I had a dreadful deliverance; for I was wet,
had no clothes to shift me, nor anything either to eat
or drink to comfort me, neither did I see any prospect
before me but that of perishing with hunger, or being
devoured by wild beasts; and that which was particularly afflicting to me was, that I had no weapon
either to hunt and kill any creature for my sustenance,

or to defend myself against any other creature that might desire to kill me for theirs. In a word, I had nothing about me but a knife, a tobacco-pipe, and a little tobacco in a box. This was all my provision; and this threw me into terrible agonies of mind, that for a while I ran about like a madman. Night coming upon me, I began, with a heavy heart, to consider what would be my lot if there were any ravenous beasts in that country, seeing at night they always come abroad for their prey.

All the remedy that offered to my thoughts at that time was, to get up into a thick bushy tree like a fir, but thorny, which grew near me, and where I resolved to sit all night, and consider the next day what death I should die, for as yet I saw no prospect of life. I walked about a furlong from the shore, to see if I could find any fresh water to drink, which I did, to my great joy; and having drank, and put a little tobacco in my mouth to prevent hunger, I went to the tree, and getting up into it, endeavoured to place myself so, as that if I should sleep I might not fall; and having cut me a short stick, like a truncheon, for my defence, I took up my lodging, and having been excessively fatigued, I fell fast asleep, and slept as comfortably as, I believe, few could have done in my condition, and found myself the most refreshed with it that I think I ever was on such an occasion.

When I waked it was broad day, the weather clear, and the storm abated, so that the sea did not rage and swell as before. But that which surprised me most was, that the ship was lifted off in the night from the sand where she lay, by the swelling of the tide, and was driven up almost as far as the rock which I first mentioned, where I had been so bruised by the dashing me against it. This being within about a mile from the shore where I was, and the ship seeming to stand upright still, I wished myself on board, that, at least, I might have some necessary things for my use.

When I came down from my apartment in the tree I looked about me again, and the first thing I found was the boat which lay as the wind and the sea had tossed her up upon the land, about two miles on my right hand. I walked as far as I could upon the shore to have got to her, but found a neck or inlet of water between me and the boat, which was about half a mile broad; so I came back for the present, being more intent upon getting at the ship, where I hoped to find something for my present subsistence.

A little after noon I found the sea very calm, and the tide ebbed so far out, that I could come within a quarter of a mile of the ship; and here I found a fresh renewing of my grief, for I saw evidently, that if we had kept on board we had been all safe, that is to say, we had all got safe on shore, and I had not been so miserable as to be left entirely destitute of all comfort and company, as I now was. This forced tears from my eyes again; but as there was little relief in that, I resolved, if possible, to get to the ship; so I pulled off my clothes, for the weather was hot to extremity, and took the water. But when I came to the ship, my difficulty was still greater to know how to get on board; for as she lay aground, and high out of the water, there was nothing within my reach to lay hold of. I swam round her twice, and the second time I spied a small piece of a rope, which I wondered I did not see at first, hang down by the fore-chains so low, as that with great difficulty I got hold of it, and by the help of that rope got up into the fore-

castle of the ship. Here I found that the ship was
bulged, and had a great deal of water in her hold,
but that she lay so on the side of a bank of hard sand,
or rather earth, that her stern lay lifted up upon the
bank, and her head low almost to the water. By this
means all her quarter was free, and all that was in
that part was dry; for you may be sure my first work
was to search and to see what was spoiled and what
was free. And first I found that all the ship's provisions
were dry and untouched by the water; and being very
well disposed to eat, I went to the bread-room and
filled my pockets with biscuit, and eat it as I went
about other things, for I had no time to lose. I also
found some rum in the great cabin, of which I took
a large dram, and which I had indeed need enough of
to spirit me for what was before me. Now I wanted
nothing but a boat, to furnish myself with many
things which I foresaw would be very necessary to me.

It was in vain to sit still and wish for what was not
to be had, and this extremity roused my application.
We had several spare yards, and two or three large
spars of wood, and a spare top-mast or two in the
ship. I resolved to fall to work with these, and flung
as many of them overboard as I could manage for
their weight, tying every one with a rope, that they
might not drive away. When this was done I went
down the ship's side, and, pulling them to me, I tied
four of them fast together at both ends as well as I
could, in the form of a raft; and laying two or three
short pieces of plank upon them crossways, I found
I could walk upon it very well, but that it was not
able to bear any great weight, the pieces being too
light. So I went to work, and with the carpenter's
saw I cut a spare top-mast into three lengths, and

added them to my raft, with a great deal of labour
and pains; but hope of furnishing myself with necessaries encouraged me to go beyond what I should have
been able to have done upon another occasion.

My raft was now strong enough to bear any reasonable weight. My next care was what to load it with,
and how to preserve what I laid upon it from the surf
of the sea; but I was not long considering this. I
first laid all the planks or boards upon it that I could
get, and having considered well what I most wanted,
I first got three of the seamen's chests, which I had
broken open, and emptied, and lowered them down
upon my raft. The first of these I filled with provisions,
viz., bread, rice, three Dutch cheeses, five pieces of
dried goat's flesh, which we lived much upon, and a
little remainder of European corn, which had been
laid by for some fowls which we brought to sea with
us, but the fowls were killed. There had been some
barley and wheat together, but, to my great disappointment, I found afterwards that the rats had
eaten or spoiled it all. As for liquors, I found several
cases of bottles belonging to our skipper, in which
were some cordial waters, and, in all, about five or
six gallons of rack. These I stowed by themselves,
there being no need to put them into the chest, nor
no room for them. While I was doing this, I found
the tide began to flow, though very calm, and I had
the mortification to see my coat, shirt, and waistcoat,
which I had left on shore upon the sand, swim away;
as for my breeches, which were only linen, and open-
kneed, I swam on board in them, and my stockings.
However, this put me upon rummaging for clothes,
of which I found enough, but took no more than
I wanted for present use; for I had other things

which my eye was more upon, as first tools to work
with on shore; and it was after long searching that
I found out the carpenter's chest, which was indeed
a very useful prize to me, and much more valuable
than a shiploading of gold would have been at that
time. I got it down to my raft, even whole as it was,
without losing time to look into it, for I knew in
general what it contained.

My next care was for some ammunition and arms;
there were two very good fowling-pieces in the great
cabin, and two pistols; these I secured first, with some
powder-horns, and a small bag of shot, and two old
rusty swords. I knew there were three barrels of
powder in the ship, but knew not where our gunner
had stowed them; but with much search I found
them, two of them dry and good, the third had taken
water; those two I got to my raft with the arms.
And now I thought myself pretty well freighted, and
began to think how I should get to shore with them,
having neither sail, oar or rudder; and the least
capful of wind would have overset all my navigation.

I had three encouragements. 1. A smooth calm sea.
2. The tide rising and setting in to the shore. 3. What
little wind there was blew me towards the land. And
thus, having found two or three broken oars belonging
to the boat, and besides the tools which were in the
chest, I found two saws, an axe, and a hammer, and
with this cargo I put to sea. For a mile or thereabouts
my raft went very well, only that I found it drive a
little distance from the place where I had landed
before, by which I perceived that there was some
indraft of the water, and consequently I hoped to
find some creek or river there, which I might make
use of as a port to get to land with my cargo.

As I imagined, so it was; there appeared before
me a little opening of the land, and I found a strong
current of the tide set into it, so I guided my raft as
well as I could to keep in the middle of the stream.
But here I had like to have suffered a second shipwreck, which, if I had, I think verily would have
broke my heart; for knowing nothing of the coast,
my raft ran aground at one end of it upon a shoal,
and not being aground at the other end, it wanted
but a little that all my cargo had slipped off towards
that end that was afloat, and so fallen into the water.
I did my utmost by setting my back against the
chests to keep them in their places, but could not
thrust off the raft with all my strength, neither durst
I stir from the posture I was in, but holding up the
chests with all my might, stood in that manner near
half-an-hour, in which time the rising of the water
brought me a little more upon a level; and a little
after, the water still rising, my raft floated again, and
I thrust her off with the oar I had into the channel,
and then driving up higher, I at length found myself
in the mouth of a little river, with land on both sides,
and a strong current or tide running up. I looked on
both sides for a proper place to get to shore, for I was
not willing to be driven too high up the river, hoping
in time to see some ship at sea, and therefore resolved
to place myself as near the coast as I could.

At length I spied a little cove on the right shore of
the creek, to which, with great pain and difficulty,
I guided my raft, and at last got so near, as that,
reaching ground with my oar, I could thrust her
directly in; but here I had like to have dipped all
my cargo in the sea again; for that shore lying pretty
steep, that is to say, sloping, there was no place to

land but where one end of my float, if it run on shore, would lie so high and the other sink lower, as before, that it would endanger my cargo again. All that I could do was to wait till the tide was at the highest, keeping the raft with my oar like an anchor to hold the side of it fast to the shore, near a flat piece of ground, which I expected the water would flow over; and so it did. As soon as I found water enough, for my raft drew about a foot of water, I thrust her on upon that flat piece of ground, and there fastened or moored her by sticking my two broken oars into the ground; one on one side near one end, and one on the other side near the other end; and thus I lay till the water ebbed away, and left my raft and all my cargo safe on shore.

CHAPTER III

CRUSOE'S ISLAND

My next work was to view the country and seek a proper place for my habitation, and where to stow my goods to secure them from whatever might happen. Where I was, I yet knew not; whether on the continent, or on an island; whether inhabited or not inhabited; whether in danger of wild beasts, or not. There was a hill, not above a mile from me, which rose up very steep and high, and which seemed to overtop some other hills, which lay as in a ridge from it, northward. I took out one of the fowling-pieces and one of the pistols, and a horn of powder; and thus armed, I travelled for discovery up to the top of that hill, where, after I had with great labour and difficulty got to the top, I saw my fate to my great

affliction, viz., that I was in an island environed every
way with the sea, no land to be seen, except some
rocks which lay a great way off, and two small islands
less than this, which lay about three leagues to the
west.

I found also that the island I was in was barren,
and, as I saw good reason to believe, uninhabited,
except by wild beasts, of whom, however, I saw none;
yet I saw an abundance of fowls, but knew not their
kinds; neither, when I killed them, could I tell what
was fit for food, and what not. At my coming back,
I shot at a great bird which I saw sitting upon a teee
on the side of a great wood. I believe it was the first
gun that had been fired there since the creation of
the world. I had no sooner fired, but from all the
parts of the wood there arose an innumerable number
of fowls of many sorts, making a confused screaming,
and crying everyone according to his usual note; but
not one of them of any kind that I knew. As for the
creature I killed, I took it to be a kind of a hawk, its
colour and beak resembling it, but had no talons or
claws more than common; its flesh was carrion, and
fit for nothing.

Contented with this discovery, I came back to my
raft, and fell to work to bring my cargo on shore,
which took me up the rest of that day; and what
to do with myself at night I knew not, nor indeed
where to rest; for I was afraid to lie down on the
ground, not knowing but some wild beast might devour
me, though, as I afterwards found, there was really
no need for those fears. However, as well as I could
I barricaded myself round with the chests and boards
that I had brought on shore, and made a kind of a
hut for that night's lodging; as for food, I yet saw

not which way to supply myself, except that I had
seen two or three creatures like hares run out of the
wood where I shot the fowl.

I now began to consider, that I might yet get a
great many things out of the ship, which would be
useful to me, and particularly some of the rigging and
sails, and such other things as might come to land;
and I resolved to make another voyage on board the
vessel, if possible. And as I knew that the first storm
that blew must necessarily break her all in pieces,
I resolved to set all other things apart till I got everything out of the ship that I could get. Then I called
a council, that is to say, in my thoughts, whether I
should take back the raft, but this appeared impracticable; so I resolved to go as before, when the tide
was down; and I did so, only that I stripped before
I went from my hut, having nothing on but a chequered
shirt and a pair of linen drawers, and a pair of pumps
on my feet.

I got on board the ship as before, and prepared a
second raft, and having had experience of the first,
I neither made this so unwieldy, nor loaded it so
hard; but yet I brought away several things very
useful to me; as, first, in the carpenter's stores I
found two or three bags of nails and spikes, a great
screw-jack, a dozen or two of hatchets, and above all,
that most useful thing called a grindstone. All these
I secured, together with several things belonging to
the gunner, particularly two or three iron crows, and
two barrels of musket bullets, seven muskets, and
another fowling-piece, with some small quantity of
powder more; a large bag full of small-shot, and a
great roll of sheet lead; but this last was so heavy,
I could not hoist it up to get it over the ship's side.

Besides these things, I took all the men's clothes that I could find, and a spare fore-top sail, a hammock, and some bedding; and with this I loaded my second raft, and brought them all safe on shore, to my very great comfort.

I was under some apprehension during my absence from the land, that at least my provisions might be devoured on shore; but when I came back, I found no sign of any visitor, only there sat a creature like a wild cat upon one of the chests, which, when I came towards it, ran away a little distance, and then stood still. She sat very composed and unconcerned, and looked full in my face, as if she had a mind to be acquainted with me. I presented my gun at her; but as she did not understand it, she was perfectly unconcerned at it, nor did she offer to stir away; upon which I tossed her a bit of biscuit, though, by the way, I was not very free of it, for my store was not great. However, I spared her a bit, I say, and she went to it, smelled of it, and ate it, and looked (as pleased) for more; but I thanked her, and could spare no more, so she marched off.

Having got my second cargo on shore, though I was fain to open the barrels of powder and bring them by parcels, for they were too heavy, being large casks, I went to work to make me a little tent with the sail and some poles which I cut for that purpose: and into this tent I brought everything that I knew would spoil either with rain or sun; and I piled all the empty chests and casks up in a circle round the tent, to fortify it from any sudden attempt, either from man or beast.

When I had done this I blocked up the door of the tent with some boards within, and an empty

chest set up on end without; and spreading one of
the beds upon the ground, laying my two pistols just
at my head, and my gun at length by me. I went to
bed for the first time, and slept very quietly all night,
for I was very weary and heavy; for the night before
I had slept little, and had laboured very hard all day,
as well to fetch all those things from the ship, as to
get them on shore.

I had the biggest magazine of all kinds now that
ever was laid up, I believe, for one man; but I was
not satisfied still, for while the ship sat upright in
that posture, I thought I ought to get everything out
of her that I could. So every day at low water I went
on board, and brought away something or other; but,
particularly, the third time I went I brought away
as much of the rigging as I could, as also all the small
ropes and rope-twine I could get, with a piece of spare
canvas, which was to mend the sails upon occasion,
the barrel of wet gunpowder; in a word, I brought
away all the sails first and last, only that I was fain
to cut them in pieces, and bring as much at a time
as I could; for they were no more useful to be sails,
but as mere canvas only.

But that which comforted me more still was, that
at last of all, after I had made five or six such voyages
as these, and thought I had nothing more to expect
from the ship that was worth my meddling with; I
say, after all this, I found a great hogshead of bread,
and three large runlets of rum or spirits, and a box
of sugar, and a barrel of fine flour; this was surprising
to me, because I had given over expecting any more
provisions, except what was spoilt by the water. I
soon emptied the hogshead of that bread, and wrapped
it up parcel by parcel in pieces of the sails, which I

cut out; and, in a word, I got all this safe on shore also.

The next day I made another voyage. And now, having plundered the ship of what was portable and fit to hand out, I began with the cables; and cutting the great cable into pieces, such as I could move, I got two cables and a hawser on shore, with all the iron-work I could get; and having cut down the sprit-sailyard, and the mizzen-yard, and everything I could to make a large raft, I loaded it with all those heavy goods, and came away. But my good luck began now to leave me; for this raft was so unwieldy, and so overladen, that after I was entered the little cove where I had landed the rest of my goods, not being able to guide it so handily as I did the other, it over-set, and threw me and all my cargo into the water. As for myself, it was no great harm, for I was near the shore; but as to my cargo, it was great part of it lost, especially the iron, which I expected would have been of great use to me. However, when the tide was out I got most of the pieces of cable ashore, and some of the iron, though with infinite labour; for I was fain to dip for it into the water, a work which fatigued me very much. After this I went every day on board, and brought away what I could get.

I had been now thirteen days on shore, and had been eleven times on board the ship; in which time I had brought away all that one pair of hands could well be supposed capable to bring, though I believe verily, had the calm weather held, I should have brought away the whole ship piece by piece. But preparing the twelfth time to go on board, I found the wind begin to rise. However, at low water I went on board, and though I thought I had rummaged the cabin so effectually as that nothing more could be found, I yet discovered a locker with drawers in it, in one of which I found two or three razors, and one pair of large scissors, with some ten or a dozen of good knives and forks; in another, I found about thirty-six pounds value in money, some European coin, some Brazil, some pieces of eight, some gold, some silver.

I smiled to myself at the sight of this money. "O drug!" said I aloud, "what art thou good for? Thou art not worth to me, no, not the taking off of the ground; one of those knives is worth all this heap I have no manner of use for thee; even remain where thou art, and go to the bottom as a creature whose life is not worth saving." However, upon second thoughts, I took it away; and wrapping all this in a piece of canvas, I began to think of making another raft; but while I was preparing this, I found the sky overcast, and the wind began to rise, and in a quarter of an hour it blew a fresh gale from the shore. It presently occurred to me that it was in vain to pretend to make a raft with the wind off shore, and that it was my business to be gone before the tide of flood began, otherwise I might not be able to reach the shore at all. Accordingly I let myself down into the water, and swam across the channel, which lay between the ship and the sands, and even that with difficulty enough, partly with the weight of the things I had about me, and partly the roughness of the water; for the wind rose very hastily, and before it was quite high water it blew a storm.

But I was gotten home to my little tent, where I lay with all my wealth about me very secure. It blew very hard all that night, and in the morning, when

I looked out, behold, no more ship was to be seen.
I was a little surprised, but recovered myself with
this satisfactory reflection, viz., that I had lost no
time, nor abated no diligence, to get everything out
of her that could be useful to me, and that indeed
there was little left in her that I was able to bring
away if I had had more time.

I now gave over any more thoughts of the ship, or
of anything out of her, except what might drive on
shore from her wreck, as indeed divers pieces of her
afterwards did; but those things were of small use to me.

My thoughts were now wholly employed about
securing myself against either savages, if any should
appear, or wild beasts, if any were in the island; and
I had many thoughts of the method how to do this,
and what kind of dwelling to make, whether I should
make me a cave in the earth, or a tent upon the earth;
and, in short, I resolved upon both, the manner and
description of which it may not be improper to give
an account of.

I soon found the place I was in was not for my
settlement, particularly because it was upon a low
moorish ground near the sea, and I believed would
not be wholesome; and more particularly because
there was no fresh water near it. So I resolved to find
a more healthy and more convenient spot of ground.

I consulted several things in my situation, which I
found would be proper for me. First, health and fresh
water, I just now mentioned. Secondly, shelter from
the heat of the sun. Thirdly, security from the ravenous
creatures, whether men or beasts. Fourthly, a view to
the sea, that if God sent any ship in sight I might
not lose any advantage for my deliverance, of which
I was not willing to banish all my expectation yet.

B

In search of a place proper for this, I found a little plain on the side of a rising hill, whose front towards this little plain was steep as a house-side, so that nothing could come down upon me from the top; on the side of this rock there was a hollow place, worn a little way in, like the entrance or door of a cave; but there was not really any cave, or way into the rock at all.

On the flat of the green, just before this hollow place, I resolved to pitch my tent. This plain was not above an hundred yards broad, and about twice as long, and lay like a green before my door, and at the end of it descended irregularly every way down into the low grounds by the seaside. It was on the N.N.W. side of the hill, so that I was sheltered from the heat every day, till it came to a W. and by S. sun, or thereabouts, which in those countries is near the setting.

Before I set up my tent, I drew a half-circle before the hollow place, which took in about ten yards in its semi-diameter from the rock, and twenty yards in its diameter from its beginning and ending. In this half-circle I pitched two rows of strong stakes, driving them into the ground till they stood very firm like piles, the biggest end being out of the ground about five feet and a half, and sharpened on the top. The two rows did not stand above six inches from one another.

Then I took the pieces of cable which I had cut in the ship, and laid them in rows one upon another, within the circle, between these two rows of stakes, up to the top, placing other stakes in the inside leaning against them, about two feet and a half high, like a spur to a post; and this fence was so strong, that

neither man or beast could get into it, or over it.
This cost me a great deal of time and labour, especially
to cut the piles in the woods, bring them to the place,
and drive them into the earth.

The entrance into this place I made to be not by
a door, but by a short ladder to go over the top;
which ladder, when I was in, I lifted over after me,
and so I was completely fenced in, and fortified, as
I thought, from all the world, and consequently slept
secure in the night, which otherwise I could not have
done; though as it appeared afterward, there was no
need of all this caution from the enemies that I
apprehended danger from.

Into this fence or fortress, with infinite labour, I
carried all my riches, all my provisions, ammunition,
and stores, of which you have the account above; and
I made me a large tent, which, to preserve me from
the rains that in one part of the year are very violent
there, I made double, viz., one smaller tent within,
and one larger tent above it, and covered the upper-
most with a large tarpaulin, which I had saved among
the sails. And now I lay no more for a while in the
bed which I had brought on shore, but in a hammock,
which was indeed a very good one, and belonged to
the mate of the ship.

Into this tent I brought all my provisions, and
everything that would spoil by the wet; and having
thus enclosed all my goods, I made up the entrance,
which, till now, I had left open, and so passed and
repassed, as I said, by a short ladder.

When I had done this, I began to work my way
into the rock; and bringing all the earth and stones
that I dug down out through my tent, I laid them up
within my fence in the nature of a terrace, so that it

raised the ground within about a foot and a half; and thus I made me a cave just behind my tent, which served me like a cellar to my house.

It cost me much labour, and many days, before all these things were brought to perfection, and therefore I must go back to some other things which took up some of my thoughts. At the same time it happened, after I had laid my scheme for the setting up my tent, and making the cave, that a storm of rain falling from a thick dark cloud, a sudden flash of lightning happened, and after that a great clap of thunder, as is naturally the effect of it. I was not so much surprised with the lightning, as I was with a thought which darted into my mind as swift as the lightning itself. Oh my powder! My very heart sunk within me when I thought, that at one blast all my powder might be destroyed, on which, not my defence only, but the providing me food, as I thought, entirely depended. I was nothing near so anxious about my own danger; though had the powder took fire, I had never known who had hurt me.

Such impression did this make upon me, that after the storm was over I laid aside all my works, my building, and fortifying, and applied myself to make bags and boxes to separate the powder, and keep it a little and a little in a parcel, in hope that whatever might come it might not all take fire at once, and to keep it so apart, that it should not be possible to make one part fire another. I finished this work in about a fortnight, and I think my powder, which in all was about 240 pounds' weight, was divided in not less than a hundred parcels. As to the barrel that had been wet, I did not apprehend any danger from that, so I placed it in my new cave, which in my fancy I called my kitchen,

and the rest I hid up and down in holes among the
rocks, so that no wet might come to it, marking very
carefully where I laid it.

In the interval of time while this was doing, I went
out once, at least, every day with my gun, as well
to divert myself, as to see if I could kill anything fit
for food, and as near as I could to acquaint myself
with what the island produced. The first time I went
out, I presently discovered that there were goats in
the island, which was a great satisfaction to me; but
then it was attended with this misfortune to me, viz.,
that they were so shy, so subtle, and so swift of foot,
that it was the difficultest thing in the world to come
at them. But I was not discouraged at this, not doubting but I might now and then shoot one, as it soon
happened; for after I had found their haunts a little,
I laid wait in this manner for them. I observed if
they saw me in the valleys, though they were upon
the rocks, they would run away in a terrible fright;
but if they were feeding in the valleys, and I was
upon the rocks, they took no notice of me, from whence
I concluded that, by the position of their optics, their
sight was so directed downward, that they did not
readily see objects that were above them. So afterward I took this method; I always climbed the rocks
first to get above them, and then had frequently a
fair mark. The first shot I made among these creatures
I killed a she-goat, which had a little kid by her, which
she gave suck to, which grieved me heartily; but
when the old one fell, the kid stood stock still by her
till I came and took her up; and not only so, but
when I carried the old one with me upon my shoulders,
the kid followed me quite to my enclosure; upon
which I laid down the dam, and took the kid in my

arms, and carried it over my pale, in hopes to have bred it up tame; but it would not eat, so I was forced to kill it, and eat it myself. These two supplied me with flesh a great while, for I eat sparingly, and saved my provisions, my bread especially, as much as possibly I could.

CHAPTER IV

CRUSOE CONSIDERS

AND now being to enter into a melancholy relation of a scene of silent life, such, perhaps, as was never heard of in the world before, I shall take it from its beginning, and continue it in its order. It was, by my account, the 30th of September when, in the manner as above said, I first set foot upon this horrid island, when the sun being to us in its autumnal equinox, was almost just over my head, for I reckoned myself, by observation, to be in the latitude of 9 degrees 22 minutes north of the line.

After I had been there about ten or twelve days, it came into my thoughts that I should lose my reckoning of time for want of books and pen and ink, and should even forget the Sabbath days from the working days; but to prevent this, I cut it with my knife upon a large post, in capital letters; and making it into a great cross, I set it up on the shore where I first landed, viz., " I came on shore here on the 30th of September 1659." Upon the sides of this square post I cut every day a notch with my knife, and every seventh notch was as long again as the rest, and every first day of the month as long again as that long one; and thus I kept my calendar, of weekly, monthly, and yearly reckoning of time.

In the next place we are to observe, that among the many things which I brought out of the ship in the several voyages, which, as above mentioned, I made to it, I got several things of less value, but not all less useful to me, which I omitted setting down before; as in particular, pens, ink, and paper, several parcels in the captain's, mate's, gunner's, and carpenter's keeping, three or four compasses, some mathematical instruments, dials, perspectives, charts, and books of navigation, all which I huddled together, whether I might want them or no. Also I found three very good Bibles, which came to me in my cargo from England, and which I had packed up among my things; some Portuguese books also, and among them two or three Popish prayer-books, and several other books, all which I carefully secured. And I must not forget, that we had in the ship a dog and two cats, of whose eminent history I may have occasion to say something in its place; for I carried both the cats with me; and as for the dog, he jumped out of the ship of himself, and swam on shore to me the day after I went on shore with my first cargo, and was a trusty servant to me many years. I wanted nothing that he could fetch me, nor any company that he could make up to me; I only wanted to have him talk to me, but that would not do. As I observed before, I found pen, ink, and paper, and I husbanded them to the utmost; and I shall show that while my ink lasted, I kept things very exact; but after that was gone, I could not, for I could not make any ink by any means that I could devise.

And this put me in mind that I wanted many things, notwithstanding all that I had amassed together; and of these, this of ink was one, as also spade, pickaxe, and shovel, to dig or remove the earth, needles, pins, and thread; as for linen, I soon learned to want that without much difficulty.

This want of tools made every work I did go on heavily; and it was near a whole year before I had entirely finished my little pale or surrounded habitation. The piles or stakes, which were as heavy as I could well lift, were a long time in cutting and preparing in the woods, and more by far in bringing home; so that I spent sometimes two days in cutting and bringing home one of those posts, and a third day in driving it into the ground; for which purpose I got a heavy piece of wood at first, but at last bethought myself of one of the iron crows, which, however, though I found it, yet it made driving those posts or piles very laborious and tedious work.

But what need I have been concerned at the tediousness of anything I had to do, seeing I had time enough to do it in? nor had I any other employment, if that had been over, at least, that I could foresee, except the ranging the island to seek for food, which I did more or less every day.

I now began to consider seriously my condition, and the circumstance I was reduced to; and I drew up the state of my affairs in writing; not so much to leave them to any that were to come after me, for I was like to have but few heirs, as to deliver my thoughts from daily poring upon them, and afflicting my mind. And as my reason began now to master my despondency, I began to comfort myself as well as I could, and to set the good against the evil, that I might have something to distinguish my case from worse; and I stated it very impartially, like debtor and creditor, the comforts I enjoyed against the miseries I suffered, thus:

Evil	Good
I am cast upon a horrible desolate island, void of all hope of recovery.	But I am alive, and not drowned, as all my ship's company was.
I am singled out and separated, as it were, from all the world to be miserable.	But I am singled out, too, from all the ship's crew to be spared from death; and He that miraculously saved me from death, can deliver me from this condition.
I am divided from mankind, a solitaire, one banished from human society.	But I am not starved and perishing on a barren place, affording no sustenance.
I have not clothes to cover me.	But I am in a hot climate, where if I had clothes I could hardly wear them.
I am without any defence or means to resist any violence of man or beast.	But I am cast on an island, where I see no wild beasts to hurt me, as I saw on the coast of Africa; and what if I had been shipwrecked there?
I have no soul to speak to, or relieve me.	But God wonderfully sent the ship in near enough to the shore, that I have gotten out so many necessary things as will either supply my wants, or enable me to supply myself even as long as I live.

Having now brought my mind a little to relish my condition, and given over looking out to sea, to see if I could spy a ship; I say, giving over these things, I began to apply myself to accommodate my way of living, and to make things as easy as I could.

*B

I have already described my habitation, which was a tent under the side of a rock, surrounded with a strong pale of posts and cables; but I might now rather call it a wall, for I raised a kind of wall up against it of turfs, about two feet thick on the outside, and after some time—I think it was a year and a half—I raised rafters from it leaning to the rock, and thatched or covered it with boughs of trees and such things as I could get to keep out the rain, which I found at some times of the year very violent.

I have already observed how I brought all my goods into this pale, and into the cave which I had made behind me. But I must observe, too, that at first this was a confused heap of goods, which as they lay in no order, so they took up all my place; I had no room to turn myself. So I set myself to enlarge my cave and works farther into the earth; for it was a loose sandy rock, which yielded easily to the labour I bestowed on it. And so, when I found I was pretty safe as to beasts of prey, I worked sideways to the right hand into the rock; and then, turning to the right again, worked quite out, and made me a door to come out on the outside of my pale or fortification. This gave me not only egress and regress, as it were a back-way to my tent and to my storehouse, but gave me room to stow my goods.

And now I began to apply myself to make such necessary things as I found I most wanted, as particularly a chair and a table; for without these I was not able to enjoy the few comforts I had in the world. I could not write or eat, or do several things with so much pleasure without a table.

I had never handled a tool in my life; and yet in time, by labour, application, and contrivance, I found

at last that I wanted nothing but I could have made
it, especially if I had had tools.   However, I made
abundance of things even without tools, and some
with no more tools than an adze and a hatchet, which
perhaps were never made that way before, and that
with infinite labour.   For example, if I wanted a
board, I had no other way but to cut down a tree,
set it on an edge before me, and hew it flat on either
side with my axe, till I had brought it to be thin as
a plank, and then dub it smooth with my adze.   It
is true, by this method I could make but one board
out of a whole tree; but this I had no remedy for
but patience, any more that I had for the prodigious
deal of time and labour which it took me up to make
a plank or board.   But my time or labour was little
worth, and so it was as well employed one way as
another.

However, I made me a table and a chair, as I
observed above, in the first place, and this I did out
of the short pieces of boards that I brought on my
raft from the ship. But when I had wrought out some
boards, as above, I made large shelves of the breadth
of a foot and a half, one over another, all along one
side of my cave, to lay all my tools, nails, and iron-
work; and, in a word, to separate everything at large
in their places, that I might come easily at them. I
knocked pieces into the wall of the rock to hang my
guns and all things that would hang up; so that had
my cave been to be seen, it looked like a general
magazine of all necessary things; and I had everything
so ready at my hand, that it was a great pleasure to
me to see all my goods in such order, and especially
to find my stock of all necessaries so great.

And now it was when I began to keep a journal of

every day's employment; for, indeed, at first, I was in too much hurry, and not only as to labour, but in too much discomposure of mind; and my journal would have been full of many dull things.

But having gotten over these things in some measure, and having settled my household stuff and habitation, made me a table and a chair, and all as handsome about me as I could, I began to keep my journal, of which I shall here give you the copy (though in it will be told all these particulars over again) as long as it lasted; for, having no more ink, I was forced to leave it off.

CHAPTER V

EXTRACTS FROM CRUSOE'S JOURNAL

Nov. 4.—This morning I began to order my times of work, of going out with my gun, time of sleep, and time of diversion, viz., every morning I walked out with my gun for two or three hours, if it did not rain; then employed myself to work till about eleven o'clock; then eat what I had to live on; and from twelve to two I lay down to sleep, the weather being excessive hot; and then in the evening to work again. The working part of this day and of the next were wholly employed in making my table; for I was yet but a very sorry workman, though time and necessity made me a complete natural mechanic soon after, as I believe it would do any one else.

Nov. 5.—This day went abroad with my gun and my dog, and killed a wild cat; her skin pretty soft, but her flesh good for nothing. Every creature I killed, I took off the skins and preserved them. Coming back by the sea-shore, I saw many sorts of sea-fowls, which I did not understand; but was surprised, and almost frighted, with two or three seals, which, while I was gazing at, not well knowing what they were, got into the sea, and escaped me for that time.

Nov. 6.—After my morning walk I went to work with my table again, and finished it, though not to my liking; nor was it long before I learned to mend it.

Nov. 7.—Now it began to be settled fair weather. The 7th, 8th, 9th, 10th, and part of the 12th (for the 11th was Sunday) I took wholly up to make me a chair, and with much ado, brought it to a tolerable shape, but never to please me; and even in the making, I pulled it in pieces several times. Note, I soon neglected my keeping Sundays; for, omitting my mark for them on my post, I forgot which was which.

Nov. 17.—This day I began to dig behind my tent into the rock, to make room for my farther conveniency. Note, three things I wanted exceedingly for this work, viz., a pick-axe, a shovel, and a wheelbarrow or basket; so I desisted from my work, and began to consider how to supply that want, and make me some tools. As for a pick-axe, I made use of the iron crows, which were proper enough, though heavy; but the next thing was a shovel or spade. This was so absolutely necessary, that indeed I could do nothing effectually without it; but what kind of one to make, I knew not.

Nov. 18.—The next day, in searching the woods, I found a tree of that wood, or like it, which in the Brazils they call the iron-tree, for its exceeding hardness; of this, with great labour, and almost spoiling my axe, I cut a piece, and brought it home, too, with difficulty enough, for it was exceeding heavy.

The excessive hardness of the wood, and having no other way, made me a long while upon this machine, for I worked it effectually, by little and little, into the form of a shovel or spade, the handle exactly shaped like ours in England, only that the broad part having no iron shod upon it at bottom, it would not last me so long.

I was still deficient, for I wanted a basket or a wheelbarrow. A basket I could not make by any means, having no such things as twigs that would bend to make wicker ware, at least none yet found out. And as to a wheelbarrow, I fancied I could make all but the wheel, but that I had no notion of, neither did I know how to go about it; besides, I had no possible way to make the iron gudgeons for the spindle or axis of the wheel to run in, so I gave it over; and so for carrying away the earth which I dug out of the cave, I made me a thing like a hod which the labourers carry mortar in, when they serve the bricklayers.

Nov. 23.—My other work having now stood still because of my making these tools, when they were finished I went on, and working every day, as my strength and time allowed, I spent eighteen days entirely in widening and deepening my cave, that it might hold my goods commodiously.

Note: During all this time I worked to make this room or cave spacious enough to accommodate me as a warehouse or magazine, a kitchen, a dining-room, and a cellar; as for my lodging, I kept to the tent, except that sometimes in the wet season of the year it rained so hard, that I could not keep myself dry, which caused me afterwards to cover all my place within my pale with long poles, in the form of rafters, leaning against the rock, and load them with flags and large leaves of trees, like a thatch.

Dec. 10.—I began now to think my cave or vault finished, when on a sudden (it seems I had made it too large) a great quantity of earth fell down from the top and one side, so much, that, in short, it frighted me, and not without reason too; for if I had been under it, I had never wanted a gravedigger. Upon this disaster I had a great deal of work to do over again; for I had the loose earth to carry out; and, which was of more importance, I had the ceiling to prop up, so that I might be sure no more would come down.

Dec. 11.—This day I went to work with it accordingly, and got two shores of posts pitched upright to the top, with two pieces of boards across over each post. This I finished the next day; and setting more posts up with boards, in about a week more I had the roof secured; and the posts standing in rows, served me for partitions to part of my house.

Dec. 17.—From this day to the twentieth I placed shelves, and knocked up nails on the posts to hang everything up that could be hung up; and now I began to be in some order within doors.

Dec. 20.—Now I carried everything into the cave, and began to furnish my house, and set up some pieces of boards, like a dresser, to order my victuals upon; but boards began to be very scarce with me; also I made me another table.

Dec. 24.—Much rain all night and all day; no stirring out.

Dec. 25.—Rain all day.

Dec. 26.—No rain, and the earth much cooler than before, and pleasanter.

Dec. 27.—Killed a young goat, and lamed another,

so that I catched it, and led it home in a string. When I had it home, I bound and splintered up its leg, which was broke. *N.B.*—I took such care of it, that it lived, and the leg grew well and as strong as ever; but by my nursing it so long it grew tame, and fed upon the little green at my door, and would not go away. This was the first time that I entertained a thought of breeding up some tame creatures, that I might have food when my powder and shot was all spent.

Dec. 28, 29, 30.—Great heats and no breeze, so that there was no stirring abroad, except in the evening, for food. This time I spent in putting all my things in order within doors.

Jan. 1.—Very hot still, but I went abroad early and late with my gun, and lay still in the middle of the day. This evening, going farther into the valleys which lay towards the centre of the island, I found there was plenty of goats, though exceeding shy, and hard to come at. However, I resolved to try if I could not bring my dog to hunt them down.

Jan. 2.—Accordingly, the next day, I went out with my dog, and set him upon the goats; but I was mistaken, for they all faced about upon the dog; and he knew his danger too well, for he would not come near them.

Jan. 3.—I began my fence or wall; which, being still jealous of my being attacked by somebody, I resolved to make very thick and strong.

N.B.—This wall being described before, I purposely omit what was said in the journal. It is sufficient to observe that I was no less time than from the 3rd of January to the 14th of April working, finishing, and perfecting the wall, though it was no more than about twenty-four yards in length, being a half circle from

one place in the rock to another place about eight
yards from it, the door of the cave being in the centre
behind it.

CHAPTER VI

THE EARTHQUAKE

ALL this time I worked very hard, the rains hindering
me many days, nay, sometimes weeks together; but I
thought I should never be perfectly secure till this wall
was finished. And it was scarce credible what inexpressible labour everything was done with, especially the
bringing piles out of the woods, and driving them into
the ground; for I made them much bigger than I
need to have done.

When this wall was finished, and the outside double-
fenced with a turf-wall raised up close to it, I persuaded myself that if any people were to come on
shore there, they would not perceive anything like a
habitation; and it was very well I did so, as may be
observed hereafter upon a very remarkable occasion.

During this time, I made my rounds in the woods
for game every day, when the rain admitted me, and
made frequent discoveries in these walks of something
or other to my advantage; particularly I found a kind
of wild pigeons, who built, not as wood pigeons in a
tree, but rather as house pigeons, in the holes of the
rocks. And taking some young ones, I endeavoured
to breed them up tame, and did so; but when they
grew older they flew all away, which, perhaps, was at
first for want of feeding them, for I had nothing to
give them. However, I frequently found their nests,
and got their young ones, which were very good meat.

And now in the managing my household affairs I found myself wanting in many things, which I thought at first it was impossible for me to make, as indeed, as to some of them, it was. For instance, I could never make a cask to be hooped; I had a small runlet or two, as I observed before, but I could never arrive to the capacity of making one by them, though I spent many weeks about it. I could neither put in the heads, or joint the staves so true to one another, as to make them hold water; so I gave that also over.

In the next place, I was at a great loss for candle; so that as soon as ever it was dark, which was generally by seven o'clock, I was obliged to go to bed. I remembered the lump of beeswax with which I made candles in my African adventure, but I had none of that now. The only remedy I had was, that when I had killed a goat I saved the tallow, and with a little dish made of clay, which I baked in the sun, to which I added a wick of some oakum, I made me a lamp; and this gave me light, though not a clear steady light like a candle.

In the middle of all my labours it happened, that rummaging my things, I found a little bag, which, as hinted before, had been filled with corn for the feeding of poultry, not for this voyage, but before, as I suppose, when the ship came from Lisbon. What little remainder of corn had been in the bag was all devoured with the rats, and I saw nothing in the bag but husks and dust; and being willing to have the bag for some other use, I think it was to put powder in, when I divided it for fear of the lightning, or some such use, I shook the husks of corn out of it on one side of my fortification, under the rock. It was a little before the great rains, just now mentioned, that

I threw this stuff away, taking no notice of anything, and not so much as remembering that I had thrown anything there; when, about a month after, or thereabout, I saw some few stalks of something green shooting out of the ground, which I fancied might be some plant I had not seen; but I was surprised, and perfectly astonished, when, after a little longer time, I saw about ten or twelve ears come out, which were perfect green barley of the same kind as our European, nay, as our English barley.

I carefully saved the ears of this corn, you may be sure, in their season, which was about the end of June; and laying up every corn, I resolved to sow them all again, hoping in time to have some quantity sufficient to supply me with bread. But it was not till the fourth year that I could allow myself the least grain of this corn to eat, and even then but sparingly, as I shall say afterwards in its order; for I lost all that I sowed the first season, by not observing the proper time; for I sowed it just before the dry season, so that it never came up at all, at least not as it would have done; of which in its place.

Besides this barley, there was, as above, twenty or thirty stalks of rice, which I preserved with the same care, and whose use was of the same kind, or to the same purpose, viz., to make me bread, or rather food; for I found ways to cook it up without baking, though I did that also after some time. But to return to my journal.

I worked excessive hard these three or four months to get my wall done; and the 14th of April I closed it up, contriving to go into it, not by a door, but over the wall by a ladder, that there might be no sign in the outside of my habitation.

April 16.—I finished the ladder, so I went up with the ladder to the top, and then pulled it up after me, and let it down on the inside. This was a complete enclosure to me; for within I had room enough, and nothing could come at me from without, unless it could first mount my wall.

The very next day after this wall was finished, I had almost had all my labour overthrown at once, and myself killed. The case was thus: As I was busy in the inside of it, behind my tent, just in the entrance into my cave, I was terribly frighted with a most dreadful surprising thing indeed; for all on a sudden I found the earth come crumbling down from the roof of my cave, and from the edge of the hill over my head, and two of the posts I had set up in the cave cracked in a frightful manner. I was heartily scared, but thought nothing of what was really the cause, only thinking that the top of my cave was falling in, as some of it had done before; and for fear I should be buried in it, I ran forward to my ladder; and not thinking myself safe there neither, I got over my wall for fear of the pieces of the hill which I expected might roll down upon me. I was no sooner stepped down upon the firm ground, but I plainly saw it was a terrible earthquake; for the ground I stood on shook three times at about eight minutes' distance, with three such shocks, as would have over-turned the strongest building that could be supposed to have stood on the earth; and a great piece of the top of a rock, which stood about half a mile from me next the sea, fell down with such a terrible noise, as I never heard in all my life. I perceived also the very sea was put into violent motion by it; and I believe the shocks were stronger under the water than on the island.

After the third shock was over, and I felt no more for some time, I began to take courage; and yet I had not heart enough to go over my wall again, for fear of being buried alive, but sat still upon the ground, greatly cast down and disconsolate, not knowing what to do. All this while I had not the least serious religious thought, nothing but the common, "Lord, have mercy upon me!" and when it was over, that went away too.

While I sat thus, I found the air overcast, and grow cloudy, as if it would rain. Soon after that the wind rose by little and little, so that in less than half-an-hour it blew a most dreadful hurricane. The sea was all on a sudden covered over with foam and froth; the shore was covered with the breach of the water; the trees were torn up by the roots; and a terrible storm it was: and this held about three hours, and then began to abate; and in two hours more it was stark calm, and began to rain very hard.

I was forced to go into my cave, though very much afraid and uneasy, for fear it should fall on my head.

This violent rain forced me to a new work, viz., to cut a hole through my new fortification, like a sink, to let the water go out, which would else have drowned my cave. After I had been in my cave some time, and found still no more shocks of the earthquake follow, I began to be more composed. And now to support my spirits, which indeed wanted it very much, I went to my little store, and took a small sup of rum, which however, I did then, and always, very sparingly, knowing I could have no more when that was gone.

It continued raining all that night and great part of the next day, so that I could not stir abroad; but my mind being more composed, I began to think of what I had best do, concluding that if the island was subject to these earthquakes, there would be no living for me in a cave, but I must consider of building me some little hut in an open place, which I might surround with a wall, as I had done here, and so make myself secure from wild beasts or men; but concluded, if I stayed where I was, I should certainly, one time or other, be buried alive.

With these thoughts I resolved to remove my tent from the place where it stood, which was just under the hanging precipice of the hill, and which, if it should be shaken again, would certainly fall upon my tent; and I spent the two next days, being the 19th and 20th of April, in contriving where and how to remove my habitation.

The fear of being swallowed up alive made me that I never slept in quiet; and yet the apprehension of lying abroad without any fence was almost equal to it. But still, when I looked about and saw how everything was put in order, how pleasantly concealed I was, and how safe from danger, it made me very loth to remove.

In the meantime it occurred to me that it would require a vast deal of time for me to do this, and that I must be contented to run the venture where I was, till I had formed a camp for myself, and had secured it so as to remove to it. So with this resolution I composed myself for a time, and resolved that I would go to work with all speed to build me a wall with piles and cables, &c., in a circle as before, and set my tent in it when it was finished, but that I would venture to stay where I was till it was finished, and fit to remove to. This was the 21st.

April 22.—The next morning I began to consider of means to put this resolve in execution; but I was at a great loss about my tools. I had three large axes, and abundance of hatchets (for we carried the hatchets for traffic with the Indians), but with much chopping and cutting knotty hard wood, they were all full of notches and dull; and though I had a grindstone, I could not turn it and grind my tools too. This cost me as much thought as a statesman would have bestowed upon a grand point of politics, or a judge upon the life and death of a man. At length I contrived a wheel with a string, to turn it with my foot, that I might have both my hands at liberty. Note, I had never seen any such thing in England, or at least not to take notice how it was done, though since I have observed it is very common there; besides that, my grindstone was very large and heavy. This machine cost me a full week's work to bring it to perfection.

April 28, 29.—These two whole days I took up in grinding my tools, my machine for turning my grindstone performing very well.

May 1.—In the morning, looking towards the seaside, the tide being low, I saw something lie on the shore bigger than ordinary, and it looked like a cask. When I came to it, I found a small barrel, and two or three pieces of the wreck of the ship, which were driven on shore by the late hurricane; and looking towards the wreck itself, I thought it seemed to lie higher out of the water than it used to do. I examined the barrel which was driven on shore, and soon found it was a barrel of gunpowder; but it had taken water, and the powder was caked as hard as a stone. However, I rolled it farther on shore for the present, and went on upon the sands as near as I could to the wreck of the ship to look for more.

When I came down to the ship I found it strangely

removed. The forecastle, which lay before buried in sand, was heaved up at least six feet; and the stern, which was broken to pieces, and parted from the rest by the force of the sea, soon after I had left rummaging her, was tossed, as it were, up, and cast on one side, and the sand was thrown so high on that side next her stern, that whereas there was a great place of water before, so that I could not come within a quarter of a mile of the wreck without swimming, I could now walk quite up to her when the tide was out. I was surprised with this at first, but soon concluded it must be done by the earthquake. And as by this violence the ship was more broken open than formerly, so many things came daily on shore, which the sea had loosened, and which the winds and water rolled by degrees to the land.

This wholly diverted my thoughts from the design of removing my habitation; and I busied myself mightily, that day especially, in searching whether I could make any way into the ship. But I found nothing was to be expected of that kind, for that all the inside of the ship was choked up with sand. However, as I had learned not to despair of anything, I resolved to pull everything to pieces that I could of the ship, concluding, that everything I could get from her would be of some use or other to me.

May 3–17.—Went every day to the wreck, and got a great deal of pieces of timber, and boards, or plank, and two or three hundredweight of iron.

May 24.—Every day to this day I worked on the wreck, and with hard labour I loosened some things so much with the crow, that the first blowing tide several casks floated out, and two of the seamen's chests. But the wind blowing from the shore, nothing came to land that day but pieces of timber, and a hogshead, which had some Brazil pork in it, but the salt water and the sand had spoiled it.

I continued this work every day to the 15th of June, except the time necessary to get food, which I always appointed, during this part of my employment, to be when the tide was up, that I might be ready when it was ebbed out. And by this time I had gotten timber, and plank, and ironwork enough to have builded a good boat, if I had known how; and also, I got at several times, and in several pieces, near one hundred-weight of the sheet lead.

June 16.—Going down to the seaside, I found a large tortoise, or turtle. This was the first I had seen, which it seems was only my misfortune, not any defect of the place, or scarcity; for had I happened to be on the other side of the island, I might have had hundreds of them every day, as I found afterwards; but, perhaps, had paid dear enough for them.

June 17 I spent in cooking the turtle. I found in her three-score eggs; and her flesh was to me, at that time, the most savoury and pleasant that ever I tasted in my life, having had no flesh, but of goats and fowls, since I landed in this horrid place.

June 18.—Rained all day, and I stayed within. I thought at this time the rain felt cold, and I was something chilly, which I knew was not usual in that latitude.

June 19.—Very ill, and shivering, as if the weather had been cold.

June 20.—No rest all night; violent pains in my head, and feverish.

June 21.—Very ill, frighted almost to death with the apprehensions of my sad condition, to be sick, and no help. Prayed to God for the first time since the

storm off Hull, but scarce knew what I said, or why;
my thoughts being all confused.

June 22.—A little better, but under dreadful apprehensions of sickness.

June 23.—Very bad again; cold and shivering, and
then a violent headache.

June 24.—Much better.

June 25.—An ague very violent; the fit held me
seven hours; cold fit, and hot with faint sweats after it.

June 26.—Better; and having no victuals to eat,
took my gun, but found myself very weak. However,
I killed a she-goat, and with much difficulty got it
home, and broiled some of it, and eat. I would fain
have stewed it, and made some broth, but had no pot.

June 27.—The ague again so violent that I lay abed
all day, and neither eat or drink. I was ready to perish
for thirst; but so weak, I had not strength to stand
up, or to get myself any water to drink. Prayed to
God again, but was light-headed; and when I was not,
I was so ignorant that I knew not what so say; only
I lay and cried, "Lord, look upon me! Lord, pity
me! Lord, have mercy upon me!" I suppose I did
nothing else for two or three hours, till the fit wearing
off, I fell asleep, and did not wake till far in the night.
When I waked, I found myself much refreshed, but
weak, and exceeding thirsty. However, as I had no
water in my whole habitation, I was forced to lie till
morning, and went to sleep again. In this second sleep
I had this terrible dream.

I thought that I was sitting on the ground, on the
outside of my wall, where I sat when the storm blew
after the earthquake, and that I saw a man descend
from a great black cloud, in a bright flame of fire,
and light upon the ground. He was all over as bright

as a flame, so that I could but just bear to look towards him. His countenance was most inexpressibly dreadful, impossible for words to describe. When he stepped upon the ground with his feet, I thought the earth trembled, just as it had done before in the earthquake, and all the air looked, to my apprehension, as if it had been filled with flashes of fire.

He was no sooner landed upon the earth, but he moved forward towards me, with a long spear or weapon in his hand, to kill me; and when he came to a rising ground, at some distance, he spoke to me, or I heard a voice so terrible, that it is impossible to express the terror of it. All that I can say I understood was this: " Seeing all these things have not brought thee to repentance, now thou shalt die "; at which words I thought he lifted up the spear that was in his hand to kill me.

No one that shall ever read this account, will expect that I should be able to describe the horrors of my soul at this terrible vision; I mean, that even while it was a dream, I even dreamed of those horrors; nor is it any more possible to describe the impression that remained upon my mind when I awaked, and found it was but a dream.

I had, alas! no divine knowledge; what I had received by the good instruction of my father was then worn out, by an uninterrupted series, for eight years, of seafaring wickedness, and a constant conversation with nothing but such as were, like myself, wicked and profane to the last degree. I do not remember that I had, in all that time, one thought that so much as tended either to looking upwards toward God, or inwards towards a reflection upon my ways.

It is true, when I got on shore first here, and found

all my ship's crew drowned, and myself spared, I was
surprised with a kind of ecstasy, and some transports
of soul, which, had the grace of God assisted, might
have come up to true thankfulness; but it ended
where it begun, in a mere common flight of joy, or,
as I may say, being glad I was alive, without the least
reflection upon the distinguishing goodness of the hand
which had preserved me, and had singled me out to
be preserved, when all the rest were destroyed; or
an inquiry why Providence had been thus merciful
to me; even just the same common sort of joy which
seamen generally have after they are got safe ashore
from a shipwreck, which they drown all in the next
bowl of punch, and forget almost as soon as it is over,
and all the rest of my life was like it.

Even the earthquake, though nothing could be more
terrible in its nature, or more immediately directing to
the invisible Power, which alone directs such things,
yet no sooner was the first fright over, but the impression it had made went off also. I had no more
sense of God or His judgments, much less of the
present affliction of my circumstances being from His
hand, than if I had been in the most prosperous
condition of life.

But now, when I began to be sick, and a leisurely
view of the miseries of death came to place itself
before me; when my spirits began to sink under the
burthen of a strong distemper, and Nature was exhausted with the violence of the fever; conscience,
that had slept so long, began to awake, and I began
to reproach myself with my past life, in which I had
so evidently, by uncommon wickedness, provoked the
justice of God to lay me under uncommon strokes,
and to deal with me in so vindictive a manner.

"Now," said I aloud, "my dear father's words are come to pass; God's justice has overtaken me, and I have none to help or hear me. I rejected the voice of Providence, which had mercifully put me in a posture or station of life wherein I might have been happy and easy; but I would neither see it myself, or learn to know the blessing of it from my parents. I refused their help and assistance, who would have lifted me into the world, and would have made everything easy to me; and now I have difficulties to struggle with, too great for even Nature itself to support, and no assistance, no help, no comfort, no advice." Then I cried out, "Lord, be my help, for I am in great distress."

This was the first prayer, if I may call it so, that I had made for many years. But I return to my journal.

June 28.—Having been somewhat refreshed with the sleep I had had, and the fit being entirely off, I got up; and though the fright and terror of my dream was very great, yet I considered that the fit of the ague would return again the next day, and now was my time to get something to refresh and support myself when I should be ill. And the first thing I did I filled a large square case-bottle with water, and set it upon my table, in reach of my bed; and to take off the chill or aguish disposition of the water, I put about a quarter of a pint of rum into it, and mixed them together. Then I got me a piece of the goat's flesh, and broiled it on the coals, but could eat very little. I walked about, but was very weak, and withal very sad and heavy-hearted in the sense of my miserable condition, dreading the return of my distemper the next day. At night I made my supper of three of the turtle's eggs, which I roasted in the

ashes, and eat, as we call it, in the shell; and this was
the first bit of meat I had ever asked God's blessing
to, even as I could remember, in my whole life.

After I had eaten, I tried to walk, but found myself
so weak, that I could hardly carry the gun (for I
never went out without that); so I went but a little
way, and sat down upon the ground, looking out upon
the sea, which was just before me, and very calm and
smooth. As I sat here, some such thoughts as these
occurred to me.

That it must needs be that God had appointed all
this to befall me; that I was brought to this miserable
circumstance by His direction, He having the sole
power, not of me only, but of everything that happened
in the world. Immediately it followed, Why has God
done this to me? What have I done to be thus used?

My conscience presently checked me in that inquiry,
as if I had blasphemed, and methought it spoke to
me like a voice: "Wretch! dost thou ask what thou
hast done? Look back upon a dreadful misspent life,
and ask thyself what thou hast not done? Ask, why
is it that thou wert not long ago destroyed? Why
wert thou not drowned in Yarmouth Roads; killed
in the fight when the ship was taken by the Sallee
man-of-war; devoured by the wild beast on the coast
of Africa? or drowned here, when all the crew perished
but thyself? Dost thou ask, What have I done?"

I was struck dumb with these reflections, as one
astonished, and had not a word to say, no, not to
answer to myself, but rose up pensive and sad, walked
back to my retreat, and went up over my wall, as if
I had been going to bed. But my thoughts were sadly
disturbed, and I had no inclination to sleep; so I sat
down in my chair, and lighted my lamp, for it began

to be dark. Now, as the apprehension of the return
of my distemper terrified me very much, it occurred
to my thought that the Brazilians take no physic but
their tobacco for almost all distempers; and I had a
piece of a roll of tobacco in one of the chests, which
was quite cured, and some also that was green, and
not quite cured.

I went, directed by Heaven no doubt; for in this
chest I found a cure both for soul and body. I opened
the chest, and found what I looked for, viz., the
tobacco; and as the few books I had saved lay there,
too, I took out one of the Bibles which I mentioned
before, and which to this time I had not found leisure,
or so much as inclination, to look into. I say, I took
it out, and brought both that and the tobacco with
me to the table.

What use to make of the tobacco I knew not, as to
my distemper, or whether it was good for it or no;
but I tried several experiments with it, as if I was
resolved it should hit one way or other. I first took
a piece of a leaf, and chewed it in my mouth, which
indeed at first almost stupified my brain, the tobacco
being green and strong, and that I had not been much
used to it. Then I took some and steeped it an hour
or two in some rum, and resolved to take a dose of it
when I lay down. And lastly, I burnt some upon a
pan of coals, and held my nose close over the smoke
of it as long as I could bear it, as well for the heat,
as almost for suffocation.

In the interval of this operation, I took up the Bible,
and began to read, but my head was too much disturbed with the tobacco to bear reading, at least that
time; only having opened the book casually, the first
words that occurred to me were these, " Call on Me in

the day of trouble, and I will deliver, and thou shalt glorify Me."

It grew now late, and the tobacco had, as I said, dozed my head so much, that I inclined to sleep; so I left my lamp burning in the cave, lest I should want anything in the night, and went to bed. But before I lay down, I did what I never had done in all my life; I kneeled down, and prayed to God to fulfil the promise to me, that if I called upon Him in the day of trouble, He would deliver me. After my broken and imperfect prayer was over, I drank the rum in which I had steeped the tobacco; which was so strong and rank of the tobacco, that indeed I could scarce get it down. Immediately upon this I went to bed. I found presently it flew up in my head violently; but I fell into a sound sleep, and waked no more, till, by the sun, it must necessarily be near three o'clock in the afternoon the next day. Nay, to this hour I am partly of the opinion that I slept all the next day and night, and till almost three that day after; for otherwise I knew not how I should lose a day out of my reckoning in the days of the week, as it appeared some years after I had done. For if I had lost it by crossing and recrossing the line, I should have lost more than one day. But certainly I lost a day in my account, and never knew which way.

Be that, however, one way or the other, when I awaked I found myself exceedingly refreshed, and my spirits lively and cheerful. When I got up, I was stronger than I was the day before, and my stomach better, for I was hungry; and, in short, I had no fit the next day, but continued much altered for the better. This was the 29th.

The 30th was my well day, of course, and I went

abroad with my gun, but did not care to travel too
far. I killed a sea-fowl or two, something like a brand-
goose, and brought them home, but was not very
forward to eat them; so I eat some more of the turtle's
eggs, which were very good. This evening I renewed
the medicine, which I had supposed did me good the
day before, viz., the tobacco steeped in rum; only
I did not take so much as before, nor did I chew any
of the leaf, or hold my head over the smoke. However,
I was not so well the next day, which was the first
of July, as I hoped I should have been; for I had a
little spice of the cold fit, but it was not much.

July 4.—In the morning I took the Bible; and
beginning at the New Testament, I began seriously
to read it, and imposed upon myself to read awhile
every morning and every night, not tying myself to
the number of chapters, but as long as my thoughts
should engage me.

Now I began to construe the words mentioned above,
" Call on Me, and I will deliver you," in a different
sense from what I had ever done before; for then I
had no notion of anything being called deliverance
but my being delivered from the captivity I was in!
for though I was indeed at large in the place, yet the
island was certainly a prison to me, and that in the
worst sense in the world. But now I learned to take
it in another sense; now I looked back upon my past
life with such horror, and my sins appeared so dreadful, that my soul sought nothing of God but deliverance
from the load of guilt that bore down all my comfort.

My condition began now to be, though not less
miserable as to my way of living, yet much easier to
my mind; and my thoughts being directed, by a constant reading the Scripture, and praying to God, to

c

things of a higher nature, I had a great deal of comfort within, which, till now, I knew nothing of. Also, as my health and strength returned, I bestirred myself to furnish myself with everything that I wanted, and make my way of living as regular as I could.

From the 4th of July to the 14th, I was chiefly employed in walking about with my gun in my hand, a little and a little at a time, as a man that was gathering up his strength after a fit of sickness; for it is hardly to be imagined how low I was, and to what weakness I was reduced. The application which I made use of was perfectly new, and perhaps what had never cured an ague before; neither can I recommend it to any one to practise, by this experiment; and though it did carry off the fit, yet it rather contributed to weakening me; for I had frequent convulsions in my nerves and limbs for some time.

I had been now in this unhappy island above ten months, all possibility of deliverance from this condition seemed to be entirely taken from me; and I firmly believed that no human shape had ever set foot upon that place. Having now secured my habitation, as I thought, fully to my mind, I had a great desire to make a more perfect discovery of the island, and to see what other productions I might find, which I yet knew nothing of.

CHAPTER VII

SURVEYING THE ISLAND

IT was the 15th of July that I began to take a more particular survey of the island itself. I went up the creek first, where, as I hinted, I brought my rafts on shore. I found after I came about two miles up, that the tide did not flow any higher, and that it was no more than a little brook of running water, and very fresh and good; but this being the dry season, there was hardly any water in some parts of it, at least, not enough to run in any stream, so as it could be perceived.

On the bank of this brook I found many pleasant savannas or meadows, plain smooth, and covered with grass; and on the rising parts of them, next to the higher grounds, where the water, as might be supposed, never overflowed, I found a great deal of tobacco, green, and growing to a great and very strong stalk. There were divers other plants, which I had no notion of, or understanding about, and might perhaps have virtues of their own which I could not find out.

I searched for the cassava root, which the Indians, in all that climate, make their bread of, but I could find none. I saw large plants of aloes, but did not then understand them. I saw several sugar-canes, but wild, and, for want of cultivation, imperfect. I contented myself with these discoveries for this time, and came back, musing with myself what course I might take to know the virtue and goodness of any of the fruits or plants which I should discover; but could bring it to no conclusion; for, in short, I had made so little observation while I was in the Brazils, that I knew little of the plants in the field, at least very little that might serve me to any purpose now in my distress.

The next day, the 16th, I went up the same way again; and after going something farther than I had gone the day before, I found the brook and the savannas began to cease, and the country became more woody

than before. In this part I found different fruits, and
particularly I found melons upon the ground in great
abundance, and grapes upon the trees. The vines had
spread indeed over the trees, and the clusters of grapes
were just now in their prime, very ripe and rich. This
was a surprising discovery, and I was exceeding glad
of them; but I was warned by my experience to eat
sparingly of them, remembering that when I was
ashore in Barbary the eating of grapes killed several
of our Englishmen, who were slaves there, by throwing
them into fluxes and fevers. But I found an excellent
use for these grapes; and that was, to cure or dry them
in the sun, and keep them as dried grapes or raisins
are kept, which I thought would be, as indeed they
were, as wholesome as agreeable to eat, when no
grapes might be to be had.

I spent all that evening there, and went not back
to my habitation; which, by the way, was the first
night, as I might say, I had lain from home. In the
night, I took my first contrivance, and got up into a
tree, where I slept well; and the next morning pro-
ceeded upon my discovery, travelling near four miles,
as I might judge by the length of the valley, keeping
still due north, with a ridge of hills on the south and
north side of me.

At the end of this march I came to an opening,
where the country seemed to descend to the west;
and a little spring of fresh water, which issued out of
the side of the hill by me, ran the other way, that is,
due east; and the country appeared so fresh, so green,
so flourishing, everything being in a constant verdure
or flourish of spring, that it looked like a planted
garden.

I descended a little on the side of that delicious

vale, surveying it with a secret kind of pleasure, though
mixed with my other afflicting thoughts, to think that
this was all my own; that I was king and lord of all
this country indefeasibly, and had a right of possession; and, if I could convey it, I might have it in in-
heritance as completely as any lord of a manor in
England. I saw here abundance of cocoa trees, orange,
and lemon, and citron trees; but all wild, and very
few bearing any fruit, at least not then. However, the
green limes that I gathered were not only pleasant to
eat, but very wholesome; and I mixed their juice
afterwards with water, which made it very wholesome,
and very cool and refreshing.

I found now I had business enough to gather and
carry home; and I resolved to lay up a store, as well
of grapes as limes and lemons to furnish myself for
the wet season, which I knew was approaching.

In order to this, I gathered a great heap of grapes
in one place, and a lesser heap in another place, and a
great parcel of limes and lemons in another place;
and, taking a few of each with me, I travelled homeward; and resolved to come again, and bring a bag
or sack, or what I could make, to carry the rest home.

Accordingly, having spent three days in this journey,
I came home (so I must now call my tent and my
cave); but before I got thither, the grapes were
spoiled; the richness of the fruits, and the weight of
the juice, having broken them and bruised them;
they were good for little or nothing: as to the limes,
they were good, but I could bring but a few.

The next day, being the 19th, I went back, having
made me two small bags to bring home my harvest;
but I was surprised, when, coming to my heap of
grapes, which were so rich and fine when I gathered

them, I found them all spread about, trod to pieces, and dragged about, some here, some there, and abundance eaten and devoured. By this I concluded there were some wild creatures thereabouts, which had done this; but what they were, I knew not.

However, as I found that there was no laying them up on heaps, and no carrying them away in a sack, but that one way they would be destroyed, and the other way they would be crushed with their own weight, I took another course; for I gathered a large quantity of the grapes, and hung them up upon the out-branches of the trees, that they might cure and dry in the sun; and as for the limes and lemons, I carried as many back as I could well stand under.

When I came home from this journey, I contemplated with great pleasure the fruitfulness of that valley, and the pleasantness of the situation; the security from storms on that side the water and the wood; and concluded that I had pitched upon a place to fix my abode, which was by far the worst part of the country. Upon the whole, I began to consider of removing my habitation, and to look out for a place equally safe as where I now was situate, if possible, in that pleasant fruitful part of the island.

This thought ran long in my head, and I was exceeding fond of it for some time, the pleasantness of the place tempting me; but when I came to a nearer view of it, and to consider that I was now by the seaside, where it was at least possible that something might happen to my advantage, and, by the same ill fate that brought me hither, might bring some other unhappy wretches to the same place; and though it was scarce probable that any such thing should ever happen, yet to enclose myself among the hills and woods in the centre of the island, was to anticipate my bondage, and to render such an affair not only improbable, but impossible; and that therefore I ought not by any means to remove.

However, I was so enamoured of this place, that I spent much of my time there for the whole remaining part of the month of July; and though, upon second thoughts, I resolved, as above, not to remove, yet I built me a little kind of bower, and surrounded it at a distance with a strong fence, being a double hedge as high as I could reach, well staked, and filled between with brushwood. And here I lay very secure, sometimes two or three nights together, always going over it with a ladder, as before; so that I fancied now I had my country house and my sea-coast house; and this work took me up to the beginning of August.

I had but newly finished my fence, and began to enjoy my labour, but the rains came on, and made me stick close to my first habitation; for though I had made me a tent like the other, with a piece of a sail, and spread it very well, yet I had not the shelter of a hill to keep me from storms, nor a cave behind me to retreat into when the rains were extraordinary.

About the beginning of August, as I said, I had finished my bower, and began to enjoy myself. The 3rd of August, I found the grapes I had hung up were perfectly dried, and indeed were excellent good raisins of the sun; so I began to take them down from the trees. And it was very happy that I did so, for the rains which followed would have spoiled them, and I had lost the best part of my winter food; for I had above two hundred large bunches of them. No sooner had I taken them all down, and carried most of them home to my cave, but it began to rain; and from hence, which was the 14th of August, it rained, more or less, every day till the middle of October, and sometimes so violently, that I could not stir out of my cave for several days.

In this season, I was much surprised with the increase of my family. I had been concerned for the loss of one of my cats, who run away from me, or, as I thought, had been dead, and I heard no more tale or tidings of her, till, to my astonishment, she came home about the end of August with three kittens. But from these three cats I afterwards came to be so pestered with cats, that I was forced to kill them like vermin, or wild beasts, and to drive them from my house as much as possible.

From the 14th of August to the 26th, incessant rain, so that I could not stir, and was now very careful not to be much wet. In this confinement, I began to be straitened for food; but venturing out twice, I one day killed a goat, and the last day, which was the 26th, found a very large tortoise, which was a treat to me, and my food was regulated thus: I eat a bunch of raisins for my breakfast, a piece of the goat's flesh, or of the turtle, for my dinner, broiled; for, to my great misfortune, I had no vessel to boil or stew anything; and two or three of the turtle's eggs for my supper.

During this confinement in my cover by the rain, I worked daily two or three hours at enlarging my cave, and by degrees worked it on towards one side, till I came to the outside of the hill, and made a door, or way out, which came beyond my fence or wall; and so I came in and out this way. But I was not perfectly easy at lying so open; for as I had managed myself before, I was in a perfect enclosure; whereas now,

I thought I lay exposed, and open for anything to come in upon me; and yet I could not perceive that there was any living thing to fear, the biggest creature that I had yet seen upon the island being a goat.

Sept. 30.—I was now come to the unhappy anniversary of my landing. I cast up the notches on my post, and found I had been on shore three hundred and sixty-five days. I kept this day as a solemn fast, setting it apart to religious exercise.

I had all this time observed no Sabbath day, for as at first I had no sense of religion upon my mind, I had, after some time, omitted to distinguish the weeks, by making a longer notch then ordinary for the Sabbath day, and so did not really know what any of the days were. But now, having cast up the days as above, I found I had been there a year, so I divided it into weeks, and set apart every seventh day for a Sabbath; though I found at the end of my account, I had lost a day or two in my reckoning.

A little after this my ink began to fail me, and so I contented myself to use it more sparingly, and to write down only the most remarkable events of my life, without continuing a daily memorandum of other things.

The rainy season and the dry season began now to appear regular to me, and I learned to divide them so as to provide for them accordingly; but I bought all my experience before I had it, and this I am going to relate was one of the most discouraging experiments that I made at all. I have mentioned that I had saved the few ears of barley and rice, which I had so surprisingly found spring up, as I thought, of themselves, and about twenty of barley; and now I thought it a proper time to sow it after the rains, the sun being in its southern position, going from me.

*C

Accordingly I dug up a piece of ground as well as I could with my wooden spade, and dividing it into two parts, I sowed my grain; but as I was sowing, it casually occurred to my thoughts that I would not sow it all at first, because I did not know when was the proper time for it, so I sowed about two-thirds of the seed, leaving about a handful of each.

It was a great comfort to me afterwards that I did so, for not one grain of that I sowed this time came to anything, for the dry months following, the earth having had no rain after the seed was sown, it had no moisture to assist its growth, and never came up at all till the wet season had come again, and then it grew as if it had been but newly sown.

Finding my first seed did not grow, which I easily imagined was by the drought, I sought for a moister piece of ground to make another trial in, and I dug up a piece of ground near my new bower, and sowed the rest of my seed in February, a little before the vernal equinox. And this having the rainy months of March and April to water it, sprung up very pleasantly, and yielded a very good crop; but having part of the seed left only, and not daring to sow all that I had, I had but a small quantity at last, my whole crop not amounting to above half a peck of each kind. But by this experiment I was made master of my business, and knew exactly when the proper season was to sow, and that I might expect two seed-times and two harvests every year.

While this corn was growing, I made a little discovery, which was of use to me afterwards. As soon as the rains were over, and the weather began to settle, which was about the month of November, I made a visit up the country to my bower, where, though I had not been some months, yet I found all things just as I left them. The circle or double hedge that I had made was not only firm and entire, but the stakes which I had cut out of some trees that grew thereabouts were all shot out, and grown with long branches, as much as a willow-tree usually shoots the first year after lopping its head. I could not tell what tree to call it that these stakes were cut from. I was surprised, and yet very well pleased to see the young trees grow, and I pruned them, and led them up to grow as much alike as I could. And it is scarce credible how beautiful a figure they grew into in three years; so that though the hedge made a circle of about twenty-five yards in diameter, yet the trees, for such I might now call them, soon covered it, and it was a complete shade, sufficient to lodge under all the dry season.

This made me resolve to cut some more stakes, and make me a hedge like this, in a semicircle round my wall (I mean that of my first dwelling), which I did; and placing the trees or stakes in a double row, at about eight yards' distance from my first fence, they grew presently, and were at first a fine cover to my habitation, and afterward served for a defence also, as I shall observe in its order.

I found now that the seasons of the year might generally be divided, not into summer and winter, as in Europe, but into the rainy seasons and the dry seasons. After I had found by experience the ill consequence of being abroad in the rain, I took care to furnish myself with provisions beforehand, that I might not be obliged to go out; and I sat within doors as much as possible during the wet months.

In this time I found much employment, and very

suitable also to the time, for I found great occasion of many things which I had no way to furnish myself with but by hard labour and constant application; particularly I tried many ways to make myself a basket; but all the twigs I could get for the purpose proved so brittle, that they would do nothing. It proved of excellent advantage to me now, that when I was a boy I used to take a great delight in standing at a basket-maker's in the town where my father lived, to see them make their wicker-ware; and being, as boys usually are, very officious to help, and a great observer of the manner how they worked those things, and sometimes lending a hand, I had by this means full knowledge of the methods of it, that I wanted nothing but the materials; when it came into my mind that the twigs of that tree from whence I cut my stakes that grew might possibly be as tough as the sallows, and willows, and osiers in England, and I resolved to try.

Accordingly, the next day, I went to my country house, as I called it; and cutting some of the smaller twigs, I found them to my purpose as much as I could desire; whereupon I came the next time prepared with a hatchet to cut down a quantity, which I soon found, for there was great plenty of them. These I set up to dry within my circle or hedge, and when they were fit for use, I carried them to my cave; and here during the next season I employed myself in making, as well as I could, a great many baskets, both to carry earth, or to carry or lay up anything as I had occasion. And though I did not finish them very handsomely, yet I made them sufficiently serviceable for my purpose. And thus, afterwards, I took care never to be without them; and as my wicker-ware decayed, I made more, especially I made strong deep baskets to place my corn in, instead of sacks, when I should come to have any quantity of it.

Having mastered this difficulty, and employed a world of time about it, I bestirred myself to see, if possible, how to supply two wants. I had no vessels to hold anything that was liquid, except two runlets, which were almost full of rum, and some glass bottles, some of the common size, and others which were case-bottles square, for the holding of waters, spirits, etc. I had not so much as a pot to boil anything, except a great kettle, which I saved out of the ship, and which was too big for such use as I desired it, viz., to make broth, and stew a bit of meat by itself. The second thing I would fain have had was a tobacco-pipe; but it was impossible to me to make one. However, I found a contrivance for that, too, at last.

I employed myself in planting my second rows of stakes or piles and in this wicker-working all the summer or dry season, when another business took me up more time than it could be imagined I could spare.

I mentioned before that I had a great mind to see the whole island, and that I had travelled up the brook, and so on to where I built my bower, and where I had an opening quite to the sea, on the other side of the island. I now resolved to travel quite across to the seashore on that side; so taking my gun, a hatchet, and my dog, and a larger quantity of powder and shot than usual, with two biscuit-cakes and a great bunch of raisins in my pouch for my store, I began my journey. When I had passed the vale where my bower stood, as above, I came within view of the sea to the west; and it being a very clear day, I fairly

descried land, whether an island or a continent I could
not tell; but it lay very high, extending from the west
to the W.S.W. at a very great distance; by my guess,
it could not be less than fifteen or twenty leagues off.

I saw abundance of parrots, and fain I would have
caught one, if possible, to have kept it to be tame,
and taught it to speak to me. I did, after some pains-
taking, catch a young parrot, for I knocked it down
with a stick, and having recovered it, I brought it
home; but it was some years before I could make him
speak. However, at last I taught him to call me by my
name very familiarly. But the accident that followed,
though it be a trifle, will be very diverting in its place.

I was exceedingly diverted with this journey. I
found in the low grounds hares, as I thought them to
be, and foxes; but they differed greatly from all the
other kinds I had met with, nor could I satisfy myself
to eat them, though I killed several. But I had no
need to be venturous, for I had no want of food, and
of that which was very good too, especially these
three sorts, viz., goats, pigeons, and turtle, or tortoise;
which, added to my grapes, Leadenhall Market could
not have furnished a table better than I, in proportion
to the company. And though my case was deplorable
enough, yet I had great cause for thankfulness, and
that I was not driven to any extremities for food,
but rather plenty, even to dainties.

I never travelled in this journey above two miles
outright in a day, or thereabouts; but I took so
many turns and returns, to see what discoveries I
could make, that I came weary enough to the place
where I resolved to sit down for all night; and then
I either reposed myself in a tree, or surrounded myself
with a row of stakes, set upright in the ground, either

from one tree to another, or so as no wild creature could come at me without waking me.

As soon as I came to the seashore, I was surprised to see that I had taken up my lot on the worst side of the island, for here indeed the shore was covered with innumerable turtles; whereas, on the other side, I had found but three in a year and a half. Here was also an infinite number of fowls of many kinds, some which I had seen, and some which I had not seen of before, and many of them very good meat, but such as I knew not the names of, except those called penguins.

I could have shot as many as I pleased, but was very sparing of my powder and shot, and therefore had more mind to kill a she-goat, if I could, which I could better feed on; and though there were many goats here, more than on my side the island, yet it was with much more difficulty that I could come near them, the country being flat and even, and they saw me much sooner than when I was on the hill.

I confess this side of the country was much pleasanter than mine; but yet I had not the least inclination to remove, for as I was fixed in my habitation, it became natural to me, and I seemed all the while I was here to be as it were upon a journey, and from home. However, I travelled along the shore of the sea towards the east, I suppose about twelve miles, and then setting up a great pole upon the shore for a mark, I concluded I would go home again; and that the next journey I took should be on the other side of the island, east from my dwelling, and so round till I came to my post again; of which in its place.

I took another way to come back than that I went, thinking I could easily keep all the island so much in my view, that I could not miss finding my first dwelling by viewing the country. But I found myself mistaken. I wandered about very uncomfortably, and at last was obliged to find out the seaside, look for my post, and come back the same way I went; and then by easy journeys I turned homeward, the weather being exceeding hot, and my gun, ammunition, hatchet, and other things very heavy.

In this journey my dog surprised a young kid, and seized upon it, and I running in to take hold of it, caught it, and saved it alive from the dog. I had a great mind to bring it home if I could, for I had often been musing whether it might not be possible to get a kid or two, and so raise a breed of tame goats, which might supply me when my powder and shot should all be spent.

I made a collar to this little creature, and with a string, which I made of some rope-yarn, which I always carried about me, I led him along, though with some difficulty, till I came to my bower, and there I enclosed him and left him, for I was very impatient to be at home, from whence I had been absent above a month.

I cannot express what a satisfaction it was to me to come into my old hutch, and lie down in my hammock-bed. This little wandering journey, without settled place of abode, had been so unpleasant to me, that my own house, as I called it to myself, was a perfect settlement to me compared to that; and it rendered everything about me so comfortable, that I resolved I would never go a great way from it again, while it should be my lot to stay on the island.

I reposed myself here a week, to rest and regale myself after my long journey; during which most of the time was taken up in the weighty affair of making a cage for my Poll, who began now to be a mere domestic, and to be mighty well acquainted with me. Then I began to think of the poor kid which I had penned in within my little circle, and resolved to go go and fetch it home, or give it some food. Accordingly I went, and found it where I left it, for indeed it could not get out, but almost starved for want of food. I went and cut boughs of trees, and branches of such shrubs as I could find, and threw it over, and having fed it, I tied it as I did before, to lead it away; but it was so tame with being hungry, that I had no need to have tied it, for it followed me like a dog. And as I continually fed it the creature became so loving, so gentle, and so fond, that it became from that time one of my domestics also, and would never leave me afterwards.

The rainy season of the autumnal equinox was now come, and I kept the 30th of September in the same solemn manner as before, being the anniversary of my landing on the island, having now been there two years, and no more prospect of being delivered than the first day I came there. I spent the whole day in humble and thankful acknowledgments of the many wonderful mercies which my solitary condition was attended with, and without which it might have been infinitely more miserable.

CHAPTER VIII

A HAPPY LIFE

IT was now that I began sensibly to feel how much more happy this life I now led was, with all its miserable circumstances, than the wicked, cursed, abominable

life I led all the past part of my days. And now
I changed both my sorrows and my joys; my very
desires altered, my affections changed their gusts,
and my delights were perfectly new from what they
were at my first coming, or indeed for the two years
past.

Thus, and in this disposition of mind, I began my
third year; and though I have not given the reader
the trouble of so particular account of my works this
year as the first, yet in general it may be observed,
that I was very seldom idle, but having regularly
divided my time, according to the several daily employ-
ments that were before me, such as, first, my duty to
God, and the reading the Scriptures, which I constantly set apart some time for, thrice every day;
secondly, the going abroad with my gun for food,
which generally took me up three hours in every
morning, when it did not rain; thirdly, the ordering,
curing, preserving, and cooking what I had killed or
catched for my supply; these took up great part of
the day; also, it is to be considered that the middle
of the day, when the sun was in the zenith, the
violence of the heat was too great to stir out; so
that about four hours in the evening was all the time
I could be supposed to work in, with this exception,
that sometimes I changed my hours of hunting and
working, and went to work in the morning, and abroad
with my gun in the afternoon.

To this short time allowed for labour, I desire may
be added the exceeding laboriousness of my work; the
many hours which, for want of tools, want of help,
and want of skill, everything I did took up out of my
time. For example, I was full two and forty days
making me a board for a long shelf, which I wanted

in my cave; whereas two sawyers, with their tools and a sawpit, would have cut six of them out of the same tree in half a day.

My case was this: it was to be a large tree which was to be cut down, because my board was to be a broad one. This tree I was three days a-cutting down, and two more cutting off the boughs, and reducing it to a log, or piece of timber. With inexpressible hacking and hewing, I reduced both the sides of it into chips till it began to be light enough to move; then I turned it, and made one side of it smooth and flat as a board from end to end; then turning that side downward, cut the other side, till I brought the plank to be about about three inches thick, and smooth on both sides. Anyone may judge the labour of my hands in such a piece of work; but labour and patience carried me through that, and many other things. I only observe this in particular, to show the reason why so much of my time went away with so little work, viz., that what might be a little to be done with help and tools, was a vast labour, and required a prodigious time to do alone, and by hand. But notwithstanding this, with patience and labour, I went through many things, and, indeed, everything that my circumstances made necessary to me to do, as will appear by what follows.

I was now, in the months of November and December, expecting my crop of barley and rice. The ground I had manured or dug up for them was not great; for as I observed, my seed of each was not above the quantity of half a peck; for I had lost one whole crop by sowing in the dry season. But now my crop promised very well, when on a sudden I found I was in danger of losing it all again by enemies of several sorts, which it was scarce possible to keep from it; as, first the goats and wild creatures which I called hares, who, tasting the sweetness of the blade, lay in it night and day, as soon as it came up, and eat it so close, that it could get no time to shoot up into stalk.

This I saw no remedy for but by making an enclosure about it with a hedge, which I did with a great deal of toil, and the more, because it required speed. However, as my arable land was but small, suited to my crop, I got it totally well fenced in about three weeks' time, and shooting some of the creatures in the daytime, I set my dog to guard it in the night, tying him up to a stake at the gate, where he would stand and bark all night long; so in a little time the enemies forsook the place, and the corn grew very strong and well, and began to ripen apace.

But as the beasts ruined me before while my corn was in the blade, so the birds were as likely to ruin me now when it was in the ear; for going along by the place to see how it throve, I saw my little crop surrounded with fowls, of I know not how many sorts, who stood, as it were, watching till I should be gone. I immediately let fly among them, for I always had my gun with me. I had no sooner shot, but there rose up a little cloud of fowls, which I had not seen at all, from among the corn itself.

This touched me sensibly, for I foresaw that in a few days they would devour all my hopes, that I should be starved, and never be able to raise a crop at all, and what to do I could not tell. However, I resolved not to lose my corn, if possible, though I should watch it night and day. In the first place I went among it to see what damage was already done, and found they had spoiled a good deal of it; but that as it was yet too green for them, the loss was not so great but that the remainder was like to be a good crop if it could be saved.

I stayed by it to load my gun, and then coming away, I could easily see the thieves sitting upon all the trees about me, as if they only waited till I was gone away. And the event proved it to be so; for as I walked off, as if I was gone, I was no sooner out of their sight but they dropped down, one by one, into the corn again. I was so provoked, that I could not have patience to stay till more came on, knowing that every grain that they eat now was, as it might be said, a peck-loaf to me in the consequence; but coming up to the hedge, I fired again, and killed three of them. This was what I wished for; so I took them up, and served them as we serve notorious thieves in England, viz., hanged them in chains, for a terror to others. It is impossible to imagine almost that this should have such an effect as it had, for the fowls would not only not come at the corn, but, in short, they forsook all that part of the island, and I could never see a bird near the place as long as my scare-crows hung there.

This I was very glad of, you may be sure; and about the latter end of December, which was our second harvest of the year, I reaped my crop.

I was sadly put to it for a scythe or a sickle to cut it down, and all I could do was to make one as well as I could out of one of the broadswords, or cutlasses, which I saved among the arms out of the ship. However, as my first crop was but small, I had no great difficulty to cut it down; in short, I reaped it my way; for I cut nothing off but the ears, and carried

it away in a great basket which I had made, and so
rubbed it out with my hands; and at the end of all
my harvesting, I found that out of my half peck of
seed I had near two bushels of rice, and above two
bushels and a half of barley, that is to say, by my
guess, for I had no measure at that time.

However, this was a great encouragement to me,
and I foresaw that, in time, it would please God to
supply with me bread. And yet here I was perplexed
again, for I neither knew how to grind or make meal
of my corn, or indeed how to clean it and part it;
nor, if made into meal, how to make bread of it, and
if how to make it, yet I knew not how to bake it.
These things being added to my desire of having a
good quantity for store, and to secure a constant
supply, I resolved not to taste any of this crop, but
to preserve it all for seed against the next season,
and, in the meantime, to employ all my study and
hours of working to accomplish this great work of
providing myself with corn and bread.

Within doors, that is, when it rained, and I could
not go out, I found employment on the following
occasions; always observing, that all the while I was
at work, I diverted myself with talking to my parrot,
and teaching him to speak, and I quickly learned him
to know his own name, and at last to speak it out
pretty loud, " Poll," which was the first word I ever
heard spoken in the island by any mouth but my own.
This, therefore, was not my work, but an assistant to
my work; for now, as I said, I had a great employment
upon my hands, as follows, viz., I had long studied,
by some means or other, to make myself some earthen
vessels, which indeed I wanted sorely, but knew not
where to come at them. However, considering the

heat of the climate, I did not doubt but if I could find out any such clay, I might botch up some such pot as might, being dried in the sun, be hard enough and strong enough to bear handling, and to hold anything that was dry, and required to be kept so; and as this was necessary in the preparing corn, meal, etc., which was the thing I was upon, I resolved to make some as large as I could, and fit only to stand like jars, to hold what should be put into them.

It would make the reader pity me, or rather laugh at me, to tell how many awkward ways I took to raise this paste; what odd, misshapen, ugly things I made; how many of them fell in, and how many fell out, the clay not being stiff enough to bear its own weight; how many cracked by the over-violent heat of the sun, being set out too hastily; and how many fell in pieces with only removing, as well before as after they were dried; and, in a word, how, after having laboured hard to find the clay, to dig it, to temper it, to bring it home, and work it, I could not make above two large earthen ugly things (I cannot call them jars) in about two months' labour.

However, as the sun baked these two very dry and hard, I lifted them very gently up, and set them down again in two great wicker baskets, which I had made on purpose for them that they might not break; and as between the pot and the basket there was a little room to spare, I stuffed it full of the rice and barley straw, and these two pots being to stand always dry, I thought would hold my dry corn, and perhaps the meal, when the corn was bruised.

Though I miscarried so much in my design for large pots, yet I made several smaller things with better success; such as little round pots, flat dishes, pitchers, and pipkins, and any things my hand turned to; and the heat of the sun baked them strangely hard. But all this would not answer my end, which was to get an earthen pot to hold what was liquid, and bear the fire, which none of these could do. It happened after some time, making a pretty large fire for cooking my meat, when I went to put it out after I had done with it, I found a broken piece of one of my earthenware vessels in the fire, burnt as hard as a stone, and red as a tile. I was agreeably surprised to see it, and said to myself, that certainly they might be made to burn whole, if they would burn broken.

This set me to studying how to order my fire, so as to make it burn me some pots. I had no notion of a kiln, such as the potters burn in, or of glazing them with lead, though I had some lead to do it with; but I placed three large pipkins, and two or three pots in a pile, one upon another, and placed my firewood all round it, with a great heap of embers under them. I plied the fire with fresh fuel round the outside, and upon the top, till I saw the pots in the inside red-hot quite through, and observed that they did not crack at all. When I saw them clear red, I let them stand in that heat about five or six hours, till I found one of them, though it did not crack, did melt or run, for the sand which was mixed with the clay melted by the violence of the heat, and would have run into glass, if I had gone on; so I slacked my fire gradually till the pots began to abate of the red colour; and watching them all night, that I might not let the fire abate too fast, in the morning I had three very good, I will not say handsome, pipkins, and two other earthen pots, as hard burnt as could be desired, and one of them perfectly glazed with the running of the sand.

After this experiment, I need not say that I wanted no sort of earthenware for my use; but I must needs say, as to the shapes of them, they were very in-different, as anyone may suppose, when I had no way of making them but as the children make dirt pies, or as a woman would make pies that never learned to raise paste.

No joy at a thing of so mean a nature was ever equal to mine, when I found I had made an earthen pot that would bear the fire; and I had hardly patience to stay till they were cold, before I set one upon the fire again, with some water in it, to boil me some meat, which it did admirably well; and with a piece of a kid I made some very good broth, though I wanted oatmeal and several other ingredients requisite to make it so good as I would have had it.

My next concern was to get me a stone mortar to stamp or beat some corn in; for as to the mill, there was no thought at arriving to that perfection of art with one pair of hands. I spent many a day to find out a great stone big enough to cut hollow, and make fit for a mortar, and could find none at all, except what was in the solid rock, and which I had no way to dig or cut out; nor indeed were the rocks in the island of hardness sufficient, but were all of a sandy crumbling stone, which neither would bear the weight of a heavy pestle, or would break the corn without filling it with sand. So, after a great deal of time lost in searching for a stone, I gave it over, and resolved to look out for a great block of hard wood, which I found indeed much easier; and getting one as big as I had strength to stir, I rounded it, and formed it in the outside with my axe and hatchet, and then, with the help of fire, and infinite labour, made a hollow

place in it, as the Indians in Brazil make their canoes.
After this, I made a great heavy pestle, or beater, of
the wood called the iron-wood; and this I prepared
and laid by against I had my next crop of corn, when
I proposed to myself to grind, or rather pound, my
corn into meal, to make my bread.

My next difficulty was to make a sieve, or search,
to dress my meal, and to part it from the bran and
the husk, without which I did not see it possible I
could have any bread. This was a most difficult thing,
so much as but to think on, for to be sure I had nothing
like the necessary thing to make it; I mean fine thin
canvas or stuff, to search the meal through. And here
I was at a full stop for many months, nor did I really
know what to do; linen I had none left, but what was
mere rags; I had goats'-hair, but neither knew I how
to weave it or spin it; and had I known how, here
was no tools to work it with. All the remedy that I
found for this was, that at last I did remember I had,
among the seamen's clothes which were saved out of
the ship, some neckcloths of calico or muslin; and
with some pieces of these I made three small sieves,
but proper enough for the work; and thus I made
shift for some years. How I did afterwards, I shall
show in its place.

The baking part was the next thing to be considered, and how I should make bread when I came
to have corn; for, first, I had not yeast. As to that
part, as there was no supplying the want, so I did
not concern myself much about it; but for an oven
I was indeed in great pain. At length I found out an
experiment for that also, which was this: I made some
earthen vessels very broad, but not deep, that is to
say, about two feet diameter, and not above nine

inches deep; these I burned in the fire, as I had done the other, and laid them by; and when I wanted to bake, I made a great fire upon my hearth, which I had paved with some square tiles, of my own making and burning also; but I should not call them square.

When the firewood was burned pretty much into embers, or live coals, I drew them forward upon this hearth, so as to cover it all over, and there I let them lie till the hearth was very hot; then sweeping away all the embers, I set down my loaf, or loaves, and whelming down the earthen pot upon them, drew the embers all round the outside of the pot, to keep in and add to the heat. And thus, as well as in the best oven in the world, I baked my barley-loaves, and became, in little time, a mere pastry-cook into the bargain; for I made myself several cakes of the rice, and puddings; indeed I made no pies, neither had I anything to put into them, supposing I had, except the flesh either of fowls or goats.

It need not be wondered at, if all these things took me up most part of the third year of my abode here; for it is to be observed, that in the intervals of these things I had my new harvest and husbandry to manage; for I reaped my corn in its season, and carried it home as well as I could, and laid it up in the ear, in my large baskets, till I had time to rub it out, for I had no floor to thrash it on, or instrument to thrash it with.

And now, indeed, my stock of corn increasing, I really wanted to build my barns bigger. I wanted a place to lay it up in, for the increase of the corn now yielded me so much, that I had of the barley about twenty bushels, and of the rice as much, or more, insomuch that now I resolved to begin to use it freely; for my bread had been quite gone a great while; also,

I resolved to see what quantity would be sufficient for me a whole year, and to sow but once a year.

Upon the whole, I found that the forty bushels of barley and rice was much more than I could consume in a year; so I resolved to sow just the same quantity every year that I sowed the last, in hopes that such a quantity would fully provide me with bread, etc.

CHAPTER IX

THE BOAT

ALL the while these things were doing, you may be sure my thoughts run many times upon the prospect of land which I had seen from the other side of the island, and I was not without secret wishes that I were on shore there, fancying the seeing the mainland, and in an inhabited country, I might find some way or other to convey myself farther, and perhaps at last find some means of escape.

But all this while I made no allowance for the dangers of such a condition, and how I might fall into the hands of savages, and perhaps such as I might have reason to think far worse than the lions and tigers of Africa; that if I once came into their power, I should run a hazard more than a thousand to one of being killed, and perhaps of being eaten; for I had heard that the people of the Caribbean coasts were cannibals, or man-eaters, and I knew by the latitude that I could not be far off from that shore. That suppose they were not cannibals, yet that they might kill me, as many Europeans who had fallen into their hands had been served, even when they had been ten or twenty together, much more I, that was but one,

and could make little or no defence; all these things,
I say, which I ought to have considered well of, and did
cast up in my thoughts afterwards, yet took up none
of my apprehensions at first, but my head ran mightily
upon the thought of getting over to the shore.

Now I wished for my boy Xury, and the long-boat
with the shoulder-of-mutton sail, with which I sailed
above a thousand miles on the coast of Africa; but
this was in vain. Then I thought I would go and look
at our ship's boat, which, as I have said, was blown
up upon the shore a great way, in the storm, when
we were first cast away. She lay almost where she did
at first, but not quite; and was turned, by the force
of the waves and the winds, almost bottom upward,
against a high ridge of beachy rough sand, but no
water about her, as before.

If I had had hands to have refitted her, and to
have launched her into the water, the boat would have
done well enough, and I might have gone back into
the Brazils with her easily enough; but I might have
foreseen that I could no more turn her and set her
upright upon her bottom, than I could remove the
island. However, I went to the woods, and cut levers
and rollers, and brought them to the boat, resolved to
try what I could do; suggesting to myself that if I
could but turn her down, I might easily repair the
damage she had received, and she would be a very
good boat, and I might go to sea in her very easily.

I spared no pains, indeed, in this piece of fruitless
toil, and spent, I think, three or four weeks about it.
At last, finding it impossible to heave it up with my
little strength, I fell to digging away the sand, to
undermine it, and so to make it fall down, setting
pieces of wood to thrust and guide it right in the

fall. But when I had done this, I was unable to stir
it up again, or to get under it, much less to move it
forward towards the water; so I was forced to give
it over. And yet, though I gave over the hopes of the
boat, my desire to venture over for the main increased,
rather than decreased, as the means for it seemed
impossible.

This at length put me upon thinking whether it
was not possible to make myself a canoe, or *periagua*,
such as the natives of those climates make, even without tools, or, as I might say, without hands, viz., of
the trunk of a great tree. This I not only thought
possible, but easy, and pleased myself extremely with
the thoughts of making it, and with my having much
more convenience for it than any of the negroes or
Indians; but not at all considering the particular
inconveniences which I lay under more than the Indians
did, viz., want of hands to move it, when it was made,
into the water, a difficulty much harder for me to
surmount than all the consequences of want of tools
could be to them. For what was it to me, that when
I had chosen a vast tree in the woods, I might with
much trouble cut it down, if, after I might be able
with my tools to hew and dub the outside into the
proper shape of a boat, and burn or cut out the inside
to make it hollow, so to make a boat of it; if, after
all this, I must leave it just there where I found it,
and was not able to launch it into the water?

One would have thought I could not have had the
least reflection upon my mind of my circumstance
while I was making this boat, but I should have
immediately thought how I should get it into the sea;
but my thoughts were so intent upon my voyage over
the sea in it, that I never once considered how I should

get it off of the land; and it was really, in its own
nature, more easy for me to guide it over forty-five
miles of sea, than about forty-five fathoms of land,
where it lay, to set it afloat in the water.

I went to work upon this boat the most like a fool
that ever man did who had any of his senses awake.
I pleased myself with the design, without determining
whether I was ever able to undertake it. Not but
that the difficulty of launching my boat came often
into my head; but I put a stop to my own inquiries
into it, by this foolish answer which I gave myself,
" Let's first make it; I'll warrant I'll find some way
or other to get it along when 'tis done."

This was a most preposterous method; but the
eagerness of my fancy prevailed, and to work I went.
I felled a cedar tree: I question much whether Solomon
ever had such a one for the building of the Temple at
Jerusalem. It was five feet ten inches diameter at the
lower part next the stump, and four feet eleven inches
diameter at the end of twenty-two feet, after which
it lessened for a while, and then parted into branches.
It was not without infinite labour that I felled this
tree. I was twenty days hacking and hewing at it at
the bottom; I was fourteen more getting the branches
and limbs, and the vast spreading head of it cut off,
which I hacked and hewed through with axe and
hatchet, and inexpressible labour. After this, it cost
me a month to shape it and dub it to a proportion,
and to something like the bottom of a boat, that it
might swim upright as it ought to do. It cost me near
three months more to clear the inside, and work it
so as to make an exact boat of it. This I did, indeed,
without fire, by mere mallet and chisel, and by the
dint of hard labour, till I had brought it to be a very

handsome *periagua*, and big enough to have carried
six and twenty men, and consequently big enough to
have carried me and all my cargo.

When I had gone through this work, I was extremely delighted with it. The boat was really much
bigger than I ever saw a canoe or *periagua*, that was
made of one tree, in my life. Many a weary stroke
it had cost, you may be sure; and there remained
nothing but to get it into the water; and had I gotten
it into the water, I make no question but I should
have begun the maddest voyage, and the most unlikely
to be performed, that ever was undertaken.

But all my devices to get it into the water failed
me, though they cost me infinite labour too. It lay
about one hundred yards from the water, and not
more; but the first inconvenience was, it was uphill
towards the creek. Well, to take away this discourage-
ment, I resolved to dig into the surface of the earth,
and so make a declivity. This I began, and it cost
me a prodigious deal of pains; but who grudges pains,
that have their deliverance in view? But when this
was worked through, and this difficulty managed, it
was still much at one, for I could no more stir the
canoe than I could the other boat.

Then I measured the distance of ground, and resolved to cut a dock or canal, to bring the water up
to the canoe, seeing I could not bring the canoe down
to the water. Well, I began this work; and when I
began to enter into it, and calculate how deep it was
to be dug, how broad, how the stuff to be thrown
out, I found that by the number of hands I had, being
none but my own, it must have been ten or twelve
years before I should have gone through with it; for
the shore lay high, so that at the upper end it must

have been at least twenty feet deep; so at length, though with great reluctancy, I gave this attempt over also.

This grieved me heartily; and now I saw, though too late, the folly of beginning a work before we count the cost, and before we judge rightly of our own strength to go through with it.

In the middle of this work I finished my fourth year in this place, and kept my anniversary with the same devotion, and with as much comfort as ever before; for, by constant study and serious application of the Word of God, and by the assistance of His grace, I gained a different knowledge from what I had before. I entertained different notions of things. I looked now upon the world as a thing remote, which I had nothing to do with, no expectation from, and, indeed, no desires about. In a word, I had nothing indeed to do with it, nor was ever like to have; so I thought it looked, as we may perhaps look upon it hereafter, viz., as a place I had lived in, but was come out of it; and well might I say, as father Abraham to Dives, " Between me and thee is a great gulf fixed."

I had now brought my state of life to be much easier in itself than it was at first, and much easier to my mind, as well as to my body. I frequently sat down to my meat with thankfulness, and admired the hand of God's providence, which had thus spread my table in the wilderness. I learned to look more upon the bright side of my condition, and less upon the dark side, and to consider what I enjoyed, rather than what I wanted; and this gave me sometimes such secret comforts, that I cannot express them; and which I take notice of here, to put those discontented people in mind of it, who cannot enjoy comfortably

D

what God has given them, because they see and covet
something that He has not given them. All our dis-
contents about what we want, appeared to me to spring
from the want of thankfulness for what we have.

I spent whole hours, I may say whole days, in re-
presenting to myself, in the most lively colours, how
I must have acted if I had got nothing out of the
ship. How I could not have so much as got any food,
except fish and turtles; and that as it was long before
I found any of them, I must have perished first; that
I should have lived, if I had not perished, like a mere
savage; that if I had killed a goat or a fowl, by any
contrivance, I had no way to flay or open them, or
part the flesh from the skin and the bowels, or to cut
it up; but must gnaw it with my teeth, and pull it
with my claws, like a beast.

These reflections made me very sensible of the goodness of Providence to me, and very thankful for my
present condition, with all its hardships and misfortunes.

In a word, as my life was a life of sorrow one way,
so it was a life of mercy another; and I wanted
nothing to make it a life of comfort, but to be able
to make my sense of God's goodness to me, and care
over me in this condition, be my daily consolation;
and after I did make a just improvement of these
things, I went away, and was no more sad.

I had not been here so long, that many things which
I brought on shore for my help were either quite gone,
or very much wasted, and near spent. My ink, as I
observed, had been gone for some time, all but a very
little, which I eked out with water, a little and a little,
till it was so pale it scarce left any appearance of black
upon the paper. As long as it lasted, I made use of

it to minute down the days of the month on which any remarkable thing happened to me. And, first, by casting up times past, I remember that there was a strange concurrence of days in the various providences which befell me, and which, if I had been superstitiously inclined to observe days as fatal or fortunate, I might have had reason to have looked upon with a great deal of curiosity.

First, I had observed that the same day that I broke away from my father and my friends, and ran away to Hull, in order to go to sea, the same day afterwards I was taken by the Sallee man-of-war, and made a slave.

The same day of the year that I escaped out of the wreck of that ship in Yarmouth Roads, that same day-year afterwards I made my escape from Sallee in the boat.

The same day of the year I was born on, viz., the 30th of September, that same day I had my life so miraculously saved twenty-six years after, when I was cast on shore in this island; so that my wicked life and my solitary life began both on a day.

The next thing to my ink's being wasted, was that of my bread; I mean the biscuit, which I brought out of the ship. This I had husbanded to the last degree, allowing myself but one cake of bread a day for above a year; and yet I was quite without bread for near a year before I got any corn of my own; and great reason I had to be thankful that I had any at all, the getting it being, as has been already observed, next to miraculous.

My clothes began to decay, too, mightily. As to linen, I had none a good while, except some chequered shirts which I found in the chests of the other seamen, and which I carefully preserved, because many times I could bear no other clothes on but a shirt; and it was a very great help to me that I had, among all the men's clothes of the ship, almost three dozen of shirts. There were also several thick watch-coats of the seamen's which were left indeed, but they were too hot to wear; and though it is true that the weather was so violent hot that there was no need of clothes, yet I could not go quite naked, no, though I had been inclined to it, which I was not, though I was all alone.

The reason why I could not go quite naked was, I could not bear the heat of the sun so well when quite naked as with some clothes on; nay, the very heat frequently blistered my skin; whereas, with a shirt on, the air itself made some motion, and whistling under that shirt, was two-fold cooler than without it. No more could I ever bring myself to go out in the heat of the sun without a cap or a hat. The heat of the sun beating with such violence, as it does in that place, would give me the headache presently, by darting so directly on my head, without a cap or hat on, so that I could not bear it; whereas, if I put on my hat, it would presently go away.

Upon those views, I began to consider about putting the few rags I had, which I called clothes, into some order. I had worn out all the waistcoats I had, and my business was now to try if I could not make jackets out of the great watch-coats which I had by me, and with such other materials as I had; so I set to work a-tailoring, or rather, indeed, a-botching, for I made most piteous work of it. However, I made shift to make two or three new waistcoats, which I hoped would serve me a great while. As for breeches, or drawers, I made but a very sorry shift indeed till afterward.

I have mentioned that I saved the skins of all the creatures that I killed, I mean four-footed ones, and I had hung them up stretched out with sticks in the sun, by which means some of them were so dry and hard that they were fit for little, but others it seems were very useful. The first thing I made of these was a great cap for my head, with the hair on the outside to shoot off the rain; and this I performed so well, that after this I made me a suit of clothes wholly of these skins, that is to say, a waistcoat, and breeches open at knees, and both loose, for they were rather wanting to keep me cool than to keep me warm. I must not omit to acknowledge that they were wretchedly made; for if I was a bad carpenter, I was a worse tailor. However, they were such as I made very good shift with; and when I was abroad, if it happened to rain, the hair of my waistcoat and cap being outermost, I was kept very dry.

After this I spent a great deal of time and pains to make me an umbrella. I was indeed in great want of one, and had a great mind to make one. I had seen them made in the Brazils, where they are very useful in the great heats, which are there; and I felt the heats every jot as great here, and greater too, being nearer the equinox. Besides, as I was obliged to be much abroad, it was a most useful thing to me, as well for the rains as the heats. I took a world of pains at it, and was a great while before I could make anything likely to hold: nay, after I thought I had hit the way, I spoiled two or three before I made one to my mind; but at last I made one that answered indifferently well. The main difficulty I found was to make it to let down. I could make it to spread; but if it did not let down too, and draw in, it was not portable

for me any way but just over my head, which would
not do. However, at last, as I said, I made one to
answer, and covered it with skins, the hair upwards,
so that it cast off the rains like a pent-house, and
kept off the sun so effectually, that I could walk out
in the hottest of the weather with greater advantage
than I could before in the coolest; and when I had
no need of it, could close it, and carry it under my
arm.

Thus I lived mighty comfortably, my mind being
entirely composed by resigning to the will of God,
and throwing myself wholly upon the disposal of His
providence.

I cannot say that after this, for five years, any
extraordinary thing happened to me; but I lived on
in the same course, in the same posture and place,
just as before. The chief things I was employed in,
besides my yearly labour of planting my barley and
rice, and curing my raisins, of both which I always
kept up just enough to have sufficient stock of one
year's provisions beforehand—I say, besides this yearly
labour, and my daily labour of going out with my gun,
I had one labour, to make me a canoe, which at last
I finished; so that by digging a canal to it of six feet
wide, and four feet deep, I brought it into the creek,
almost half a mile. As for the first, which was so
vastly big, as I made it without considering beforehand, as I ought to do, how I should be able to launch
it; so, never being able to bring it to the water, or
bring the water to it, I was obliged to let it lie where
it was, as a memorandum to teach me to be wiser
next time. Indeed, the next time, though I could not
get a tree proper for it, and in a place where I could
not get the water to it at any less distance than, as

I have said, near half a mile, yet as I saw it was practicable at last, I never gave it over; and though I was near two years about it, yet I never grudged my labour, in hopes of having a boat to go off to sea at last.

However, though my little *periagua* was finished, yet the size of it was not at all answerable to the design which I had in view when I made the first; I mean, of venturing over to the *terra firma*, where it was about forty miles broad. Accordingly, the smallness of my boat assisted to put an end to that design, and now I thought no more of it. But as I had a boat, my next design was to make a tour round the island; for as I had been on the other side in one place, crossing, as I have already described it, over the land, so the discoveries I made in that little journey made me very eager to see other parts of the coast; and now I had a boat, I thought of nothing but sailing round the island.

For this purpose, that I might do everything with discretion and consideration, I fitted up a little mast to my boat, and made a sail to it out of some of the pieces of the ship's sail, which lay in store, and of which I had a great stock by me.

Having fitted my mast and sail, and tried the boat, I found she would sail very well. Then I made little lockers, or boxes, at either end of my boat, to put provisions, necessaries, and ammunition, etc., into, to be kept dry, either from rain or the spray of the sea; and a little long hollow place I cut in the inside of the boat, where I could lay my gun, making a flap to hang down over it to keep it dry.

I fixed my umbrella also in a step at the stern, like a mast, to stand over my head, and keep the heat of the sun off of me, like an awning; and thus I every now and then took a little voyage upon the sea, but never went far out, not far from the little creek. But at last, being eager to view the circumference of my little kingdom, I resolved upon my tour; and accordingly I victualled my ship for the voyage, putting in two dozen of my loaves (cakes I should rather call them) of barley bread, an earthen pot full of parched rice, a food I eat a great deal of, a little bottle of rum, half a goat, and powder and shot for killing more, and two large watch-coats, of those which, as I mentioned before, I had saved out of the seamen's chests; these I took, one to lie upon, and the other to cover me in the night.

It was the 6th of November, in the sixth year of my reign, or my captivity, which you please, that I set out on this voyage, and I found it much longer than I expected; for though the island itself was not very large, yet when I came to the east side of it I found a great ledge of rocks lie out above two leagues into the sea, some above water, some under it, and beyond that a shoal of sand, lying dry half a league more; so that I was obliged to go a great way out to sea to double the point.

When first I discovered them, I was going to give over my enterprise and come back again, not knowing how far it might oblige me to go out to sea, and, above all, doubting how I should get back again, so I came to an anchor; for I had made me a kind of an anchor with a piece of a broken grappling which I got out of the ship.

Having secured my boat, I took my gun and went on shore, climbing up upon a hill, which seemed to overlook that point, where I saw the full extent of it, and resolved to venture.

In my viewing the sea from that hill, where I stood, I perceived a strong, and indeed a most furious current, which run to the east, and even came close to the point; and I took the more notice of it, because I saw there might be some danger that when I came into it I might be carried out to sea by the strength of it, and not be able to make the island again. And indeed, had I not gotten first up upon this hill, I believe it would have been so; for there was the same current on the other side the island, only that it set off at a farther distance; and I saw there was a strong eddy under the shore; so I had nothing to do but to get in out of the first current, and I should presently be in an eddy.

I lay here, however, two days; because the wind, blowing pretty fresh at E.S.E., and that being just contrary to the said current, made a great breach of the sea upon the point; so that it was not safe for me to keep too close to the shore for the breach, nor to go too far off because of the stream.

The third day, in the morning, the wind having abated overnight, the sea was calm, and I ventured. But I am a warning piece again to all rash and ignorant pilots; for no sooner was I come to the point, when even I was not my boat's length from the shore, but I found myself in a great depth of water, and a current like the sluice of a mill. It carried my boat along with it with such violence, that all I could do could not keep her so much as on the edge of it, but I found it hurried me farther and farther out from the eddy, which was on my left hand. There was no wind stirring to help me, and all I could do with my paddlers signified nothing. And now I began to give myself over for lost; for as the current was on both sides the

*D

island, I knew in a few leagues' distance they must join again, and then I was irrecoverably gone. Nor did I see any possibility of avoiding it; so that I had no prospect before me but of perishing; not by the sea, for that was calm enough, but of starving for hunger. I had indeed found a tortoise on the shore, as big almost as I could lift, and had tossed it into the boat; and I had a great jar of fresh water, that is to say, one of my earthen pots; but what was all this to being driven into the vast ocean, where, to be sure, there was no shore, no mainland or island, for a thousand leagues at least.

And now I saw how easy it was for the providence of God to make the most miserable condition mankind could be in worse. Now I looked back upon my desolate solitary island as the most pleasant place in the world, and all the happiness my heart could wish for was to be but there again. However, I worked hard, till indeed my strength was almost exhausted, and kept my boat as much to the northward, that is, towards the side of the current which the eddy lay on, as possibly I could; when about noon, as the sun passed the meridian, I thought I felt a little breeze of wind in my face, springing up from the S.S.E. This cheered my heart a little, and especially when, in about half-an-hour more, it blew a pretty small gentle gale. By this time I was gotten at a frightful distance from the island; and had the least cloud or hazy weather intervened, I had been undone another way too; for I had no compass on board, and should never have known how to have steered towards the island if I had but once lost sight of it. But the weather continuing clear, I applied myself to get up my mast again, and spread my sail, standing away to the north as much as possible, to get out of the current, north-west; and in about an hour came within about a mile of the shore, where, it being smooth water, I soon got to land.

When I was on shore, I fell on my knees, and gave God thanks for my deliverance, resolving to lay aside all thoughts of my deliverance by my boat; and refreshing myself with such things as I had, I brought my boat close to the shore, in a little cove that I had spied under some trees, and laid me down to sleep, being quite spent with the labour and fatigue of the voyage.

I was now at a great loss which way to get home with my boat. I had run so much hazard, and knew too much the case, to think of attempting it by the way I went out; and what might be at the other side (I mean the west side) I knew not, nor had I any mind to run any more ventures. So I only resolved in the morning to make my way westward along the shore, and to see if there was no creek where I might lay up my frigate in safety, so as to have her again if I wanted her. In about three miles, or thereabouts, coasting the shore, I came to a very good inlet or bay, about a mile over, which narrowed till it came to a very little rivulet or brook, where I found a very convenient harbour for my boat, and where she lay as if she had been in a little dock made on purpose for her. Here I put in, and having stowed my boat very safe, I went on shore to look about me, and see where I was.

I soon found I had but a little passed by the place where I had been before, when I travelled on foot to that shore; so taking nothing out of my boat but my gun and my umbrella, for it was exceedingly hot, I began my march. The way was comfortable enough after such a voyage as I had been upon, and I reached my old bower in the evening, where I found everything standing as I left it; for I always kept it in good order, being, as I said before, my country house.

I got over the fence, and laid me down in the shade to rest my limbs, for I was very weary, and fell asleep. But judge you, if you can, that read my story, what a surprise I must be in, when I was waked out of my sleep by a voice calling me by my name several times, " Robin, Robin, Robin Crusoe, poor Robin Crusoe! Where are you, Robin Crusoe? Where are you? Where have you been? "

I was so dead asleep at first, being fatigued with rowing, or paddling, as it is called, the first part of the day, and with walking the latter part, that I did not wake thoroughly; but dozing between sleeping and waking, thought I dreamed that somebody spoke to me. But as the voice continued to repeat " Robin Crusoe, Robin Crusoe," at last I began to wake more perfectly, and was at first dreadfully frighted, and started up in the utmost consternation. But no sooner were my eyes open, but I saw my Poll sitting on the top of the hedge, and immediately knew that it was he that spoke to me; for just in such bemoaning language I had used to talk to him, and teach him; and he had learned it so perfectly, that he would sit upon my finger, and lay his bill close to my face, and cry, " Poor Robin Crusoe! Where are you? Where have you been? How come you here? " and such things as I had taught him.

However, even though I knew it was the parrot, and that indeed it could be nobody else, it was a good while before I could compose myself. First, I was amazed how the creature got thither, and then, how he should just keep about the place, and nowhere else. But as I was well satisfied it could be nobody but honest Poll, I got it over; and holding out my hand, and calling him by his name, Poll, the sociable creature came to me, and sat upon my thumb, as he used to do, and continued talking to me, " Poor Robin Crusoe! and how did I come here? and where had I been? " just as if he had been overjoyed to see me again; and so I carried him home along with me.

I had now had enough of rambling to sea for some time, and had enough to do for many days to sit still, and reflect upon the danger I had been in. I would have been very glad to have had my boat again on my side of the island; but I knew not how it was practicable to get it about. As to the east side of the island, which I had gone round, I knew well enough there was no venturing that way; my very heart would shrink, and my very blood run chill, but to think of it. And as to the other side of the island, I did not know how it might be there; but supposing the current ran with the same force against the shore at the east as it passed by it on the other, I might run the same risk of being driven down the stream, and carried by the island, as I had been before of being carried away from it. So, with these thoughts, I contented myself to be without any boat, though it had been the product of so many months' labour to make it, and of so many more to get it unto the sea.

CHAPTER X

THE DAILY TASK

IN this government of my temper I remained near a year, lived a very sedate, retired life, as you may well suppose; and my thoughts being very much composed as to my condition, and fully comforted in resigning myself to the dispositions of Providence, I thought I lived really very happily in all things, except that of society.

I improved myself in this time in all the mechanic exercises which my necessities put me upon applying myself to, and I believe could, upon occasion, make a very good carpenter, especially considering how few tools I had. Besides this, I arrived at an unexpected perfection in my earthenware, and contrived well enough to make them with a wheel, which I found infinitely easier and better, because I made things round and shapable which before were filthy things indeed to look on. But I think I was never more vain of my own performance, or more joyful for anything I found out, than for my being able to make a tobacco-pipe. And though it was a very ugly clumsy thing when it was done, and only burnt red, like other earthenware, yet as it was hard and firm, and would draw the smoke, I was exceedingly comforted with it; for I had been always used to smoke, and there were pipes in the ship, but I forgot them at first, not knowing that there was tobacco in the island; and afterwards, when I searched the ship again, I could not come at any pipes at all.

In my wicker-ware also I improved much, and made abundance of necessary baskets, as well as my invention showed me; though not very handsome, yet they were such as were very handy and convenient for my laying things up in, or fetching things home in. For example, if I killed a goat abroad, I could hang it up in a tree, flay it, and dress it, and cut it in pieces, and bring it home in a basket; and the like by a turtle; I could cut it up, take out the eggs, and a piece or two of the flesh, which was enough for me, and bring them home in a basket, and leave the rest behind me. Also large deep baskets were my receivers for my corn, which I always rubbed out as soon as it was dry, and cured, and kept it in great baskets.

I began now to perceive my powder abated considerably, and this was a want which it was impossible for me to supply, and I began seriously to consider what I must do when I should have no more powder; that is to say, how I should do to kill any goats. I had, as is observed, in the third year of my being here kept a young kid, and bred her up tame. I could never find in my heart to kill her, till she died at last of mere age.

But being now in the eleventh year of my residence, and, as I have said, my ammunition growing low, I set myself to study some art to trap and snare the goats, to see whether I could not catch some of them alive.

To this purpose, I made snares to hamper them, and I do believe they were more than once taken in them; but my tackle was not good, for I had no wire, and I always found them broken, and my bait devoured. At length I resolved to try a pitfall; so I dug several large pits in the earth, in places where I had observed the goats used to feed, and over these pits I placed hurdles, of my own making too, with a great weight upon them; and several times I put ears of barley and dry rice, without setting the trap, and I could easily perceive that the goats had gone in and eaten up the corn, for I could see the mark of their feet. At length I set three traps in one night, and going the next morning, I found them all standing, and yet the bait eaten and gone; this was very discouraging. However, I altered my trap; and, not to trouble you with particulars, going one morning to see my trap, I found in one of them a large old he-goat, and in one of the other three kids.

As to the old one, I knew not what to do with him, he was so fierce I durst not go into the pit to him; that is to say, to go about to bring him away alive, which is was what I wanted. So I even let him out, and he ran away, as if he had been frighted out of his wits. But I had forgot then what I learned afterwards, that hunger will tame a lion. If I had let him stay there three or four days without food, and then have carried him some water to drink, and then a little corn, he would have been as tame as one of the kids, for they are mighty sagacious, tractable creatures where they are well used.

However, for the present I let him go, knowing no better at that time. Then I went to the three kids, and taking them one by one, I tied them with strings together, and with some difficulty brought them all home.

It was a good while before they would feed, but throwing them some sweet corn, it tempted them, and they began to be tame. And now I found that if I expected to supply myself with goat-flesh when I had no powder or shot left, breeding some up tame was my only way, when perhaps I might have them about my house like a flock of sheep.

But then it presently occurred to me that I must keep the tame from the wild, or else they would always run wild when they grew up; and the only way for this was to have some enclosed piece of ground, well fenced either with hedge or pale, to keep them in so effectually, that those within might not break out, or those without break in.

This was a great undertaking for one pair of hands; yet as I saw there was an absolute necessity of doing it, my first piece of work was to find out a proper piece of ground, viz., where there was likely to be herbage for them to eat, water for them to drink, and cover to keep them from the sun.

For the first beginning, I resolved to enclose a piece of about 150 yards in length, and 100 yards in breadth; which, as it would maintain as many as I should have in any reasonable time, so, as my flock increased, I could add more ground to my enclosure.

This was acting with some prudence, and I went to work with courage. I was about three months hedging in the first piece, and, till I had done it, I tethered the three kids in the best part of it, and used them to feed as near me as possible, to make them familiar; and very often I would go and carry them some ears of barley, or a handful of rice, and feed them out of my hand; so that after my enclosure was finished, and I let them loose, they would follow me up and down, bleating after me for a handful of corn.

This answered my end, and in about a year and half I had a flock of about twelve goats, kids, and all; and in two years more I had three and forty, besides several that I took and killed for my food. And after that I enclosed five several pieces of ground to feed them in, with little pens to drive them into, to take them as I wanted, and gates out of one piece of ground into another.

But this was not all, for now I not only had goat's flesh to feed on when I pleased, but milk too, a thing which, indeed, in my beginning, I did not so much as think of, and which, when it came into my thoughts, was really an agreeable surprise. For now I set up my dairy, and had sometimes a gallon or two of milk in a day; and as Nature, who gives supplies of food to every creature, dictates even naturally how to make use of it, so I, that had never milked a cow, much less a goat, or seen butter or cheese made, very readily and handily, though after a great many essays and miscarriages, made me both butter and cheese at last, and never wanted it afterwards.

It would have made a stoic smile, to have seen me and my little family sit down to dinner. There was my majesty, the prince and lord of the whole island; I had the lives of all my subjects at my absolute command. I could hang, draw, give liberty, and take it away; and no rebels among all my subjects.

Then to see how like a king I dined, too, all alone, attended by my servants. Poll, as if he had been my favourite, was the only person permitted to talk to me. My dog, who was now grown very old and crazy, sat always at my right hand, and two cats, one on one side the table, and one on the other, expecting now and then a bit from my hand, as a mark of special favour.

With this attendance, and in this plentiful manner, I lived; neither could I be said to want anything but society; and of that in some time after this, I was like to have too much.

I was something impatient, as I have observed, to have the use of my boat, though very loth to run any more hazards; and therefore sometimes I sat contriving ways to get her about the island, and at other times I sat myself down contented enough without her. But I had a strange uneasiness in my mind to go down to the point of the island where, as I have said, in my last ramble, I went up the hill to see how the shore lay, and how the current set, that I might see what I had to do. This inclination increased upon me every day, and at length I resolved to travel thither by land, following the edge of the shore. I did so; but had anyone in England been to meet such a man as I was, it must either have frightened them, or raised a great deal of laughter; and as I frequently stood still to look at myself, I could not but smile at the notion of my travelling through Yorkshire, with such an equipage, and in such a dress. Be pleased to take a sketch of my figure, as follows.

I had a great high shapeless cap, made of a goat's skin, with a flap hanging down behind, as well to keep the sun from me, as to shoot the rain off from running into my neck; nothing being so hurtful in these climates as the rain upon the flesh, under the clothes. I had a short jacket of goat-skin, the skirts coming down to about the middle of my thighs; and a pair of open-kneed breeches of the same. The breeches were made of the skin of an old he-goat, whose hair hung down such a length on either side, that, like pantaloons, it reached to the middle of my legs. Stockings and shoes I had none, but had made me a pair of somethings, I scarce know what to call them, like buskins, to flap over my legs, and lace on either side like spatterdashes; but of a most barbarous shape, as indeed were all the rest of my clothes.

I had on a broad belt of goat's skin dried which

I drew together with two thongs of the same, instead of buckles; and in a kind of a frog on either side of this, instead of a sword and a dagger, hung a little saw and a hatchet, one on one side, one on the other. I had another belt, not so broad, and fastened in the same manner, which hung over my shoulder; and at the end of it, under my left arm, hung two pouches, both made of goat's skin too; in one of which hung my powder, in the other my shot. At my back I carried my basket, on my shoulder my gun, and over my head a great clumsy ugly goat-skin umbrella, but which, after all, was the most necessary thing I had about me, next to my gun. As for my face, the colour of it was really not so mulatto-like as one might expect from a man not at all careful of it, and living within nineteen degrees of the equinox. My beard I had once suffered to grow till it was about a quarter of a yard long; but as I had both scissors and razors sufficient, I had cut it pretty short, except what grew on my upper lip, which I had trimmed into a large pair of Mahometan whiskers, such as I had seen worn by some Turks whom I saw at Sallee; for the Moors did not wear such, though the Turks did. Of these mustachios or whiskers, I will not say they were long enough to hang my hat upon them, but they were of a length and shape monstrous enough, and such as, in England, would have passed for frightful.

But all this is by-the-bye; for, as to my figure, I had so few to observe me, that it was of no manner of consequence; so I say no more to that part. In this kind of figure I went my new journey, and was out five or six days. I travelled first along the sea-shore, directly to the place where I first brought my boat to an anchor, to get up upon the rocks. And having no boat now to take care of, I went over the land, a nearer way, to the same height that I was upon before; when, looking forward to the point of the rocks which lay out, and which I was obliged to double with my boat, as is said above, I was surprised to see the sea all smooth and quiet, no rippling, no motion, no current, any more there than in other places.

I was at a strange loss to understand this, and resolved to spend some time in the observing it, to see if nothing from the sets of the tide had occasioned it.

My observation convinced me that I had nothing to do but to observe the ebbing and the flowing of the tide, and I might very easily bring my boat about the island again. But when I began to think of putting it in practice, I had such a terror upon my spirits at the remembrance of the danger I had been in, that I could not think of it again with any patience; but, on the contrary, I took up another resolution, which was more safe, though more laborious; and this was that I would build, or rather make me another *periagua* or canoe; and so have one for one side of the island, and one for the other.

You are to understand that now I had, as I may call it, two plantations in the island; one, my little fortification or tent, with the wall about it, under the rock, with the cave behind me, which, by this time, I had enlarged into several apartments or caves, one within another. One of these which was the driest and largest, and had a door out beyond my wall of fortification, that is to say, beyond where my wall joined to the rock, was all filled up with the large earthen pots, of which I have given an account, and with fourteen or fifteen great baskets, which would hold five or six bushels each, where I laid up my stores of provision, especially my corn, some in the ear, cut off short from the straw, and the other rubbed out with my hand.

As for my wall, made, as before, with long stakes or piles, those piles grew all like trees, and were by this time grown so big, and spread so very much, that there was not the least appearance, to any one's view, of any habitation behind them.

Near this dwelling of mine, but a little further within the land, and upon lower ground, lay my two pieces of corn ground, which I kept duly cultivated and sowed, and which duly yielded me their harvest in its season; and whenever I had occasion for more corn, I had more land adjoining as fit as that.

Besides this, I had my country seat, and I had now a tolerable plantation there also; for, first, I had my little bower, as I called it, which I kept in repair; that is to say, I kept the hedge which circled it in constantly fitted up to its usual height, the ladder standing always in the inside. I kept the trees, which at first were no more than my stakes, but were now grown very firm and tall, I kept them always so cut, that they might spread and grow thick and wild, and make the more agreeable shade, which they did effectually to my mind. In the middle of this, I had my tent always standing, being a piece of sail spread over poles, set up for that purpose, and which never wanted any repair or renewing; and under this I had made me a squab or couch, with the skins of the creatures I had killed, and with other soft things, and a blanket laid on them, such as belonged to our sea-bedding, which I had saved, and a great watch-coat to cover me; and here, whenever I had occasion to be absent from my chief seat, I took up my country habitation.

Adjoining to this I had my enclosures for my cattle, that is to say, my goats. And as I had taken an inconceivable deal of pains to fence and enclose this ground, so I was so uneasy to see it kept entire, lest the goats should break through, that I never left off till, with infinite labour, I had stuck the outside of the hedge so full of small stakes, and so near to one another, that it was rather a pale than a hedge, and there was scarce room to put a hand through between them; which afterwards, when those stakes grew, as they all did in the next rainy season, made the enclosure strong like a wall, indeed, stronger than any wall.

This will testify for me that I was not idle, and that I spared no pains to bring to pass whatever appeared necessary for my comfortable support; for I considered the keeping up a breed of tame creatures thus at my hand would be a living magazine of flesh, milk, butter, and cheese for me as long as I lived in the place, if it were to be forty years; and that keeping them in my reach depended entirely upon my perfecting my enclosures to such a degree, that I might be sure of keeping them together, which, by this method, indeed, I so effectually secured, that when these little stakes began to grow, I had planted them so very thick, I was forced to pull some of them up again.

In this place also I had my grapes growing, which I principally depended on for my winter store of raisins, and which I never failed to preserve carefully, as the best and most agreeable dainty of my whole diet. And indeed they were not agreeable only, but physical, wholesome, nourishing, and refreshing to the last degree.

As this was also about half-way between my other habitation and the place where I had laid up my

boat, I generally stayed and lay here in my way
thither; for I used frequently to visit my boat, and
I kept all things about, or belonging to her, in very
good order. Sometimes I went out in her to divert
myself, but no more hazardous voyages would I go,
not scarce ever above a stone's cast or two from the
shore, I was so apprehensive of being hurried out of
my knowledge again by the currents or winds, or any
other accident. But now I come to a new scene of
my life.

CHAPTER XI

THE FOOTPRINT

It happened one day, about noon, going towards
my boat, I was exceedingly surprised with the print
of a man's naked foot on the shore, which was very
plain to be seen in the sand. I stood like one thunder-
struck, or as if I had seen an apparition. I listened,
I looked round me, I could hear nothing, nor see
anything. I went up to a rising ground, to look farther.
I went up the shore, and down the shore, but it was
all one; I could see no other impression but that one.
I went to it again to see if there were any more, and
to observe if it might not be my fancy; but there
was no room for that, for there was exactly the very
print of a foot—toes, heel, and every part of a foot.
How it came thither I knew not, nor could in the least
imagine. But after innumerable fluttering thoughts,
like a man perfectly confused and out of myself, I
came home to my fortification, not feeling, as we say,
the ground I went on, but terrified to the last degree,
looking behind me at every two or three steps,

mistaking every bush and tree, and fancying every stump at a distance to be a man; nor is it possible to describe how many various shapes affrighted imagination represented things to me in, how many wild ideas were found every moment in my fancy, and what strange unaccountable whimsies came into my thoughts, by the way.

When I came to my castle, for so I think I called it ever after this, I fled into it like one pursued. Whether I went over by the ladder, as first contrived, or went in at the hole in the rock, which I called a door, I cannot remember; no, nor could I remember the next morning, for never frighted hare fled to cover, or fox to earth, with more terror of mind than I to this retreat.

I slept none that night. The farther I was from the occasion of my fright, the greater my apprehensions were; which is something contrary to the nature of such things, and especially to the usual practice of all creatures in fear. But I was so embarrassed with my own frightful ideas of the thing, that I formed nothing but dismal imaginations to myself, even though I was now a great way off it. Sometimes I fancied it must be the devil, and reason joined in with me upon this supposition; for how should any other thing in human shape come into the place? Where was the vessel that brought them? What marks was there of any other footsteps? And how was it possible a man should come there? But then to think that Satan should take human shape upon him in such a place, where there could be no manner of occasion for it, but to leave the print of his foot behind him, and that even for no purpose too, for he could not be sure I should see it; this was an amusement the other way.

I considered that the devil might have found out abundance of other ways to have terrified me than this of the single print of a foot; that as I live quite on the other side of the island, he would never have been so simple to leave a mark in a place where it was ten thousand to one whether I should ever see it or not, and in the sand too, which the first surge of the sea, upon a high wind, would have defaced entirely. All this seemed inconsistent with the thing itself, and with all the notions we usually entertain of the subtilty of the devil.

Abundance of such things as these assisted to argue me out of all apprehensions of its being the devil; and I presently concluded then, that it must be some more dangerous creature, viz., that it must be some of the savages of the mainland over against me, who had wandered out to sea in their canoes, and, either driven by the currents or by contrary winds, had made the island, and had been on shore, but were gone away again to sea, being as loth, perhaps, to have stayed in this desolate island as I would have been to have had them.

While these reflections were rolling upon my mind, I was very thankful in my thoughts that I was so happy as not to be thereabouts at that time, or that they did not see my boat, by which they would have concluded that some inhabitants had been in the place, and perhaps have searched farther for me. Then terrible thoughts racked my imagination about their having found my boat, and that there were people here; and that if so, I should certainly have them come in greater numbers, and devour me; that if it should happen so that they should not find me, yet they would find my enclosure, destroy all my corn, carry away all my flock of tame goats, and I should perish at last for mere want.

Thus my fear banished all my religious hope. All that former confidence in God, which was founded upon such wonderful experience as I had had of His goodness, now vanished, as if He that had fed me by miracle hitherto could not preserve, by His power, the provision which He had made for me by His goodness. I reproached myself with my easiness, that would not sow any more corn one year than would just serve me till the next season, as if no accident could intervene to prevent my enjoying the crop that was upon the ground. And this I thought so just a reproof, that I resolved for the future to have two or three years' corn beforehand, so that, whatever might come, I might not perish for want of bread.

I then reflected that God, who was not only righteous, but omnipotent, as He had thought fit thus to punish and afflict me, so He was able to deliver me; that if He did not think fit to do it, 'twas my unquestioned duty to resign myself absolutely and entirely to His will; and, on the other hand, it was my duty also to hope in Him, pray to Him, and quietly to attend the dictates and directions of His daily providence.

These thoughts took me up many hours, days, nay, I may say, weeks and months; and one particular effect of my cogitations on this occasion I cannot omit, viz., one morning early, lying in my bed, and filled with thought about my danger from the appearance of savages, I found it discomposed me very much; upon which those words of the Scripture came into my thoughts, " Call upon Me in the day of trouble, and I will deliver, and thou shalt glorify Me."

In the middle of these cogitations, apprehensions, and reflections, it came into my thought one day, that all this might be a mere chimera of my own; and that this foot might be the print of my own foot, when I came on shore from my boat. This cheered me up a little too, and I began to persuade myself it was all a delusion, that it was nothing else but my own foot; and why might not I come that way from the boat, as well as I was going that way to the boat? Again, I considered also, that I could by no means tell, for certain, where I had trod, and where I had not; and that if, at last, this was only the print of my own foot, I had played the part of those fools who strive to make stories of spectres and apparitions, and then are frighted at them more than anybody.

Now I began to take courage, and to peep abroad again, for I had not stirred out of my castle for three days and nights, so that I began to starve for provision; for I had little or nothing within doors but some barley-cakes and water. Then I knew that my goats wanted to be milked too, which usually was my evening diversion; and the poor creatures were in great pain and inconvenience for want of it; and, indeed, it almost spoiled some of them, and almost dried up their milk.

Heartening myself, therefore, with the belief that this was nothing but the print of one of my own feet, and so I might be truly said to start at my own shadow, I began to go abroad again, and went to my country house to milk my flock. But to see with what fear I went forward, how often I looked behind me, how I was ready, every now and then, to lay down my basket, and run for my life, it would have made any one have thought I was haunted with an evil conscience, or that I had been lately most terribly frighted; and so, indeed, I had.

However, as I went down thus two or three days, and having seen nothing, I began to be a little bolder, and to think there was really nothing in it but my own imagination. But I could not persuade myself fully of this till I should go down to the shore again, and see this print of a foot, and measure it by my own, and see if there was any similitude or fitness, that I might be assured it was my own foot. But when I came to the place, first, it appeared evidently to me, that when I laid up my boat, I could not possibly be on shore anywhere thereabout; secondly, when I came to measure the mark with my own foot, I found my foot not so large by a great deal. Both these things filled my head with new imaginations, and gave me the vapours again to the highest degree; so that I shook with cold, like one in an ague; and I went home again, filled with the belief that some man or men had been on shore there; or, in short, that the island was inhabited, and I might be surprised before I was aware. And what course to take for my security, I knew not.

The confusion of my thoughts kept me waking all night, but in the morning I fell asleep; and having, by the amusement of my mind, been, as it were, tired, and my spirits exhausted, I slept very soundly, and waked much better composed than I had ever been before. And now I began to think sedately; and upon the utmost debate with myself, I concluded that this island, which was so exceeding pleasant, fruitful, and no farther from the mainland than as I had seen, was not so entirely abandoned as I might imagine; that although there were no stated inhabitants who lived on the spot, yet that there might sometimes come boats off from the shore, who, either with design, or perhaps never but when they were driven by cross winds, might come to this place; that I had lived here fifteen years now, and had not met with the least shadow or figure of any people yet; and that if at any time they should be driven here, it was probable they went away again as soon as ever they could, seeing they had never thought fit to fix there upon any occasion to this time; that the most I could suggest any danger from, was from any such casual accidental landing of straggling people from the main, who, as it was likely, if they were driven hither, were here against their wills; so they made no stay here, but went off again with all possible speed, seldom staying one night on shore, lest they should not have the help of the tides and daylight back again; and that, therefore, I had nothing to do but to consider of some safe retreat, in case I should see any savages land upon the spot.

Now I began sorely to repent that I had dug my cave so large as to bring a door through again, which door, as I said, came out beyond where my fortification joined to the rock. Upon maturely considering this, therefore, I resolved to draw me a second fortification, in the same manner of a semicircle, at a distance from my wall, just where I had planted a double row of trees about twelve years before, of which I made mention. These trees having been planted so thick before, they wanted but a few piles to be driven between them, that they should be thicker and stronger, and my wall would be soon finished.

So that I had now a double wall; and my outer wall was thickened with pieces of timber, old cables, and everything I could think of, to make it strong, having in it seven little holes, about as big as I might put my arm out at. In the inside of this I thickened my wall to above ten feet thick with continual bringing earth out of my cave, and laying it at the foot of the wall, and walking upon it; and through the seven holes I contrived to plant the muskets, of which I took notice that I got seven on shore out of the ship. These, I say, I planted like my cannon, and fitted them into frames, that held them like a carriage, that so I could fire all the seven guns in two minutes' time. This wall I was many a weary month a-finishing, and yet never thought myself safe till it was done.

When this was done, I stuck all the ground without my wall, for a great way every way, as full with stakes, or sticks, of the osier-like wood, which I found so apt to grow, as they could well stand; insomuch, that I believe I might set in near twenty thousand of them, leaving a pretty large space between them and my wall, that I might have room to see an enemy, and they might have no shelter from the young trees, if they attempted to approach my outer-wall.

Thus in two years' time I had a thick grove; and in five or six years' time I had a wood before my dwelling, growing so monstrous thick and strong, that it was indeed perfectly impassable; and no men, of what kind soever, would ever imagaine that there was any thing beyond it, much less a habitation. As for the way which I proposed to myself to go in and out, for I left no avenue, it was by setting two ladders, one to a part of the rock which was low, and then broke in, and left room to place another ladder upon that; so when the two ladders were taken down, no man living could come down to me without mischieving himself; and if they had come down, they were still on the outside of my outer wall.

Thus I took all the measures human prudence could suggest for my own preservation; and it will be seen, at length, that they were not altogether without just reason; though I foresaw nothing at that time more than my mere fear suggested to me.

While this was doing, I was not altogether careless of my other affairs; for I had a great concern upon me for my little herd of goats. They were not only a present supply to me upon every occasion, and began to be sufficient to me, without the expense of powder and shot, but also without the fatigue of hunting after the wild ones; and I was loth to lose the advantage of them, and to have them all to nurse up over again

To this purpose, after long consideration, I could think of but two ways to preserve them. One was, to find another convenient place to dig a cave under ground, and to drive them into it every night; and the other was, to enclose two or three little bits of land, remote from one another, and as much concealed as I could, where I might keep about half-a-dozen young goats in each place; so that if any disaster happened to the flock in general, I might be able to raise them again with little trouble and time. And this, though it would require a great deal of time and labour, I thought was the most rational design.

Accordingly I spent some time to find out the most retired parts of the island; and I pitched upon one which was as private indeed as my heart could wish for. It was a little damp piece of ground in the middle of the hollow and thick woods, where, as is observed, I almost lost myself once before, endeavouring to come back that way from the eastern part of the island.

Here I found a clear piece of land, near three acres, so surrounded with woods, that it was almost an enclosure by Nature; at least, it did not want near so much labour to make it so as the other pieces of ground I had worked so hard at.

I immediately went to work with this piece of ground, and in less than a month's time I had so fenced it round that my flock, or herd, call it which you please, who were not so wild now as at first they might be supposed to be, were well enough secured in it. So, without any farther delay, I removed ten young she-goats and two he-goats to this piece. And when they were there, I continued to perfect the fence, till I had made it as secure as the other, which, however, I did at more leisure, and it took me up more time by a great deal.

All this labour I was at the expense of, purely from my apprehensions on the account of the print of a man's foot which I had seen; for, as yet, I never saw any human creature come near the island. And I had now lived two years under these uneasinesses, which, indeed, made my life much less comfortable than it was before, as may well be imagined by any who know what it is to live in the constant snare of the fear of man. And this I must observe, with grief too, that the discomposure of my mind had too great impressions also upon the religious part of my thoughts; for the dread and terror of falling into the hands of savages and cannibals lay so upon my spirits, that I seldom found myself in a due temper for application to my Maker, at least not with the sedate calmness and resignation of soul which I was wont to do.

But to go on. After I had thus secured one part of my little living stock, I went about the whole

E

island, searching for another private place to make such another deposit; when, wandering more to the west point of the island than I had ever done yet, and looking out to sea, I thought I saw a boat upon the sea, at a great distance. I had found a prospective glass or two in one of the seamen's chests, which I saved out of our ship, but I had it not about me; and this was so remote, that I could not tell what to make of it, though I looked at it till my eyes were not able to hold to look any longer. Whether it was a boat or not, I do not know; but as I descended from the hill, I could see no more of it, so I gave it over; only I resolved to go no more out without a prospective glass in my pocket.

When I was come down the hill to the end of the island, where, indeed, I had never been before, I was presently convinced that the seeing the print of a man's foot was not such a strange thing in the island as I imagined. And, but that it was a special providence that I was cast upon the side of the island where the savages never came, I should easily have known that nothing was more frequent than for the canoes from the main, when they happened to be a little too far out at sea, to shoot over to that side of the island for harbour; likewise, as they often met and fought in their canoes, the victors having taken any prisoners would bring them over to this shore, where, according to their dreadful customs, being all cannibals, they would kill and eat them; of which hereafter.

When I was come down the hill to the shore, as I said above, being the S.W. point of the island, I was perfectly confounded and amazed; nor is it possible for me to express the horror of my mind at seeing the shore spread with skulls, hands, feet, and other bones of human bodies; and particularly, I observed a place where there had been a fire made, and a circle dug in the earth, like a cockpit, where it is supposed the savage wretches had sat down to their inhuman feastings upon the bodies of their fellow-creatures.

I was so astonished with the sight of these things, that I entertained no notion of any danger to myself from it for a long while. All my apprehensions were buried in the thoughts of such a pitch of inhuman, hellish brutality, and the horror of the degeneracy of human nature, which, though I had heard of often, yet I never had so near a view of before. In short, I turned away my face from the horrid spectacle. I got me up the hill again with all the speed I could, and walked on towards my own habitation.

When I came a little out of that part of the island, I stood still a while, as amazed; and then recovering myself, I looked up with the utmost affection of my soul, and with a flood of tears in my eyes, gave God thanks, that had cast my first lot in a part of the world where I was distinguished from such dreadful creatures as these.

In this frame of thankfulness I went home to my castle, and began to be much easier now, as to the safety of my circumstances, than ever I was before; for I observed that these wretches never came to this island in search of what they could get; perhaps not seeking, not wanting, or not expecting, anything here; and having often, no doubt, been up in the covered, woody part of it, without finding anything to their purpose. I knew I had been here now almost eighteen years, and never saw the least footsteps of human creature there before; and I might be here eighteen more as entirely concealed as I was now, if I did not discover myself to them, which I had no manner of occasion to do; it being my only business to keep myself entirely concealed where I was, unless I found a better sort of creatures than cannibals to make myself known to.

Yet I entertained such an abhorrence of the savage wretches that I have been speaking of, and of the wretched inhuman custom of their devouring and eating one another up, that I continued pensive and sad, and continued close within my own circle for almost two years after this. When I say my own circle, I mean by it my three plantations, viz., my castle, my country seat, which I called my bower, and my enclosure in the woods. Nor did I look after this for any other use than as an enclosure for my goats; for the aversion which Nature gave me to these hellish wretches was such, that I was fearful of seeing them as of seeing the devil himself.

Time, however, and the satisfaction I had that I was in no danger of being discovered by these people, began to wear off my uneasiness about them; and I began to live just in the same composed manner as before; only with this difference, that I used more caution, and kept my eyes more about me, than I did before, lest I should happen to be seen by any of them; and particularly, I was more cautious of firing my gun, lest any of them being on the island should happen to hear of it. And it was, therefore, a very good providence to me that I had furnished myself with a tame breed of goats, that I needed not hunt any more about the woods, or shoot at them. And if I did catch any of them after this, it was by traps and snares, as I had done before; so that for

two years after this I believe I never fired my gun
once off, though I never went out without it; and,
which was more, as I had saved three pistols out of
the ship, I always carried them out with me, or at least
two of them, sticking them in my goat-skin belt. Also
I furbished up one of the great cutlasses that I had
out of the ship, and made me a belt to put it on also;
so that I was now a most formidable fellow to look at
when I went abroad, if you add to the former description of myself the particular of two pistols and a great
broadsword hanging at my side in a belt, but without
a scabbard.

Things going on thus, as I have said, for some time,
I seemed, excepting these cautions, to be reduced to
my former calm, sedate way of living. All these
things tended to showing me, more and more, how far
my condition was from being miserable, compared to
some others; nay, to many other particulars of life,
which it might have pleased God to have made my
lot. It put me upon reflecting how little repining there
would be among mankind at any condition of life, if
people would rather compare their condition with those
that are worse, in order to be thankful, than be always
comparing them with those which are better, to assist
their murmurings and complainings.

CHAPTER XII

FEAR OF SAVAGES

As in my present condition there were not really
many things which I wanted, so indeed I thought that
the frights I had been in about these savage wretches,
and the concern I had been in for my own preservation,

had taken off the edge of my invention for my own conveniences. And I had dropped a good design, which I had once bent my thoughts too much upon; and that was, to try if I could not make some of my barley into malt, and then try to brew myself some beer.

But my invention now run quite another way; for, night and day, I could think of nothing but how I might destroy some of these monsters in their cruel, bloody entertainment, and, if possible, save the victim they should bring hither to destroy. It would take up a larger volume than this whole work is intended to be, to set down all the contrivances I hatched, or rather brooded upon, in my thought, for the destroying these creatures, or at least frighting them so as to prevent their coming hither any more. But all was abortive; nothing could be possible to take effect, unless I was to be there to do it myself. And what could one man do among them, when perhaps there might be twenty or thirty of them together, with their darts, or their bows and arrows, with which they could shoot as true to a mark as I could with my gun?

Sometimes I contrived to dig a hole under the place where they made their fire, and put in five or six pound of gunpowder, which, when they kindled their fire, would consequently take fire, and blow up all that was near it. But as, in the first place, I should be very loth to waste so much powder upon them, my store being now within the quantity of one barrel, so neither could I be sure of its going off at any certain time, when it might surprise them; and, at best, that it would do little more than just blow the fire about their ears, and fright them, but not sufficient to make them forsake the place. So I laid it aside, and then proposed that I would place myself in ambush in some convenient place, with my three guns all double-loaded, and, in the middle of their bloody ceremony, let fly at them, when I should be sure to kill or wound perhaps two or three at every shot; and then falling in upon them with my three pistols and my sword, I made no doubt but that if there was twenty I should kill them all. This fancy pleased my thoughts for some weeks; and I was so full of it, that I often dreamed of it, and sometimes that I was just going to let fly at them in my sleep.

I went so far with it in my imagination, that I employed myself several days to find out proper places to put myself in ambuscade, as I said, to watch for them; and I went frequently to the place itself, which was now grown more familiar to me; and especially while my mind was thus filled with thoughts of revenge, and of a bloody putting twenty or thirty of them to the sword, as I may call it, the horror I had at the place, and at the signals of the barbarous wretches devouring one another, abated my malice.

Well, at length I found a place in the side of the hill, where I was satisfied I might securely wait till I saw any of their boats coming; and might then, even before they would be ready to come on shore, convey myself, unseen, into thickets of trees, in one of which there was a hollow large enough to conceal me entirely; and where I might sit and observe all their bloody doings, and take my full aim at their heads, when they were so close together, as that it would be next to impossible that I should miss my shot, or that I could fail wounding three or four of them at the first shot.

In this place, then, I resolved to fix my design; and,

accordingly, I prepared two muskets and my ordinary fowling-piece. The two muskets I loaded with a brace of slugs each, and four or five smaller bullets, about the size of pistol-bullets; and the fowling-piece I loaded with near a handful of swan-shot, of the largest size. I also loaded my pistols with about four bullets each; and in this posture, well provided with ammunition for a second or third charge, I prepared myself for my expedition.

After I had thus laid the scheme of my design, and in my imagination put it in practice, I continually made my tour every morning up to the top of the hill, which was from my castle, as I called it, about three miles, or more, to see if I could observe any boats upon the sea coming near the island, or standing over towards it. But I began to tire of this hard duty, after I had, for two or three months, constantly kept my watch, but came always back without any discovery; there having not, in all that time, been the least appearance, not only on or near the shore, but not on the whole ocean, so far as my eyes or glasses could reach every way.

As long as I kept up my daily tour to the hill to look out, so long also I kept up the vigour of my design, and my spirits seemed to be all the while in a suitable form for so outrageous an execution as the killing twenty or thirty naked savages for an offence which I had not at all entered into a discussion of in my thoughts, any farther than my passions were at first fired by the horror I conceived at the unnatural custom of that people of the country.

But when I had considered a little, it followed necessarily that I was certainly in the wrong in it; that these people were not murderers in the sense that I had before condemned them in my thoughts, any more than those Christians were murderers who often put to death the prisoners taken in battle; or more frequently, upon many occasions, put whole troops of men to the sword, without giving quarter, though they threw down their arms and submitted.

In the next place it occurred to me, that albeit the usage they thus gave one another was thus brutish and inhuman, yet it was really nothing to me; these people had done me no injury. That if they attempted me, or I saw it necessary for my immediate preservation to fall upon them, something might be said for it; but that as I was yet out of their power, and they had really no knowledge of me, and consequently no design upon me, and therefore it could not be just for me to fall upon them.

These considerations really put me to a pause, and to a kind of a full stop; and I begun, by little and little, to be off of my design, and to conclude, I had taken wrong measures in my resolutions to attack the savages; that it was not my business to meddle with them, unless they first attacked me; and this it was my business, if possible, to prevent; but that if I were discovered and attacked, then I knew my duty.

On the other hand, I argued with myself that this really was the way not to deliver myself, but entirely to ruin and destroy myself; for unless I was sure to kill every one that not only should be on shore at that time, but that should ever come on shore afterwards, if but one of them escaped to tell their country people what had happened, they would come over again by thousands to revenge the death of their fellows, and I should only bring upon myself a certain destruction, which, at present, I had no manner of occasion for.

*E

Upon the whole, I concluded that neither in principles nor in policy I ought, one way or other, to concern myself in this affair. That my business was, by all possible means, to conceal myself from them, and not to leave the least signal to them to guess by, that there were any living creatures upon the island; I mean of human shape.

Religion joined in with this prudential, and I was convinced now, many ways, that I was perfectly out of my duty when I was laying all my bloody schemes for the destruction of innocent creatures; I mean innocent as to me. As to the crimes they were guilty of towards one another, I had nothing to do with them. They were national, and I ought to leave them to the justice of God, who is the Governor of nations, and knows how, by national punishments, to make a just retribution for national offences, and to bring public judgments upon those who offend in a public manner by such ways as best please Him.

In this disposition I continued for near a year after this; and so far was I from desiring an occasion for falling upon these wretches, that in all that time I never once went up the hill to see whether there were any of them in sight, or to know whether any of them had been on shore there or not, that I might not be tempted to renew any of my contrivances against them, or be provoked, by any advantage which might present itself, to fall upon them. Only this I did, I went and removed my boat, which I had on the other side the island, and carried it down to the east end of the whole island, where I ran it into a little cove, which I found under some high rocks and where I knew, by reason of the currents, the savages durst not, at least would not come, with their boats, upon any account whatsoever.

With my boat I carried away everything that I had left there belonging to her, though not necessary for the bare going thither, viz., a mast and sail which I had made for her and a thing like an anchor, but indeed which could not be called either anchor or grappling; however, it was the best I could make of its kind. All these I removed, that there might not be the least shadow of any discovery, or any appearance of any boat, or of any human habitation, upon the island.

Besides this, I kept myself, as I said, more retired than ever, and seldom went from my cell, other than upon my constant employment, viz., to milk my she-goats, and manage my little flock in the wood, which, as it was quite on the other part of the island, was quite out of danger; for certain it is, that these savage people, who sometimes haunted this island, never came with any thoughts of finding anything here, and consequently never wandered off from the coast; and I doubt not but they might have been several times on shore after my apprehensions of them had made me cautious, as well as before; and indeed, I looked back with some horror upon the thoughts of what my condition would have been if I had chopped upon them and been discovered before that, when, naked and unarmed, except with one gun, and that loaded often only with small shot, I walked everywhere, peeping and peeping about the island to see what I could get. What a surprise should I have been in if, when I discovered the print of a man's foot, I had, instead of that, seen fifteen or twenty savages and found them pursuing me, and by the swiftness of their running, no possibility of my escaping them!

I believe the reader of this will not think it strange if

I confess that these anxieties, these constant dangers I
lived in, and the concern that was now upon me, put
an end to all invention, and to all the contrivances
that I had laid for my future accommodations and
conveniences. I had the care of my safety more now
upon my hands than that of my food. I cared not to
drive a nail, or chop a stick of wood now, for fear the
noise I should make should be heard; much less would
I fire a gun, for the same reason; and, above all, I was
intolerably uneasy at making any fire, lest the smoke,
which is visible at a great distance in the day, should
betray me; and for this reason I removed that part
of my business which required fire, such as burning
of pots and pipes, etc., into my new apartment in the
woods; where, after I had been some time, I found,
to my unspeakable consolation, a mere natural cave
in the earth, which went in a vast way, and where,
I dare say, no savage, had he been at the mouth of
it, would be so hardy as to venture in; nor, indeed,
would any man else, but one who, like me, wanted
nothing so much as a safe retreat.

The mouth of this hollow was at the bottom of a
great rock, where, by mere accident I would say (if
I did not see abundant reason to ascribe all such
things now to Providence), I was cutting down some
thick branches of trees to make charcoal; and before
I go on, I must observe the reason of my making this
charcoal, which was thus.

I was afraid of making a smoke about my habitation,
as I said before; and yet I could not live there without
baking my bread, cooking my meat, etc. So I contrived to burn some wood here, as I had seen done in
England under turf, till it became chark, or dry coal;
and then putting the fire out, I preserved the coal to

carry home, and perform the other services which fire was wanting for at home, without danger of smoke.

But this is by-the-bye. While I was cutting down some wood here, I perceived that behind a very thick branch of low brushwood, or underwood, there was a kind of hollow place. I was curious to look into it; and getting with difficulty into the mouth of it, I found it was pretty large; that is to say, sufficient for me to stand upright in it, and perhaps another with me. But I must confess to you I made more haste out than I did in when, looking farther into the place, and which was perfectly dark, I saw two broad shining eyes of some creature, whether devil or man I knew not, which twinkled like two stars, the dim light from the cave's mouth shining directly in, and making the reflection.

But plucking up my spirits as well as I could, and encouraging myself a little with considering that the power and presence of God was everywhere, and was able to protect me, upon this I stepped forward again, and by the light of a firebrand, holding it up a little over my head, I saw lying on the ground a most monstrous, frightful, old he-goat, just making his will, as we say, and gasping for life; and dying indeed, of mere old age.

I stirred him a little to see if I could get him out, and he essayed to get up, but was not able to raise himself; and I thought with myself he might even lie there; for if he had frighted me so, he would certainly fright any of the savages, if any of them should be so hardy as to come in there while he had any life in him.

I was now recovered from my surprise, and began to look round me when I found the cave was but very small; that is to say, it might be about twelve feet over, but in no manner of shape, either round or square, no hands having ever been employed in making it but for those of mere Nature. I observed also that there was a place at the farther side of it that went in farther, but was so low, that it required me to creep upon my hands and knees to go into it, and whither I went I knew not; so having a candle, I gave it over for some time, but resolved to come again the next day, provided with candles and a tinder-box, which I had made of the lock of one of the muskets, with some wild-fire in the pan.

Accordingly the next day I came provided with six large candles of my own making, for I made very good candles now of goat's tallow; and going into this low place, I was obliged to creep upon all fours, as I have said, almost ten yards; which, by the way, I thought was a venture bold enough, considering that I knew not how far it might go, nor what was beyond it. When I was got through the straight, I found the roof rose higher up, I believe near twenty feet. But never was such a glorious sight seen in the island, I dare say, as it was, to look round the sides and roof of this vault or cave; the walls reflected a hundred thousand lights to me from my two candles. What it was in the rock, whether diamonds, or any other precious stones, or gold, which I rather supposed it to be, I knew not.

The place I was in was a most delightful cavity or grotto of its kind, as could be expected, though perfectly dark. The floor was dry and level, and had a sort of small loose gravel upon it, so that there was no nauseous or venomous creature to be seen; neither was there any damp or wet on the sides or roof. The only difficulty in it was the entrance, which, however, as it was a place of security, and such a retreat as I wanted, I thought that was a convenience; so that I was really rejoiced at the discovery, and resolved, without any delay, to bring some of those things which I was most anxious about to this place; particularly, I resolved to bring hither my magazine of powder, and all my spare arms, viz., two fowling-pieces, for I had three in all, and three muskets, for of them I had eight in all. So I kept at my castle only five, which stood ready-mounted, like pieces of cannon, on my outmost fence; and were ready also to take out upon any expedition.

Upon this occasion of removing my ammunition, I took occasion to open the barrel of powder, which I took out of the sea, and which had been wet; and I found that the water had penetrated about three or four inches into the powder on every side, which caking, and growing hard, had preserved the inside like a kernel in a shell; so that I had near sixty pounds of very good powder in the centre of the cask. And this was an agreeable discovery to me at that time; so I carried all away thither, never keeping above two or three pounds of powder with me in my castle, for fear of a surprise of any kind. I also carried thither all the lead I had left for bullets.

I fancied myself now like one of the ancient giants, which were said to live in caves and holes in the rocks, where none could come at them; for I persuaded myself, while I was here, if five hundred savages were to hunt me, they could never find me out; or, if they did, they would not venture to attack me here.

The old goat, whom I found expiring, died in the

mouth of the cave the next day after I made this
discovery; and I found it much easier to dig a great
hole there, and throw him in and cover him with
earth, than to drag him out.

CHAPTER XIII

THE WRECK

I WAS now in my twenty-third year of residence in
this island; and was so naturalised to the place, and
to the manner of living, that could I have but enjoyed
the certainty that no savages would come to the
place to disturb me, I could have been content to have
capitulated for spending the rest of my time there,
even to the last moment, till I had laid me down and
died, like the old goat in the cave. I had also arrived
to some little diversions and amusements, which made
the time pass more pleasantly with me a great deal
than it did before. As, first, I had taught my Poll,
as I noted before, to speak; and he did it so familiarly,
and talked so articulately and plain, that it was very
pleasant to me; and he lived with me no less than
six and twenty years. How long he might live afterwards I know not, though I know they have a notion
in the Brazils that they live a hundred years. Perhaps
poor Poll may be alive there still, calling after poor
Robin Crusoe to this day. I wish no Englishman the
ill luck to come there and hear him; but if he did,
he would certainly believe it was the devil. My dog
was a very pleasant and loving companion to me for
no less than sixteen years of my time, and then died
of mere old age. As for my cats, they multiplied, as

I have observed, to that degree, that I was obliged to shoot several of them at first to keep them from devouring me and all I had; but at length, when the two old ones I brought with me were gone, and after some time continually driving them from me, and letting them have no provision with me, they all ran wild into the woods, except two or three favourites, which I kept tame, and whose young, when they had any, I always drowned; and these were part of my family. Besides these, I always kept two or three household kids about me, whom I taught to feed out of my hand. And I had two more parrots, which talked pretty well, and would all call " Robin Crusoe," but none like my first; nor, indeed, did I take the pains with any of them that I had done with him. I had also several tame sea-fowls, whose names I know not, whom I caught upon the shore, and cut their wings; and the little stakes which I had planted before my castle wall being now grown up to a good thick grove, these fowls all lived among these low trees, and bred there, which was very agreeable to me; so that, as I said above, I began to be very well contented with the life I led, if it might but have been secure from the dread of the savages.

But it was otherwise directed; and it may not be amiss for all people who shall meet with my story, to make this just observation from it, viz., how frequently, in the course of our lives, the evil which in itself we seek most to shun, and which, when we are fallen into it, is the most dreadful to us, is oftentimes the very means or door of our deliverance, by which alone we can be raised again from the affliction we are fallen into. I could give many examples of this in the course of my unaccountable life; but in nothing was it more particularly remarkable, than in the circumstances of my last years of solitary residence in this island.

It was now the month of December, as I said above, in my twenty-third year; and this, being the southern solstice (for winter I cannot call it), was the particular time of my harvest, and required my being pretty much abroad in the fields; when, going out pretty early in the morning, even before it was thorough daylight, I was surprised with seeing a light of some fire upon the shore, at a distance from me of about two miles, towards the end of the island, where I had observed some savages had been, as before. But not on the other side; but, to my great affliction, it was on my side of the island.

I was indeed terribly surprised at the sight, and stopped short within my grove, not daring to go out, lest I might be surprised; and yet I had no more peace within, from the apprehensions I had that if these savages, in rambling over the island, should find my corn standing or cut, or any of my works and improvements, they would immediately conclude that there were people in the place, and would then never give over till they had found me out. In this extremity I went back directly to my castle, pulled up the ladder after me, and made all things without look as wild and natural as I could.

Then I prepared myself within, putting myself in a posture of defence. I loaded all my cannon, as I called them, that is to say, my muskets, which were mounted upon my new fortification, and all my pistols, and resolved to defend myself to the last gasp; not forgetting seriously to commend myself to the Divine protection, and earnestly to pray to God to deliver me out the hands of the barbarians. And in this posture I continued about two hours; but began to be mighty impatient for intelligence abroad, for I had no spies to send out.

After sitting a while longer, and musing what I should do in this case, I was not able to bear sitting in ignorance any longer; so setting up my ladder to the side of the hill where there was a flat place, as I observed before, and then pulling the ladder up after me, I set it up again, and mounted to the top of the hill; and pulling out my perspective-glass, which I had taken on purpose, I laid me down flat on my belly on the ground, and began to look for the place. I presently found there was no less than nine naked savages sitting round a small fire they had made, not to warm them, for they had no need of that, the weather being extreme hot, but, as I supposed, to dress some of their barbarous diet of human flesh which they had brought with them, whether alive or dead, I could not know.

They had two canoes with them, which they had hauled up upon the shore; and as it was then tide of ebb, they seemed to me to wait for the return of the flood to go away again. It is not easy to imagine what confusion this sight put me into, especially seeing them come on my side of the island, and so near me too. But when I observed their coming must be always with the current of the ebb, I began afterwards to be more sedate in my mind, being satisfied that I might go abroad with safety all the time of the tide of flood, if they were not on shore before; and having made this observation, I went abroad about my harvest-work with the more composure.

As I expected, so it proved; for as soon as the tide made to the westward, I saw them all take boat, and

row (or paddle, as we call it) all away. I should have
observed, that for an hour and more before they went
off, they went to dancing; and I could easily discern
their postures and gestures by my glasses.

As soon as I saw them shipped and gone, I took
two guns upon shoulders, and two pistols at my
girdle, and my great sword by my side, without a
scabbard, and with all the speed I was able to make
I went away to the hill where I had discovered the
first appearance of all. And as soon as I got thither,
which was not less than two hours (for I could not go
apace, being so loden with arms as I was), I perceived
there had been three canoes more of savages on that
place; and looking out farther, I saw they were all
at sea together, making over for the main.

This was a dreadful sight to me, especially when,
going down to the shore, I could see the marks of
horror which the dismal work they had been about
had left behind it, viz., the blood, the bones, and
part of the flesh of human bodies, eaten and devoured
by those wretches with merriment and sport. I was
so filled with indignation at the sight, that I began
now to premeditate the destruction of the next that
I saw there, let them be who or how many soever.

However, I wore out a year and three months more
before I ever saw any more of the savages, and then I
found them again, as I shall soon observe. It is true
they might have been there once or twice, but either
they made no stay, or at least I did not hear them;
but in the month of May, as near as I could calculate,
and in my four and twentieth year, I had a very
strange encounter with them; of which in its place.

The perturbation of my mind, during this fifteen or
sixteen months' interval, was very great. I slept

unquiet, dreamed always frightful dreams, and often started out of my sleep in the night. In the day great troubles overwhelmed my mind, and in the night I dreamed often of killing the savages, and of the reasons why I might justify the doing of it. But, to waive all this for a while, it was in the middle of May, on the sixteenth day, I think, as well as my poor wooden calendar would reckon, for I marked all upon the post still; I say, it was the sixteenth of May that it blew a very great storm of wind all day, with a great deal of lightning and thunder, and a very foul night it was after it. I know not what was the particular occasion of it, but as I was reading in the Bible, and taken up with very serious thoughts about my present condition, I was surprised with a noise of a gun, as I thought, fired at sea.

This was, to be sure, a surprise of a quite different nature from any I had met with before; for the notions this put into my thoughts were quite of another kind. I started up in the greatest haste imaginable, and, in a trice, clapped my ladder to the middle place of the rock, and pulled it after me; and mounting it the second time, got to the top of the hill the very moment that a flash of fire bid me listen for a second gun, which accordingly, in about half a minute, I heard; and, by the sound, knew that it was from that part of the sea where I was driven down the current in my boat.

I immediately considered that this must be some ship in distress, and that they had some comrade, or some other ship in company, and fired these guns for signals of distress, and to obtain help. I had this presence of mind, at that minute, as to think that though I could not help them, it may be they might help me; so I brought together all the dry wood I could get at hand, and, making a good handsome pile, I set it on fire upon the hill. The wood was dry, and blazed freely; and though the wind blew very hard, yet it burnt fairly out; so that I was certain, if there was any such thing as a ship, they must needs see it, and no doubt they did; for as soon as ever my fire blazed up I heard another gun, and after that several others, all from the same quarter. I plied my fire all night long till day broke; and when it was broad day, and the air cleared up, I saw something at a great distance at sea, full east of the island, whether a sail or a hull I could not distinguish, no, not with my glasses, the distance was so great, and the weather still something hazy also; at least it was so out at sea.

I looked frequently at it all that day, and soon perceived that it did not move; so I presently concluded that it was a ship at an anchor. And being eager, you may be sure, to be satisfied, I took my gun in my hand and ran toward the south side of the island, to the rocks where I had formerly been carried away with the current; and getting up there, the weather by this time being perfectly clear, I could plainly see, to my great sorrow, the wreck of a ship, cast away in the night upon those concealed rocks which I found when I was out in my boat; and which rocks, as they checked the violence of the stream, and made a kind of counter-stream or eddy, were the occasion of my recovering from the most desperate, hopeless condition that ever I had been in in all my life.

Thus, what is one man's safety is another man's destruction; for it seems these men, whoever they were, being out of their knowledge, and the rocks

being wholly under water, had been driven upon them
in the night, the wind blowing hard at E. and E.N.E.
Had they seen the island, as I must necessarily suppose
they did not, they must, as I thought, have endeavoured to have saved themselves on shore by the help
of their boat; but their firing of guns for help, especially
when they saw, as I imagined, my fire, filled me with
many thoughts. First, I imagined that upon seeing
my light, they might have put themselves into their
boat, and have endeavoured to make the shore; but
that the sea going very high, they might have been
cast away. Other times I imagined that they might
have lost their boat before, as might be the case
many ways; as, particularly, by the breaking of the
sea upon their ship, which many times obliges men
to stave, or take in pieces their boat, and sometimes
to throw it overboard with their own hands. Other
times I imagined they had some other ship or ships
in company, who, upon the signals of distress they
had made, had taken them up and carried them off.
Other whiles I fancied they were all gone off to sea
in their boat, and being hurried away by the current
that I had been formerly in, were carried out into
the great ocean, where there was nothing but misery
and perishing; and that, perhaps, they might by this
time think of starving, and of being in a condition to
eat one another.

As all these were but conjectures at best, so, in the
condition I was in, I could do no more than look on
upon the misery of the poor men, and pity them;
which had still this good effect on my side, that it
gave me more and more cause to give thanks to God,
who had so happily and comfortably provided for
me in my desolate condition: and that of two ships'

companies who were now cast away upon this part of the world, not one life should be spared but mine. I learned here again to observe, that it is very rare that the providence of God casts us into any condition of life so low, or any misery so great, but we may see something or other to be thankful for, and may see others in worse circumstances than our own.

I cannot explain, by any possible energy of words, what a strange longing or hankering of desires I felt in my soul upon this sight, breaking out sometimes thus: " Oh that there had been but one or two, nay, or but one soul, saved out of this ship, to have escaped to me, that I might but have had one companion, one fellow-creature, to have spoken to me, and to have conversed with! " In all the time of my solitary life, I never felt so earnest, so strong a desire after the society of my fellow-creatures, or so deep a regret at the want of it.

But it was not to be. Either their fate or mine, or both, forbid it; for, till the last year of my being on this island, I never knew whether any were saved out of that ship or no; and had only the affliction, some days after, to see the corpse of a drowned boy come on shore at the end of the island which was next the shipwreck. He had on no clothes but a seaman's waistcoat, a pair of open-kneed linen drawers, and a blue linen shirt; but nothing to direct me so much as to guess what nation he was of. He had nothing in his pocket but two pieces of eight and a tobacco-pipe. The last was to me of ten times more value than the first.

It was now calm, and I had a great mind to venture out in my boat to this wreck, not doubting but I might find something on board that might be useful to me. But that did not altogether press me so much as the possibility that there might be yet some living creature on board, whose life I might not only save, but might, by saving that life, comfort my own to the last degree. And this thought clung so to my heart, that I could not be quiet night nor day, but I must venture out in my boat on board this wreck; and committing the rest to God's providence, I thought, the impression was so strong upon my mind that it could not be resisted, that it must come from some invisible direction, and that I should be wanting to myself if I did not go.

Under the power of this impression, I hastened back to my castle, prepared everything for my voyage, took a quantity of bread, a great pot for fresh water, a compass to steer by, a bottle of rum (for I had still a great deal of that left), and a basket full of raisins. And thus, loading myself with everything necessary, I went down to my boat, got the water out of her, and got her afloat, loaded all my cargo in her and then went home again for more. My second cargo was a great bag full of rice, the umbrella to set up over my head for shade, another large pot full of fresh water, and about two dozen of my small loaves, or barley-cakes, more than before, with a bottle of goat's milk and a cheese; all which, with great labour and sweat, I brought to my boat. And praying to God to direct my voyage, I put out; and rowing, or paddling, the canoe along the shore, I came at last to the utmost point of the island on that side, viz., N.E. And now I was to launch out into the ocean, and either to venture or not to venture. I looked on the rapid currents which ran constantly on both sides of the island at a distance, and which were very terrible to me, from the remembrance of the hazard I had been in before, and my heart began to fail me; for I foresaw that if I was driven into either of those currents, I should be carried a vast way out to sea, and perhaps out of my reach, or sight of the island again; and that then, as my boat was but small, if any little gale of wind should rise, I should be inevitably lost.

These thoughts so oppressed my mind, that I began to give over my enterprise; and having hauled my boat into a little creek on the shore, I stepped out, and sate me down upon a little rising bit of ground, very pensive and anxious, between fear and desire, about my voyage; when, as I was musing, I could perceive that the tide was turned, and the flood come on; upon which my going was for so many hours impracticable. Upon this, presently it occurred to me that I should go up to the highest piece of ground I could find and observe, if I could, how the sets of the tide, or currents, lay when the flood came in, that I might judge whether, if I was driven one way out, I might not expect to be driven another way home, with the same rapidness of the currents. This thought was no sooner in my head but I cast my eye upon a little hill, which sufficiently overlooked the sea both ways, and from whence I had a clear view of the currents, or sets of the tide, and which way I was to guide myself in my return. Here I found, that as the current of the ebb set out close by the south point of the island, so the current of the flood set in close by the shore of the north side; and that I had nothing to do but to keep to the north of the island in my return, and I should do well enough.

Encouraged with this observation, I resolved the next morning to set out with the first of the tide, and reposing myself for the night in the canoe, under the great watch-coat I mentioned, I launched out. I made first a little out to sea full north, till I began to feel the benefit of the current which set eastward, and which carried me at a great rate; and yet did not so hurry me as the southern side current had done before, and so as to take from me all government of the boat; but having a strong steerage with my paddle, I went at a great rate directly for the wreck, and in less than two hours I came up to it.

It was a dismal sight to look at. The ship, which, by its building, was Spanish, stuck fast, jammed in between two rocks. All the stern and quarter of her was beaten to pieces with the sea; and as her fore-castle, which stuck in the rocks, had run on with great violence, her mainmast and foremast were brought by the board; that is to say, broken short off; but her bowsprit was sound, and the head and bow appeared firm. When I came close to her a dog appeared upon her, who, seeing me coming, yelped and cried; and as soon as I called him, jumped into the sea to come to me, and I took him into the boat, but found him almost dead for hunger and thirst. I gave him a cake of my bread, and he ate it like a ravenous wolf that had been starving a fortnight in the snow. I then gave the poor creature some fresh water, with which, if I would have let him, he would have burst himself.

After this I went on board; but the first sight I met with was two men drowned in the cook-room, or forecastle of the ship, with their arms fast about one another. I concluded, as is indeed probable, that when the ship struck, it being in a storm, the sea broke so high, and so continually over her, that the men were not able to bear it, and were strangled with the constant rushing in of the water, as much as if they had been under water. Besides the dog, there was nothing left in the ship that had life; nor any goods that I could see, but what were spoiled by the water. There were some casks of liquor, whether wine or brandy I knew not, which lay lower in the hold, and which, the water being ebbed out, I could see; but they were too big to meddle with. I saw several chests, which I believed belonged to some of the seamen; and I got two of them into the boat, without examining what was in them.

Had the stern of the ship been fixed, and the fore-part broken off, I am persuaded I might have made a good voyage; for by what I found in these two chests, I had room to suppose the ship had a great deal of wealth on board; and if I may guess by the course she steered, she must have been bound from the Buenos Ayres, or the Rio de la Plata, in the south part of America, beyond the Brazils, to the Havana, in the Gulf of Mexico, and so perhaps to Spain. She had, no doubt, a great treasure in her, but of no use, at that time, to anybody; and what became of the rest of her people, I then knew not.

I found, besides these chests, a little cask full of liquor, of about twenty gallons, which I got into my boat with much difficulty. There were several muskets in a cabin, and a great powder-horn, with about four pounds of powder in it. As for the muskets, I had no occasion for them, so I left them, but took the powder-horn. I took a fire-shovel and tongs, which I wanted extremely; as also two little brass kettles, a copper pot to make chocolate, and a gridiron. And with this cargo, and the dog, I came away, the tide beginning to make home again; and the same evening, about an hour within night, I reached the island again, weary and fatigued to the last degree.

I reposed that night in the boat; and in the morning I resolved to harbour what I had gotten in my new cave, not to carry it home to my castle. After refreshing myself, I got all my cargo on shore, and began to examine the particulars. The cask of liquor I found to be a kind of rum, but not such as we had at the Brazils, and, in a word, not at all good. But when I came to open the chests, I found several things of great use to me. For example, I found in one a fine case of bottles, of an extraordinary kind, and filled with cordial waters, fine, and very good; the bottles held about three pints each, and were tipped with silver. I found two pots of very good succades, or sweetmeats, so fastened also on top, that the salt water had not hurt them; and two more of the same, which the water had spoiled. I found some very good shirts, which were very welcome to me; and about a dozen and a half of linen white handkerchiefs and coloured neckcloths. The former were also very welcome, being exceeding refreshing to wipe my face in a hot day. Besides this, when I came to the till in the chest, I found there three great bags of pieces of eight, which held about eleven hundred pieces in all; and in one of them, wrapped up in a paper, six doubloons of gold, and some small bars or wedges of gold. I suppose they might all weigh near a pound.

The other chest I found had some clothes in it, but of little value; but by the circumstances, it must have belonged to the gunner's mate; though there was no powder in it, but about two pounds of fine glazed powder, in three small flasks, kept, I suppose, for charging their fowling-pieces, on occasion. Upon the whole, I got very little by this voyage that was of any use to me; for as to the money, I had no manner of occasion for it; 'twas to me as the dirt under my feet; and I would have given it all for three of four pair of English shoes and stockings, which were things I greatly wanted, but had not had on my feet now for many years. I had indeed gotten two pairs of shoes now, which I took off the feet of the two drowned men whom I saw in the wreck, and I found two pair more in one of the chests, which were very welcome to me; but they were not like our English shoes, either for ease or service, being rather what we call pumps than shoes. I found in this seaman's chest about fifty pieces of eight in royals, but no gold. I suppose this belonged to a poorer man than the other, which seemed to belong to some officer.

Well, however, I lugged this money home to my cave, and laid it up, as I had done that before which I brought from our own ship; but it was great pity, as I said, that the other part of this ship had not come to my share, for I am satisfied I might have loaded my canoe several times over with money, which, if I had ever escaped to England, would have lain here safe enough till I might have come again and fetched it.

Having now brought all my things on shore, and secured them, I went back to my boat, and rowed or paddled her along the shore to her old harbour, where I laid her up, and made the best of my way to my old habitation, where I found everything safe and quiet. So I began to repose myself, live after my old fashion, and take care of my family affairs; and, for a while, I lived easy enough, only that I was more vigilant than I used to be, looked out oftener, and did not go abroad so much; and if at any time I did stir

with any freedom, it was always to the east part of
the island, where I was pretty well satisfied the savages
never came, and where I could go without so many
precautions, and such a load of arms and ammunition
as I always carried with me if I went the other way.

I lived in this condition near two years more; but
my unlucky head, that was always to let me know it
was born to make my body miserable, was all this
two years filled with projects and designs, how, if it
were possible, I might get away from this island; for
sometimes I was for making another voyage to the
wreck, though my reasons told me that there was
nothing left there worth the hazard of my voyage;
sometimes for a ramble one way sometimes another;
and I believe verily, if I had had the boat that I went
from Sallee in, I should have ventured to sea, bound
anywhere, I knew not whither.

I have been, in all my circumstances, a memento
to those who are touched with the general plague of
mankind, whence, for aught I know, one-half of their
miseries flow; I mean, that of not being satisfied with
the station wherein God and Nature has placed them.

CHAPTER XIV

MAN FRIDAY

IT was one of the nights in the rainy season in
March, the four and twentieth year of my first setting
foot in this island of solitariness. I was lying in my
bed, or hammock, awake, very well in health, had no
pain, no distemper, no uneasiness of body, no, nor
any uneasiness of mind, more than ordinary, but could

by no means close my eyes, that is, so as to sleep; no, not a wink all night long, otherwise than as follows.

It is as impossible, as needless, to set down the innumerable crowd of thoughts that whirled through that great thoroughfare of the brain, the memory, in this night's time. I ran over the whole history of my life in miniature, or by abridgment, as I may call it, to my coming to this island, and also of the part of my life since I came to this island.

My head was for some time taken up in considering the nature of these wretched creatures, I mean the savages, and how it came to pass in the world that the wise Governor of all things should give up any of His creatures to such inhumanity; nay, to something so much below even brutality itself, as to devour its own kind. But as this ended in some (at that time fruitless) speculations, it occurred to me to inquire what part of the world these wretches lived in? how far off the coast was from whence they came? what they ventured over so far from home for? what kind of boats they had? and why I might not order myself and my business so, that I might be as able to go over thither, as they were to come to me.

I never so much as troubled myself to consider what I should do with myself when I came thither; what would become of me, if I fell into the hands of the savages; or how I should escape from them, if they attempted me; no, nor so much as how it was possible for me to reach the coast, and not be attempted by some or other of them, without any possibility of delivering myself; and if I should not fall into their hands, what I should do for provision, or whither I should bend my course. None of these thoughts, I say, so much as came in my way; but my mind was

wholly bent upon the notion of my passing over in
my boat to the mainland. I looked back upon my
present condition as the most miserable that could
possibly be; that I was not able to throw myself into
anything, but death, that could be called worse; that
if I reached the shore of the main, I might perhaps
meet with relief, or I might coast along, as I did on
the shore of Africa, till I came to some inhabited
country, and where I might find some relief; and after
all, perhaps I might fall in with some Christian ship
that might take me in; and if the worse came to the
worst, I could but die, which would put an end to all
these miseries at once.

When this had agitated my thoughts for two hours,
or more, with such violence that it set my very blood
into a ferment, and my pulse beat as high as if I had
been in a fever, merely with the extraordinary fervour
of my mind about it, Nature, as if I had been fatigued
and exhausted with the very thought of it, threw me
into a sound sleep. One would have thought I should
have dreamed of it, but I did not, nor of anything
relating to it; but I dreamed that as I was going out
in the morning, as usual, from my castle, I saw upon
the shore two canoes and eleven savages coming to
land, and that they brought with them another savage,
whom they were going to kill in order to eat him;
when, on a sudden, the savage that they were going
to kill jumped away and ran for his life. And I thought
in my sleep, that he came running into my little thick
grove before my fortification to hide himself; and that
I, seeing him alone, and not perceiving that the other
sought him that way, showed myself to him, and
smiling upon him, encouraged him; that he kneeled
down to me, seeming to pray me to assist him; upon

F

which I showed my ladder, made him go up, and
carried him into my cave, and he became my servant;
and that as soon as I had gotten this man, I said to
myself, " Now I may certainly venture to the mainland; for this fellow will serve me as a pilot, and will
tell me what to do, and whither to go for provisions,
and whither not to go for fear of being devoured;
what places to venture into, and what to escape." I
waked with this thought, and was under such inexpressible impressions of joy at the prospect of my
escape in my dream, that the disappointments which
I felt upon coming to myself and finding it was no
more than a dream were equally extravagant the other
way, and threw me into a very dejection of spirit.

Upon this, however, I made this conclusion; that
my only way to go about an attempt for an escape
was, if possible, to get a savage into my possession;
and, if possible, it should be one of their prisoners,
whom they had condemned to be eaten, and should
bring hither to kill. But these thoughts still were
attended with this difficulty, that it was impossible
to effect this without attacking a whole caravan of
them, and killing them all; and this was not only a
very desperate attempt, and might miscarry, but, on
the other hand, I had greatly scrupled the lawfulness
of it to me; and my heart trembled at the thoughts
of shedding so much blood, though it was for my
deliverance. I need not repeat the arguments which
occurred to me against this, they being the same mentioned before. But though I had other reasons to offer
now, viz., that those men were enemies to my life,
and would devour me if they could; that it was self-
preservation, in the highest degree, to deliver myself
from this death of a life, and was acting in my own

defence as much as if they were actually assaulting
me, and the like; I say, though these things argued
for it, yet the thoughts of shedding human blood for
my deliverance were very terrible to me, and such as
I could by no means reconcile myself to a great while.

However, at last, after many secret disputes with
myself, and after great perplexities about it, for all
these arguments, one way and another, struggled in
my head a long time, the eager prevailing desire of
deliverance at length mastered all the rest, and I
resolved, if possible, to get one of those savages into
my hands, cost what it would. My next thing then
was to contrive how to do it, and this indeed was very
difficult to resolve on. But as I could pitch upon no
probable means for it, so I resolved to put myself
upon the watch, to see them when they came on shore,
and leave the rest to the event, taking such measures
as the opportunity should present, let be what would be.

With these resolutions in my thoughts, I set myself
upon the scout as often as possible, and indeed so
often, till I was heartily tired of it; for it was above
a year and half that I waited; and for great part of
that time went out to the west end, and to the south-
west corner of the island, almost every day, to seek for
canoes, but none appeared. This was very discouraging,
and began to trouble me much; though I cannot say
that it did in this case, as it had done some time before
that, viz., wear off the edge of my desire to the thing.
But the longer it seemed to be delayed, the more eager
I was for it. In a word, I was not at first so careful
to shun the sight of these savages, and avoid being
seen by them, as I was now eager to be upon them.

Besides, I fancied myself able to manage one, nay,
two or three savages, if I had them, so as to make

them entirely slaves to me, to do whatever I should direct them, and to prevent their being able at any time to do me any hurt. It was a great while that I pleased myself with this affair; but nothing still presented. All my fancies and schemes came to nothing, for no savages came near me for a great while.

About a year and half after I had entertained these notions, and by long musing had, as it were, resolved them all into nothing, for want of an occasion to put them in execution, I was surprised, one morning early, with seeing no less than five canoes all on shore together on my side the island, and the people who belonged to them all landed, and out of my sight. The number of them broke all my measures; for seeing so many, and knowing that they always came four, or six, or sometimes more, in a boat, I could not tell what to think of it, or how to take my measures to attack twenty or thirty men single-handed; so I lay still in my castle, perplexed and discomforted. However, I put myself into all the postures for an attack if anything had presented. Having waited a good while, listening to hear if they made any noise, at length, being very impatient, I set my guns at the foot of my ladder, and clambered up to the top of the hill, by my two stages, as usual; standing so, however, that my head did not appear above the hill, so that they could not perceive me by any means. Here I observed, by the help of my perspective glass, that they were no less than thirty in number, that they had a fire kindled, that they had had meat dressed. How they had cooked it, that I knew not, or what it was; but they were all dancing, in I know not how many barbarous gestures and figures, their own way, round the fire.

While I was thus looking on them, I perceived by my perspective two miserable wretches dragged from the boats, where, it seems, they were laid by, and were now brought out for the slaughter. I perceived one of them immediately fell, being knocked down, I suppose, with a club or wooden sword, for that was their way, and two or three others were at work immediately, cutting him open for their cookery, while the other victim was left standing by himself, till they should be ready for him. In that very moment this poor wretch seeing himself a little at liberty, Nature inspired him with hopes of life, and he started away from them, and ran with incredible swiftness along the sands directly towards me, I mean towards that part of the coast where my habitation was.

I was dreadfully frighted (that I must acknowledge) when I perceived him to run my way, and especially when, as I thought, I saw him pursued by the whole body; and now I expected that part of my dream was coming to pass, and that he would certainly take shelter in my grove; but I could not depend, by any means, upon my dream for the rest of it, viz., that the other savages would not pursue him thither, and find him there. However, I kept my station, and my spirits began to recover when I found that there was not above three men that followed him; and still more was I encouraged when I found that he out-stripped them exceedingly in running, and gained ground of them; so that if he could but hold it for half-an-hour, I saw easily he would fairly get away from them all.

There was between them and my castle the creek, which I mentioned often at the first part of my story, when I landed my cargoes out of the ship; and this

I saw plainly he must necessarily swim over, or the poor wretch would be taken there. But when the savage escaping came thither he made nothing of it, though the tide was then up; but plunging in, swam through in about thirty strokes or thereabouts, landed, and ran on with exceeding strength and swiftness. When the three persons came to the creek, I found that two of them could swim, but the third could not, and that, standing on the other side, he looked at the other, but went no further, and soon after went softly back, which, as it happened, was very well for him in the main.

I observed, that the two who swam were yet more than twice as long swimming over the creek as the fellow was that fled from them. It came now very warmly upon my thoughts, and indeed irresistibly, that now was my time to get me a servant, and perhaps a companion or assistant, and that I was called plainly by Providence to save this poor creature's life. I immediately ran down the ladders with all possible expedition, fetched my two guns, for they were both but at the foot of the ladders, as I observed above, and getting up again, with the same haste, to the top of the hill, I crossed toward the sea, and having a very short cut, and all down hill, clapped myself in the way between the pursuers and the pursued, hallooing aloud to him that fled, who, looking back, was at first perhaps as much frighted at me as at them; but I beckoned with my hand to him to come back; and, in the meantime, I slowly advanced towards the two that followed; then rushing at once upon the foremost, I knocked him down with the stock of my piece. I was loth to fire, because I would not have the rest hear; though, at that distance, it would not have been easily heard, and being out of sight of the smoke too, they would not have easily known what to make of it. Having knocked this fellow down, the other who pursued with him stopped, as if he had been frighted, and I advanced apace towards him; but as I came nearer, I perceived presently he had a bow and arrow, and was fitting it to shoot at me; so I was then necessitated to shoot at him first, which I did, and killed him at the first shot.

The poor savage who fled, but had stopped, though he saw both his enemies fallen and killed, as he thought, yet was so frighted with the fire and noise of my piece, that he stood stock-still, and neither came forward or went backward, though he seemed rather inclined to fly still, than to come on. I hallooed again to him, and made signs to come forward, which he easily understood, and came a little way, then stopped again, and then a little further, and stopped again; and I could then perceive that he stood trembling, as if he had been taken prisoner, and had just been to be killed, as his two enemies were. I beckoned him again to come to me, and gave him all the signs of encouragement that I could think of; and he came nearer and nearer, kneeling down every ten or twelve steps, in token of acknowledgment for my saving his life. I smiled at him, and looked pleasantly, and beckoned to him to come still nearer. At length he came close to me, and then he kneeled down again, kissed the ground, and laid his head upon the ground, and taking me by the foot, set my foot upon his head. This, it seems, was in token of swearing to be my slave for ever. I took him up, and made much of him, and encouraged him all I could. But there was more work to do yet; for I perceived the savage whom I knocked down was not killed, but stunned with the blow, and began to come to himself; so I pointed to him, and showing him the savage, that he was not dead, upon this he spoke some words to me; and though I could not understand them, yet I thought they were pleasant to hear; for they were the first sound of a man's voice that I had heard, my own excepted, for above twenty-five years. But there was no time for such reflections now. The savage who was knocked down recovered himself so far as to sit up upon the ground, and I perceived that my savage began to be afraid; but when I saw that, I presented my other piece at the man, as if I would shoot him. Upon this my savage, for so I call him now, made a motion to me to lend him my sword, which hung naked in a belt by my side; so I did. He no sooner had it but he runs to his enemy, and, at one blow, cut off his head as cleverly, no executioner in Germany could have done it sooner or better; which I thought very strange for one who, I had reason to believe, never saw a sword in his life before, except their own wooden swords. However, it seems, as I learned afterwards, they make their wooden swords so sharp, so heavy, and the wood is so hard, that they will cut off heads even with them, ay, and arms, and that at one blow too. When he had done this, he comes laughing to me in sign of triumph, and brought me the sword again, and with abundance of gestures, which I did not understand, laid it down, with the head of the savage that he had killed, just before me.

But that which astonished him most was to know how I had killed the other Indian so far off; so pointing to him, he made signs to me to let him go to him; so I bade him go, as well as I could. When he came to him, he stood like one amazed, looking at him, turned him first on one side, then on t'other, looked at the wound the bullet had made, which, it seems, was just in his breast, where it had made a hole, and no great quantity of blood had followed; but he had bled inwardly, for he was quite dead. He took up his bow and arrows and came back; so I turned to go away, and beckoned to him to follow me, making signs to him that more might come after them.

Upon this he signed to me that he should bury them with sand, that they might not be seen by the rest if they followed; and so I made signs again to him to do so. He fell to work, and in an instant he had scraped a hole in the sand with his hands big enough to bury the first in, and then dragged him into it, and covered him, and did so also by the other. I believe he had buried them both in a quarter of an hour. Then calling him away, I carried him, not to my castle, but quite away to my cave, on the farthest part of the island; so I did not let my dream come to pass in that part, viz., that he came into my grove for shelter.

Here I gave him bread and a bunch of raisins to eat, and a draught of water, which I found he was indeed in great distress for, by his running; and having refreshed him, I made signs for him to go lie down and sleep, pointing to a place where I had laid a great parcel of rice-straw, and a blanket upon it, which I used to sleep upon myself sometimes; so the poor creature laid down, and went to sleep.

He was a comely, handsome fellow, perfectly well made, with straight strong limbs, not too large, tall, and well-shaped, and, as I reckon, about twenty-six years of age. He had a very good countenance, not a fierce and surly aspect, but seemed to have something

*F

very manly in his face; and yet he had all the sweetness and softness of an European in his countenance
too, especially when he smiled. His hair was long and
black, not curled like wool; his forehead very high
and large; and a great vivacity and sparkling sharp-
ness in his eyes. The colour of his skin was not quite
black, but very tawny; and yet not of an ugly,
yellow, nauseous tawny as the Brazilians and Virgin-
ians and other natives of America are, but of a bright
kind of a dun olive colour, that had in it something
very agreeable, though not very easy to describe. His
face was round and plump; his nose small, not flat
like the negroes; a very good mouth, thin lips, and
his fine teeth well set, and white as ivory.

After he had slumbered, rather than slept, about
half-an-hour, he waked again, and comes out of the
cave to me, for I had been milking my goats, which
I had in the enclosure just by. When he espied me,
he came running to me, laying himself down again
upon the ground, with all the possible signs of an
humble, thankful disposition, making a many antic
gestures to show it. At last he lays his head flat upon
the ground close to my foot, and sets my other foot
upon his head, as he had done before, and after this
made all the signs to me of subjection, servitude, and
submission imaginable, to let me know how he would
serve me as long as he lived. I understood him in
many things, and let him know I was very well pleased
with him. In a little time I began to speak to him,
and teach him to speak to me; and, first, I made
him know his name should be Friday, which was the
day I saved his life. I called him so for the memory
of the time. I likewise taught him to say master, and
then let him know that was to be my name. I like-

wise taught him to say Yes and No, and to know the meaning of them. I gave him some milk in an earthen pot, and let him see me drink it before him, and sop my bread in it; and I gave him a cake of bread to do the like, which he quickly complied with, and made signs that it was very good for him.

I kept there with him all that night; but as soon as it was day, I beckoned to him to come with me, and let him know I would give him some clothes; at which he seemed very glad, for he was stark naked. As we went by the place where he had buried the two men, he pointed exactly to the place, and showed me the marks that he had made to find them again, making signs to me that we should dig them up again, and eat them. At this I appeared very angry, expressed my abhorrence of it, and beckoned with my hand to him to come away; which he did immediately, with great submission. I then led him up to the top of the hill, to see if his enemies were gone; and pulling out my glass, I looked, and saw plainly the place where they had been, but no appearance of them or of their canoes; so that it was plain that they were gone, and had left their two comrades behind them, without any search after them.

But I was not content with this discovery; but having now more courage, and consequently more curiosity, I takes my man Friday with me, giving him the sword in his hand, with the bow and arrows at his back, which I found he could use very dexterously, making him carry one gun for me, and I two for myself, and away we marched to the place where these creatures had been; for I had a mind now to get some fuller intelligence of them. When I came to the place, my very blood ran chill in my veins, and my heart sunk within me, at the horror of the spectacle. Indeed, it was a dreadful sight, at least it was so to me, though Friday made nothing of it. The place was covered with human bones, the ground dyed with their blood, great pieces of flesh left here and there, half-eaten, mangled, and scorched; and, in short, all the tokens of the triumphant feast they had been making there, after a victory over their enemies. I saw three skulls, five hands, and the bones of three or four legs and feet, and abundance of other parts of the bodies; and Friday, by his signs, made me understand that they brought over four prisoners to feast upon; that three of them were eaten up, and that he, pointing to himself, was the fourth; that there had been a great battle between them and their next king, whose subjects it seems he had been one of, and that they had taken a great number of prisoners; all which were carried to several places by those that had taken them in the fight, in order to feast upon them, as was done here by these wretches upon those they brought hither.

I caused Friday to gather all the skulls, bones, flesh, and whatever remained, and lay them together on a heap, and make a great fire upon it, and burn them all to ashes. I found Friday had still a hankering stomach after some of the flesh, and was still a cannibal in his nature; but I discovered so much abhorrence at the very thoughts of it, and at the least appearance of it, that he durst not discover it; for I had, by some means let him know that I would kill him if he offered it.

When we had done this we came back to our castle, and there I fell to work for my man Friday; and, first of all, I gave him a pair of linen drawers, which I had out of the poor gunner's chest I mentioned,

and which I found in the wreck; and which, with a
little alteration, fitted him very well. Then I made
him a jerkin of goat's-skin, as well as my skill would
allow, and I was now grown a tolerable good tailor;
and I gave him a cap, which I made of a hare-skin,
very convenient and fashionable enough; and thus he
was clothed for the present tolerably well, and was
mighty well pleased to see himself almost as well clothed
as his master. It is true he went awkwardly in these
things at first; wearing the drawers was very awkward
to him, and the sleeves of the waistcoat galled his
shoulders, and the inside of his arms; but a little easing
them where he complained they hurt him, and using
himself to them, at length he took to them very well.

The next day after I came home to my hutch with
him, I began to consider where I should lodge him.
And that I might do well for him, and yet be perfectly
easy myself, I made a little tent for him in the vacant
place between my two fortifications, in the inside of
the last and in the outside of the first; and as there
was a door or entrance there into my cave, I made
a formal framed door-case, and a door to it of boards,
and set it up in the passage, a little within the entrance;
and causing the door to open on the inside, I barred
it up in the night, taking in my ladders too; so that
Friday could no way come at me in the inside of my
innermost wall without making so much noise in
getting over, that it must needs waken me; for my
first wall had now a complete roof over it of long
poles, covering all my tent, and leaning up to the side
of the hill, which was again laid across with smaller
sticks instead of laths, and then thatched over a great
thickness with the rice-straw, which was strong, like
reeds; and at the hole or place which was left to go

in or out by the ladder, I had placed a kind of trap-
door, which, if it had been attempted on the outside,
would not have opened at all, but would have fallen
down, and made a great noise; and as to weapons,
I took them all into my side every night.

But I needed none of all this precaution; for never
man had a more faithful, loving, sincere servant than
Friday was to me; without passions, sullenness, or
designs, perfectly obliged and engaged; his very affections were tied to me, like those of a child to a father;
and I dare say he would have sacrificed his life for
the saving mine, upon any occasion whatsoever. The
many testimonials he gave me of this put it out of
doubt, and soon convinced me that I needed to use
no precautions as to my safety on his account.

This frequently gave me occasion to observe, and
that with wonder, that however it had pleased God,
in His providence, and in the government of the
works of His hands, to take from so great a part of
the world of His creatures the best uses to which their
faculties and the powers of their souls are adapted,
yet that He has bestowed upon them the same powers,
the same reason, the same affections, the same senti-
ments of kindness and obligation, the same passions
and resentments of wrongs, the same sense of gratitude, sincerity, fidelity, and all the capacities of doing
good, and receiving good, that He has given to us;
and that when He pleases to offer to them occasions
of exerting these, they are as ready, nay, more ready,
to apply them to the right uses for which they were
bestowed than we are.

But to return to my new companion. I was greatly
delighted with him, and made it my business to teach
him everything that was proper to make him useful,

handy, and helpful; but especially to make him speak,
and understand me when I spake. And he was the
aptest scholar that ever was; and particularly was so
merry, so constantly diligent, and so pleased when he
could but understand me, or make me understand him,
that it was very pleasant to me to talk to him. And
now my life began to be so easy, that I began to say
to myself, that could I but have been safe from more
savages, I cared not if I was never to remove from
the place while I lived.

After I had been two or three days returned to my
castle, I thought that, in order to bring Friday off
from his horrid way of feeding, and from the relish
of a cannibal's stomach, I ought to let him taste
other flesh; so I took him out with me one morning
to the woods. I went, indeed, intending to kill a kid
out of my own flock, and bring him home and dress
it; but as I was going, I saw a she-goat lying down
in the shade, and two young kids sitting by her. I
catched hold of Friday. "Hold," says I, "stand still,"
and made signs to him not to stir. Immediately I
presented my piece, shot and killed one of the kids.
The poor creature, who had, at a distance indeed,
seen me kill the savage, his enemy, but did not know,
or could imagine, how it was done, was sensibly surprised and shook, and looked so amazed, that I thought
he would have sunk down. He did not see the kid I
had shot at, or perceive I had killed it, but ripped up
his waistcoat to feel if he was not wounded; and, as
I found presently, thought I was resolved to kill him;
for he came and kneeled down to me, and embracing
my knees, said a great many things I did not understand; but I could easily see that the meaning was to
pray me not to kill him.

I soon found a way to convince him that I would do him no harm; and taking him up by the hand, laughed at him, and pointing to the kid which I had killed, beckoned to him to run and fetch it, which he did; and while he was wondering, and looking to see how the creature was killed, I loaded my gun again; and by-and-by I saw a great fowl, like a hawk, sit upon a tree, within shot; so, to let Friday understand a little what I would do, I called him to me again, pointing at the fowl, which was indeed a parrot, though I thought it had been a hawk; I say, pointing to the parrot, and to my gun, and to the ground under the parrot, to let him see I would make it fall, I made him understand that I would shoot and kill that bird. Accordingly I fired, and bade him look, and immediately he saw the parrot fall. He stood like one frighted again, notwithstanding all I had said to him; and I found he was the more amazed, because he did not see me put anything into the gun, but thought that there must be some wonderful fund of death and destruction in that thing, able to kill man, beast, bird, or anything near or far off; and the astonishment this created in him was such as could not wear off for a long time; and I believe, if I would have let him, he would have worshipped me and my gun. As for the gun itself, he would not so much as touch it for several days after; but would speak to it, and talk to it, as if it had answered him, when he was by himself; which, as I afterwards learned of him, was to desire it not to kill him.

Well, after his astonishment was a little over at this, I pointed to him to run and fetch the bird I had shot, which he did, but stayed some time; for the parrot, not being quite dead, was fluttered a good

way off from the place she fell. However, he found
her, took her up, and brought her to me; and as I
had perceived his ignorance about the gun before, I
took this advantage to charge the gun again, and not
let him see me do it, that I might be ready for any
mark that might present. But nothing more offered
at that time; so I brought home the kid, and the
same evening I took the skin off, and cut it out as well
as I could; and having a pot for that purpose, I
boiled or stewed some of the flesh, and made some
very good broth; and after I had begun to eat some,
I gave some to my man, who seemed very glad of it,
and liked it very well; but that which was strangest
to him, was to see me eat salt with it. He made a
sign to me that the salt was not good to eat, and
putting a little into his own mouth, he seemed to
nauseate it, and would spit and splutter at it, washing
his mouth with fresh water after it. On the other hand,
I took some meat in my mouth without salt, and I
pretended to spit and splutter for want of salt, as fast
as he had done at the salt. But it would not do; he
would never care for salt with his meat or in his
broth; at least, not a great while, and then but a very
little.

Having thus fed him with boiled meat and broth,
I was resolved to feast him the next day with roasting
a piece of the kid. This I did by hanging it before
the fire in a string, as I had seen many people do in
England, setting two poles up, one on each side of
the fire, and one across on the top, and tying the string
to the cross stick, letting the meat turn continually.
This Friday admired very much. But when he came
to taste the flesh, he took so many ways to tell me
how well he liked it, that I could not but understand

him; and at last he told me he would never eat man's flesh any more, which I was very glad to hear.

The next day I set him to work to beating some corn out, and sifting it in the manner I used to do, as I observed before; and he soon understood how to do it as well as I, especially after he had seen what the meaning of it was, and that it was to make bread of; for after that I let him see me make my bread, and bake it too; and in a little time Friday was able to do all the work for me, as well as I could do it myself.

CHAPTER XV

LIFE WITH FRIDAY

I BEGAN now to consider that, having two mouths to feed instead of one, I must provide more ground for my harvest, and plant a larger quantity of corn than I used to do; so I marked out a larger piece of land, and began the fence in the same manner as before, in which Friday not only worked very willingly and very hard, but did it very cheerfully; and I told him what it was for; that it was for corn to make more bread, because he was now with me, and that I might have enough for him and myself too. He appeared very sensible of that part, and let me know that he thought I had much more labour upon me on his account, than I had for myself; and that he would work the harder for me, if I would tell him what to do.

This was the pleasantest year of all the life I led in this place. Friday began to talk pretty well, and understand the names of almost everything I had occasion to call for, and of every place I had to send him to, and talk a great deal to me; so that, in short,

I began now to have some use for my tongue again,
which, indeed, I had very little occasion for before,
that is to say, about speech. Besides the pleasure of
talking to him, I had a singular satisfaction in the
fellow himself. His simple, unfeigned honesty appeared
to me more and more every day, and I began really
to love the creature; and, on his side, I believe he
loved me more than it was possible for him ever to
love anything before.

I had a mind once to try if he had any hankering
inclination to his own country again; and having
learned him English so well that he could answer me
almost any questions, I asked him whether the nation
that he belonged to never conquered in battle? At
which he smiled, and said, " Yes, yes, we always fight
the better "; that is, he meant, always get the better
in fight; and so we began the following discourse:
" You always fight the better," said I. " How came
you to be taken prisoner then, Friday? "

Friday. My nation beat much for all that.

Master. How beat? If your nation beat them, how
came you to be taken?

Friday. They more many than my nation in the
place where me was; they take one, two, three, and
me. My nation overbeat them in the yonder place,
where me no was; there my nation take one, two,
great thousand.

Master. But why did not your side recover you from
the hands of your enemies then?

Friday. They run one, two, three, and me, and make
go in the canoe; my nation have no canoe that time.

Master. Well, Friday, and what does your nation
do with the men they take? Do they carry them
away and eat them, as these did?

Friday. Yes, my nation eats mans too; eat all up.

Master. Where do they carry them?

Friday. Go to other place, where they think.

Master. Do they come hither?

Friday. Yes, yes, they come hither; come other else place.

Master. Have you been here with them?

Friday. Yes, I been here. (*Points to the N.W. side of the island which, it seems, was their side.*)

By this I understood that my man Friday had formerly been among the savages who used to come on shore on the farther part of the island, on the same man-eating occasions that he was now brought for; and, some time after, when I took the courage to carry him to that side, being the same I formerly mentioned, he presently knew the place, and told me he was there once when they eat up twenty men, two women, and one child. He could not tell twenty in English, but he numbered them by laying so many stones on a row, and pointing to me to tell them over.

I have told this passage, because it introduces what follows; that after I had had this discourse with him, I asked him how far it was from our island to the shore, and whether the canoes were not often lost. He told me there was no danger, no canoes ever lost; but that, after a little way out to the sea, there was a current and a wind, always one way in the morning, the other in the afternoon.

This I understood to be no more than the sets of the tide, as going out or coming in; but I afterwards understood it was occasioned by the great draught and reflux of the mighty river Oroonoko, in the mouth of the gulf of which river, as I found afterwards, our island lay; and this land which I perceived to the

W. and N.W. was the great island Trinidad, on the
north point of the mouth of the river. I asked Friday
a thousand questions about the country, the inhabitants, the sea, the coast, and what nations were near.
He told me all he knew, with the greatest openness
imaginable. I asked him the names of the several
nations of his sort of people, but could get no other
name than Caribs; from whence I easily understood
that these were the Caribbees, which our maps place
on the part of America which reaches from the mouth
of the river Oroonoko to Guiana, and onwards to St.
Martha. He told me that up a great way beyond the
moon, that was, beyond the setting of the moon, which
must be W. from their country, there dwelt white-
bearded men, like me, and pointed to my great
whiskers, which I mentioned before; and that they
had killed much mans, that was his word; by all
which I understood he meant the Spaniards, whose
cruelties in America had been spread over the whole
countries, and was remembered by all the nations
from father to son.

I inquired if he could tell me how I might come
from this island and get among those white men. He
told me, " Yes, yes, I might go in two canoe." I could
not understand what he meant, or make him describe
to me what he meant by two canoe; till at last, with
great difficulty, I found he meant it must be in a
large great boat, as big as two canoes.

This part of Friday's discourse began to relish with
me very well; and from this time I entertained some
hopes that, one time or other, I might find an opportunity to make my escape from this place, and that
this poor savage might be a means to help me to do it.

During the long time that Friday had now been

with me, and that he began to speak to me, and understand me, I was not wanting to lay a foundation of religious knowledge in his mind; particularly I asked him one time, Who made him? The poor creature did not understand me at all, so I took it by another handle, and asked him who made the sea, the ground we walked on, and the hills and woods? He told me it was one old Benamuckee, that lived beyond all. He could describe nothing of this great person, but that he was very old, much older, he said, than the sea or the land, than the moon or the stars. I asked him then, if this old person had made all things, why did not all things worship him? He looked very grave, and with a perfect look of innocence said, " All things do say O to him." I asked him if the people who die in his country went away anywhere? He said, " Yes, they all went to Benamuckee." Then I asked him whether these they eat up went thither too? He said " Yes."

From these things I began to instruct him in the knowledge of the true God. I told him that the great Maker of all things lived up there, pointing up towards heaven; that He governs the world by the same power and providence by which He had made it; that He was omnipotent, could do everything for us, give everything to us, take everything from us; and thus, by degrees, I opened his eyes. He listened with great attention, and received with pleasure the notion of Jesus Christ being sent to redeem us, and of the manner of making our prayers to God, and His being able to hear us, even into heaven. He told me one day that if our God could hear us up beyond the sun, He must needs be a greater God than their Benamuckee, who lived but a little way off, and yet could not hear till they went up to the great mountains where he dwelt to speak to him. I asked him if he ever went thither to speak to him? He said, No; they never went that were young men; none went thither but the old men, whom he called their Oowokakee, that is, as I made him explain it to me, their religious, or clergy; and that they went to say O (so he called saying prayers), and then came back, and told them what Benamuckee said. By this I observed that there is priestcraft even amongst the most blinded, ignorant pagans in the world; and the policy of making a secret religion in order to preserve the veneration of the people to the clergy is not only to be found in the Roman, but perhaps among all religions in the world, even among the most brutish and barbarous savages.

I endeavoured to clear up this fraud to my man Friday, and told him that the pretence of their old men going up to the mountains to say O to their god Benamuckee was a cheat, and their bringing word from thence what he said was much more so; that if they met with any answer, or spoke with any one there, it must be with an evil spirit; and then I entered into a long discourse with him about the devil, the original of him, his rebellion against God, his enmity to man, the reason of it, his setting himself up in the dark parts of the world to be worshipped instead of God, and as God, and the many stratagems he made use of to delude mankind to their ruin; how he had a secret access to our passions and to our affections, to adapt his snares so to our inclinations, as to cause us even to be our own tempters, and to run upon our destruction by our own choice.

I had been telling him how the devil was God's enemy in the hearts of men, and used all his malice and skill to defeat the good designs of Providence, and to ruin the kingdom of Christ in the world, and the like. "Well," says Friday, "but you say God is so strong, so great; is He not much strong, much might as the devil?" "Yes, yes," says I, "Friday, God is stronger than the devil; God is above the devil, and therefore we pray to God to tread him down under our feet, and enable us to resist his temptations, and quench his fiery darts." "But," says he again, "if God much strong, much might as the devil, why God no kill the devil, so make him no more do wicked?"

I was strangely surprised at his question; and after all, though I was now an old man, yet I was but a young doctor, and ill enough qualified for a casuist, or a solver of difficulties; and at first I could not tell what to say; so I pretended not to hear him, and asked him what he said? But he was too earnest for an answer to forget his question, so that he repeated it in the very same broken words as above. By this time I had recovered myself a little, and I said, "God will at last punish him severely; he is reserved for the judgment, and is to be cast into the bottomless pit, to dwell with everlasting fire." This did not satisfy Friday; but he returns upon me, repeating my words, "Reserve at last! me no understand; but why not kill the devil now? not kill great ago?" "You may as well ask me," said I, "why God does not kill you and me, when we do wicked things here that offend Him; we are preserved to repent and be pardoned." He muses awhile at this. "Well, well," says he, mighty affectionately, "that well; so you, I, devil, all wicked, all preserve, repent, God pardon all."

I therefore diverted the present discourse between

me and my man, rising up hastily, as upon some
sudden occasion of going out; then sending him for
something a good way off, I seriously prayed to God
that He would enable me to instruct savingly this
poor savage, and would guide me to speak so to him
from the Word of God as his conscience might be
convinced, his eyes opened, and his soul saved. When
he came again to me, I entered into a long discourse
with him upon the subject of the redemption of man
by the Saviour of the world, and of the doctrine of
the Gospel preached from heaven, viz., of repentance
towards God, and faith in our blessed Lord Jesus.
I then explained to him as well as I could why our
blessed Redeemer took not on Him the nature of
angels, but the seed of Abraham; and how, for that
reason, the fallen angels had no share in the redemption; that He came only to the lost sheep of the house
of Israel, and the like.

In this thankful frame I continued all the remainder
of my time, and the conversation which employed the
hours between Friday and I was such as made the
three years which we lived there together perfectly
and completely happy, if any such thing as complete
happiness can be formed in a sublunary state. The
savage was now a good Christian, a much better than
I; though I have reason to hope, and bless God for
it, that we were equally penitent, and comforted,
restored penitents. We had here the Word of God to
read, and no farther off from His Spirit to instruct
than if we had been in England.

As to all the disputes, wranglings, strife, and con-
tention which has happened in the world about religion,
whether niceties in doctrines, or schemes of Church
government, they were all perfectly useless to us; as,

for aught I can yet see, they have been to all the rest
in the world. We had the sure guide to heaven, viz.,
the Word of God; and we had, blessed be God, comfortable views of the Spirit of God teaching and in-
structing us by His Word, leading us into all truth,
and making us both willing and obedient to the
instruction of His Word; and I cannot see the least
use that the greatest knowledge of the disputed points
in religion, which have made such confusions in the
world, would have been to us if we could have obtained
it. But I must go on with the historical part of things,
and take every part in its order.

After Friday and I became more intimately acquainted, and that he could understand almost all I
said to him, and speak fluently, though in broken
English, to me, I acquainted him with my own story,
or at least so much of it as related to my coming into
the place; how I had lived there, and how long. I
let him into the mystery, for such it was to him, of
gunpowder and bullet, and taught him how to shoot;
I gave him a knife, which he was wonderfully delighted
with, and I made him a belt, with a frog hanging to
it, such as in England we wear hangers in; and in the
frog, instead of a hanger, I gave him a hatchet, which
was not only as good a weapon, in some cases, but
much more useful upon other occasions.

I described to him the country of Europe, and particularly England, which I came from; how we lived,
how we worshipped God, how we behaved to one
another, and how we traded in ships to all parts of
the world. I gave him an account of the wreck which
I had been on board of, and showed him, as near as
I could, the place where she lay; but she was all
beaten in pieces before, and gone.

I showed him the ruins of our boat, which we lost when we escaped, and which I could not stir with my whole strength then, but was now fallen almost all to pieces. Upon seeing this boat, Friday stood musing a great while, and said nothing. I asked him what it was he studied upon. At last says he, " Me see such boat like come to place at my nation."

I did not understand him a good while; but at last, when I had examined further into it, I understood by him that a boat such as that had been, came on shore upon the country where he lived; that is, as he explained it, was driven thither by stress of weather. I presently imagined that some European ship must have been cast away upon their coast, and the boat might get loose and drive ashore; but was so dull, that I never once thought of men making escape from a wreck thither, much less whence they might come; so I only inquired after a description of the boat.

Friday described the boat to me well enough; but brought me better to understand him when he added with some warmth, " We save the white mans from drown." Then I presently asked him if there was any white mans, as he called them, in the boat. " Yes," he said, " the boat full of white mans." I asked him how many. He told upon his fingers seventeen. I asked him then what became of them. He told me, " They live, they dwell at my nation."

This put new thoughts into my head; for I presently imagined that these might be the men belonging to the ship that was cast away in sight of my island, as I now call it; and who, after the ship was struck on the rock, and they saw her inevitably lost, had saved themselves in their boat, and were landed upon that wild shore among the savages.

Upon this I inquired of him more critically what
was become of them. He assured me they lived still
there; that they had been there about four years;
that the savages let them alone, and gave them
victuals to live. I asked him how it came to pass they
did not kill them, and eat them. He said, "No, they
make brother with them"; that is, as I understood
him, a truce; and then he added, "They no eat mans
but when make the war fight"; that is to say, they
never eat any men but such as come to fight with them
and are taken in battle.

It was after this some considerable time, that being
on the top of the hill, at the east side of the island
(from whence, as I have said, I had in a clear day
discovered the main or continent of America), Friday,
the weather being very serene, looks very earnestly
towards the mainland, and, in a kind of surprise, falls
a-jumping and dancing, and calls out to me, for I was
at some distance from him. I asked him what was
the matter? "O joy!" says he, "O glad! there see
my country, there my nation!"

I observed an extraordinary sense of pleasure
appeared in his face, and his eyes sparkled, and his
countenance discovered a strange eagerness, as if he
had a mind to be in his own country again; and this
observation of mine put a great many thoughts into
me, which made me at first not so easy about my new
man Friday as I was before; and I made no doubt
but that if Friday could get back to his own nation
again, he would not only forget all his religion, but
all his obligation to me; and would be forward enough
to give his countrymen an account of me, and come
back perhaps with a hundred or two of them, and
make a feast upon me, at which he might be as merry

as he used to be with those of his enemies, when they were taken in war.

But I wronged the poor honest creature very much, for which I was very sorry afterwards. However, as my jealousy increased, and held me some weeks, I was a little more circumspect, and not so familiar and kind to him as before; in which I was certainly in the wrong too, the honest, grateful creature having no thought about it but what consisted with the best principles, both as a religious Christian and as a grateful friend, as appeared afterwards to my full satisfaction.

While my jealousy of him lasted, you may be sure I was every day pumping him, to see if he would discover any of the new thoughts which I suspected were in him; but I found everything he said was so honest and so innocent, that I could find nothing to nourish my suspicion; and, in spite of all my uneasiness, he made me at last entirely his own again, nor did he in the least perceive that I was uneasy, and therefore I could not suspect him of deceit.

One day, walking up the same hill, but the weather being hazy at sea, so that we could not see the continent, I called to him, and said, " Friday, do not you wish yourself in your own country, your own nation? " " Yes," he said, " I be much O glad to be at my own nation." " What would you do there? " said I. " Would you turn wild again, eat men's flesh again, and be a savage as you were before? " He looked full of concern, and shaking his head said, " No, no; Friday tell them to live good; tell them to pray God; tell them to eat corn-bread, cattle-flesh, milk, no eat man again." " Why then," said I to him, " they will kill you." He looked grave at that, and then said, " No, they no kill me, they willing love

learn." He meant by this they would be willing to
learn. He added, they learned much of the bearded
mans that come in the boat. Then I asked him if he
would go back to them? He smiled at that, and told
me he could not swim so far. I told him I would make
a canoe for him. He told me he would go, if I would
go with him. "I go!" says I; "why, they will eat
me if I come there." "No, no," says he, "me make
they no eat you; me make they much love you."
He meant, he would tell them how I had killed his
enemies, and saved his life, and so he would make
them love me. Then he told me, as well as he could,
how kind they were to the seventeen white men, or
bearded men, as he called them, who came on shore
there in distress.

CHAPTER XVI

THE ISLAND PEOPLED

FROM this time I confess I had a mind to venture
over, and see if I could possibly join with these bearded
men, who, I made no doubt, were Spaniards or Portuguese; not doubting but, if I could, we might find
some method to escape from thence, being upon the
continent, and a good company together, better than
I could from an island forty miles off the shore, and
alone, without help. So, after some days, I took
Friday to work again, by way of discourse, and told
him I would give him a boat to go back to his own
nation; and accordingly I carried him to my frigate,
which lay on the other side of the island, and having
cleared it of water, for I always kept it sunk in the
water, I brought it out, showed it him, and we both
went into it.

I found he was a most dexterous fellow at managing it, would make it go almost as swift and fast again as I could. So when he was in I said to him, " Well now, Friday, shall we go to your nation? " He looked very dull at my saying so, which, it seems, was because he thought the boat too small to go so far. I told him then I had a bigger; so the next day I went to the place where the first boat lay which I had made, but which I could not get into water. He said that was big enough; but then, as I had taken no care of it, and it had lain two or three and twenty years there, the sun had split and dried it, and it was in a manner rotten. Friday told me such a boat would do very well, and would carry " much enough victual, drink, bread "; that was his way of talking.

Upon the whole, I was by this time so fixed upon my design of going over with him to the continent, that I told him we would go and make one as big as that, and he should go home in it. He answered not one word, but looked very grave and sad. I asked him what was the matter with him? He asked me again thus, " Why you angry mad with Friday? what me done? " I asked him what he meant. I told him I was not angry with him at all. " No angry! no angry! " says he, repeating the words several times. " Why send Friday home away to my nation? " " Why," says I, " Friday, did you not say you wished you were there? " " Yes, yes," says he, " wish be both there, no wish Friday there, no master there ! " In a word, he would not think of going there without me. " I go there, Friday? " says I; " what shall I do there? " He turned very quick upon me at this: " You do great deal much good," says he; " you teach wild mans to be good, sober, tame mans; you

tell them know God, pray God, and live new life."
"Alas! Friday," says I, "thou knowest not what
thou sayest. I am but an ignorant man myself."
"Yes, yes," says he, "you teachee me good, you
teachee them good." "No, no, Friday," says I, "you
shall go without me; leave me here to live by myself,
as I did before." He looked confused again at that
word, and running to one of the hatchets which he
used to wear, he takes it up hastily, comes and gives
it me. "What must I do with this?" says I to him.
"You take kill Friday," said he. "What must I kill
you for?" said I again. He returns very quick,
"What you send Friday away for? Take kill Friday,
no send Friday away." This he spoke so earnestly,
that I saw tears stand in his eyes. In a word, I so
plainly discovered the utmost affection in him to me,
and a firm resolution in him, that I told him then,
and often after, that I would never send him away
from me if he was willing to stay with me.

Upon the whole, as I found by all his discourse a
settled affection to me, and that nothing should part
him from me, so I found all the foundation of his
desire to go to his own country was laid in his ardent
affection to the people, and his hopes of my doing
them good; a thing which, as I had no notion of
myself, so I had not the least thought or intention
or desire of undertaking it. But still I found a strong
inclination to my attempting an escape, as above,
founded on the supposition gathered from the discourse, viz., that there were seventeen bearded men
there; and, therefore, without any more delay I
went to work with Friday to find out a great tree
proper to fell, and make a large *periagua*, or canoe,
to undertake the voyage. There were trees enough in

the island to have built a little fleet, not of *periaguas*
and canoes, but even of good large vessels. But the
main thing I looked at was, to get one so near the
water that we might launch it when it was made, to
avoid the mistake I committed at first.

At last Friday pitched upon a tree, for I found he
knew much better than I what kind of wood was
fittest for it; nor can I tell, to this day, what wood
to call the tree we cut down, except that it was very
like the tree we call fustic, or between that and the
Nicaragua wood, for it was much of the same colour
and smell. Friday was for burning the hollow or
cavity of this tree out, to make it for a boat, but I
showed him how rather to cut it out with tools; which,
after I had showed him how to use, he did very handily;
and in about a month's hard labour we finished it, and
made it very handsome; especially when, with our
axes, which I showed him how to handle, we cut and
hewed the outside into the true shape of a boat. After
this, however, it cost us near a fortnight's time to get
her along, as it were inch by inch, upon great rollers
into the water; but when she was in, she would have
carried twenty men with great ease.

When she was in the water, and though she was so
big, it amazed me to see with what dexterity, and
how swift my man Friday would manage her, turn
her, and paddle her along. So I asked him if he would,
and if we might venture over in her. " Yes," he said,
" he venture over in her very well, though great blow
wind." However, I had a farther design that he knew
nothing of, and that was to make a mast and sail,
and to fit her with an anchor and cable. As to a
mast, that was easy enough to get; so I pitched upon
a straight young cedar tree, which I found near the

G

place, and which there was great plenty of in the island; and I set Friday to work to cut it down, and gave him directions how to shape and order it. But as to the sail, that was my particular care. I knew I had old sails, or rather pieces of old sails enough; but as I had had them now twenty-six years by me, and had not been very careful to preserve them, not imagining that I should ever have this kind of use for them, I did not doubt but they were all rotten, and, indeed, most of them were so. However, I found two pieces which appeared pretty good, and with these I went to work, and with a great deal of pains, and awkward tedious stitching (you may be sure) for want of needles, I, at length, made a three-corner ugly thing, like what we call in England a shoulder-of-mutton sail, to go with a boom at bottom, and a little short sprit at the top, such as usually our ships' long-boats sail with, and such as I best know how to manage; because it was such a one as I had to the boat in which I made my escape from Barbary, as related in the first part of my story.

I was near two months performing this last work, viz., rigging and fitting my mast and sails; for I finished them very complete, making a small stay, and a sail, or foresail, to it, to assist, if we should turn to windward; and, which was more than all, I fixed a rudder to the stern of her to steer with; and though I was but a bungling shipwright, yet as I knew the usefulness, and even necessity, of such a thing, I applied myself with so much pains to do it, that at last I brought it to pass; though, considering the many dull contrivances I had for it that failed, I think it cost me almost as much labour as making the boat.

After all this was done too, I had my man Friday

to teach as to what belonged to the navigation of my
boat; for though he knew very well how to paddle
a canoe, he knew nothing what belonged to a sail and
a rudder; and was the most amazed when he saw me
work the boat to and again in the sea by the rudder,
and how the sail jibbed, and filled this way, or that
way, as the course we sailed changed; I say, when
he saw this, he stood like one astonished and amazed.
However, with a little use I made all these things
familiar to him, and he became an expert sailor, except
that as to the compass I could make him understand
very little of that.   On the other hand, as there was
very little cloudy weather, and seldom or never any fogs
in those parts, there was the less occasion for a compass,
seeing the stars were always to be seen by night, and
the shore by day, except in the rainy seasons, and then
nobody cared to stir abroad, either by land or sea.

I was now entered on the seven and twentieth year
of my captivity in this place; though the three last
years that I had this creature with me ought rather
to be left out of the account, my habitation being quite
of another kind than in all the rest of the time. I kept
the anniversary of my landing here with the same
thankfulness to God for His mercies as at first; and
if I had such cause of acknowledgment at first, I had
much more so now, having such additional testimonies
of the care of Providence over me, and the great hopes
I had of being effectually and speedily delivered; for
I had an invincible impression upon my thoughts that
my deliverance was at hand, and that I should not
be another year in this place. However, I went on
with my husbandry, digging, planting, fencing, as
usual. I gathered and cured my grapes, and did
every necessary thing as before.

The rainy season was, in the meantime, upon me, when I kept more within doors than at other times; so I had stowed our new vessel as secure as we could, bringing her up into the creek, where, as I said in the beginning, I landed my rafts from the ship; and hauling her up to the shore at high-water mark, I made my man Friday dig a little dock, just big enough to hold her, and just deep enough to give her water enough to float in; and then, when the tide was out, we made a strong dam across the end of it, to keep the water out; and so she lay dry, as to the tide, from the sea; and to keep the rain off, we laid a great many boughs of trees, so thick, that she was as well thatched as a house; and thus we waited for the month of November and December, in which I designed to make my adventure.

When the settled season began to come in, as the thought of my design returned with the fair weather, I was preparing daily for the voyage; and the first thing I did was to lay by a certain quantity of provisions, being the stores for our voyage; and intended, in a week or a fortnight's time, to open the dock, and launch out our boat. I was busy one morning upon something of this kind, when I called to Friday, and bid him go to the sea-shore and see if he could find a turtle, or tortoise, a thing which we generally got once a week, for the sake of the eggs as well as the flesh. Friday had not been long gone when he came running back, and flew over my outer wall, or fence, like one that felt not the ground, or the steps he set his feet on; and before I had time to speak to him, he cries out to me, " O master! O master! O sorrow! O bad!" "What's the matter, Friday?" says I. "O yonder, there," says he, " one, two, three canoe! one,

two, three!" By his way of speaking, I concluded
there were six; but, on inquiry, I found it was but
three. "Well, Friday," says I, "do not be frighted."
So I heartened him up as well as I could. However,
I saw the poor fellow was most terribly scared; for
nothing ran in his head but that they were come to
look for him, and would cut him in pieces, and eat
him; and the poor fellow trembled so, that I scarce
knew what to do with him. I comforted him as well
as I could, and told him I was in as much danger
as he, and that they would eat me as well as him.
"But," says I, "Friday, we must resolve to fight them.
Can you fight, Friday?" "Me shoot," says he; "but
there come many great number." "No matter for
that," said I again, "our guns will fright them that
we do not kill." So I asked him whether, if I resolved
to defend him, he would defend me, and stand by me,
and do just as I bid him. He said, "Me die when you
bid die, master." So I went and fetched a good dram
of rum, and gave him; for I had been so good a husband
of my rum, that I had a great deal left. When he had
drank it, I made him take the two fowling-pieces,
which we always carried, and load them with large
swan-shot, as big as small pistol-bullets. Then I took
four muskets, and loaded them with two slugs and five
small bullets each; and my two pistols I loaded with
a brace of bullets each. I hung my great sword, as
usual, naked by my side, and gave Friday his hatchet.

When I had thus prepared myself, I took my perspective glass, and went up to the side of the hill to
see what I could discover; and I found quickly, by
my glass, that there were one and twenty savages,
three prisoners, and three canoes, and that their whole
business seemed to be the triumphant banquet upon

these three human bodies; a barbarous feast indeed, but nothing more than, as I had observed, was usual with them.

I observed also that they were landed, not where they had done when Friday made his escape, but nearer to my creek, where the shore was low, and where a thick wood came close almost down to the sea. This, with the abhorrence of the inhuman errand these wretches came about, filled me with such indignation, that I came down again to Friday, and told him I was resolved to go down to them, and kill them all, and asked him if he would stand by me. He was now gotten over his fright, and his spirits being a little raised with the dram I had given him, he was very cheerful, and told me, as before, he would die when I bid die.

In this fit of fury, I took first and divided the arms which I had charged, as before, between us. I gave Friday one pistol to stick in his girdle, and three guns upon his shoulder; and I took one pistol, and the other three myself, and in this posture we marched out. I took a small bottle of rum in my pocket, and gave Friday a large bag with more powder and bullet; and as to orders, I charged him to keep close behind me, and not to stir, or shoot, or do anything, till I bid him, and in the meantime not to speak a word. In this posture I fetched a compass to my right hand of near a mile, as well to get over the creek as to get into the wood, so that I might come within shot of them before I should be discovered, which I had seen, by my glass, it was easy to do.

While I was making this march, my former thoughts returning, I began to abate my resolution. I do not mean that I entertained any fear of their number;

for as they were naked, unarmed wretches, 'tis certain
I was superior to them; nay, though I had been alone.
But it occurred to my thoughts what call, what
occasion, much less what necessity, I was in to go
and dip my hands in blood, to attack people who had
neither done or intended me any wrong; that whenever God thought fit, He would take the cause into
His own hands, and by national vengeance, punish
them, as a people, for national crimes; but that, in
the meantime, it was none of my business; that, it
was true, Friday might justify it, because he was a
declared enemy, and in a state of war with those very
particular people, and it was lawful for him to attack
them; but I could not say the same with respect to
me. These things were so warmly pressed upon my
thoughts all the way as I went, that I resolved I
would only go and place myself near them, that I
might observe their barbarous feast, and that I would
act then as God should direct; but that, unless something offered that was more a call to me than yet
I knew of, I would not meddle with them.

With this resolution I entered the wood, and with
all possible wariness and silence, Friday following close
at my heels, I marched till I came to the skirt of the
wood, on the side which was next to them; only that
one corner of the wood lay between me and them.
Here I called softly to Friday, and showing him a
great tree, which was just at the corner of the wood,
I bade him go to the tree and bring me word if he
could see there plainly what they were doing. He did
so, and came immediately back to me, and told me
they might be plainly viewed there; that they were
all about their fire, eating the flesh of one of their
prisoners, and that another lay bound upon the sand,

a little from them, which, he said, they would kill next; and, which fired all the very soul within me, he told me it was not one of their nation, but one of the bearded men, whom he had told me of, that came to their country in the boat. I was filled with horror at the very naming the white, bearded man; and going to the tree, I saw plainly, by my glass, a white man, who lay upon the beach of the sea, with his hands and feet tied with flags, or things like rushes, and that he was an European, and had clothes on.

There was another tree, and a little thicket beyond it, about fifty yards nearer to them than the place where I was, which, by going a little way about, I saw I might come at undiscovered, and that then I should be within half shot of them; so I withheld my passion, though I was indeed enraged to the highest degree; and going back about twenty paces, I got behind some bushes, which held all the way till I came to the other tree; and then I came to a little rising ground, which gave me a full view of them, at the distance of about eighty yards.

I had now not a moment to lose, for nineteen of the dreadful wretches sat upon the ground, all close huddled together, and had just sent the other two to butcher the poor Christian, and bring him, perhaps limb by limb, to their fire; and they were stooped down to untie the bands at his feet. I turned to Friday: "Now, Friday," said I, "do as I bid thee." Friday said he would. "Then, Friday," says I, "do exactly as you see me do; fail in nothing." So I set down one of the muskets and the fowling-piece upon the ground, and Friday did the like by his; and with the other musket I took my aim at the savages, bidding him do the like. Then asking him if he was ready, he

said, " Yes," " Then fire at them," said I; and the
same moment I fired also.

Friday took his aim so much better than I, that on
the side that he shot he killed two of them, and
wounded three more; and on my side I killed one,
and wounded two. They were, you may be sure, in a
dreadful consternation; and all of them who were not
hurt jumped up upon their feet, but did not immediately know which way to run, or which way to look,
for they knew not from whence their destruction
came. Friday kept his eyes close upon me, that, as I
had bid him, he might observe what I did; so as
soon as the first shot was made I threw down the
piece, and took up the fowling-piece, and Friday did
the like. He sees me cock and present; he did the same
again. " Are you ready, Friday? " said I. " Yes,"
says he. " Let fly, then," says I, " in the name of
God! " and with that I fired again among the amazed
wretches, and so did Friday; and as our pieces were
now loaded with what I called swan-shot, or small
pistol-bullets, we found only two drop, but so many
were wounded, that they ran about yelling and screaming like mad creatures, all bloody, and miserably
wounded most of them; whereof three more fell
quickly after, though not quite dead.

" Now, Friday," says I, laying down the discharged
pieces, and taking up the musket which was yet loaded,
" follow me," says I, which he did with a great deal
of courage; upon which I rushed out of the wood,
and showed myself, and Friday close at my foot. As
soon as I perceived they saw me, I shouted as loud
as I could, and bade Friday do so too; and running
as fast as I could, which, by the way, was not very
fast, being loaded with arms as I was, I made directly

*G

towards the poor victim, who was, as I said, lying upon the beach, or shore, between the place where they sat and the sea. The two butchers, who were just going to work with him, had left him at the surprise of our first fire, and fled in a terrible fright to the seaside, and had jumped into a canoe, and three more of the rest made the same way. I turned to Friday, and bid him step forwards and fire at them. He understood me immediately, and running about forty yards, to be near them, he shot at them, and I thought he had killed them all, for I saw them all fall of a heap into the boat; though I saw two of them up again quickly. However, he killed two of them, and wounded the third, so that he lay down in the bottom of the boat as if he had been dead.

While my man Friday fired at them, I pulled out my knife and cut the flags that bound the poor victim; and loosing his hands and feet, I lifted him up, and asked him in the Portuguese tongue what he was. He answered in Latin, Christianus; but was so weak and faint, that he could scarce stand or speak. I took my bottle out of my pocket and gave it him, making signs that he should drink, which he did; and I gave him a piece of bread, which he ate. Then I asked him what countryman he was; and he said, Espagniole; and being a little recovered, let me know, by all the signs he could possibly make, how much he was in my debt for his deliverance. "Seignior," said I, with as much Spanish as I could make up, "we will talk afterwards, but we must fight now. If you have any strength left, take this pistol and sword, and lay about you." He took them very thankfully, and no sooner had he the arms in his hands but, as if they had put new vigour into him, he flew upon his murderers like a fury, and had cut two of them in pieces in an instant; for the truth is, as the whole was a surprise to them, so the poor creatures were so much frighted with the noise of our pieces, that they fell down for mere amazement and fear, and had no more power to attempt their own escape, than their flesh had to resist our shot; and that was the case of those five that Friday shot at in the boat; for as three of them fell with the hurt they received, so the other two fell with the fright.

I kept my piece in my hand still without firing, being willing to keep my charge ready, because I had given the Spaniard my pistol and sword. So I called to Friday, and bade him run up to the tree from whence we first fired, and fetch the arms which lay there that had been discharged, which he did with great swiftness; and then giving him my musket, I sat down myself to load all the rest again, and bade them come to me when they wanted. While I was loading these pieces, there happened a fierce engagement between the Spaniard and one of the savages, who made at him with one of their great wooden swords, the same weapon that was to have killed him before if I had not prevented it. The Spaniard, who was as bold and as brave as could be imagined, though weak, had fought this Indian a good while, and had cut him two great wounds on his head; but the savage being a stout, lusty fellow, closing in with him, had thrown him down, being faint, and was wringing my sword out of his hand, when the Spaniard, though undermost, wisely quitting the sword, drew the pistol from his girdle, shot the savage through the body, and killed him upon the spot, before I, who was running to help him, could come near him.

Friday being now left to his liberty, pursued the
flying wretches with no weapon in his hand but his
hatchet; and with that he despatched those three
who, as I said before, were wounded at first, and
fallen, and all the rest he could come up with; and the
Spaniard coming to me for a gun, I gave him one of
the fowling-pieces, with which he pursued two of the
savages, and wounded them both; but as he was not
able to run, they both got from him into the wood,
where Friday pursued them, and killed one of them;
but the other was too nimble for him, and though he
was wounded, yet had plunged himself into the sea
and swam with all his might off to those two who were
left in the canoe; which three in the canoe, with one
wounded, who we know not whether he died or no,
were all that escaped out hands of one and twenty.
The account of the rest is as follows:

3 killed at our first shot from the tree.
2 killed at the next shot.
2 killed by Friday in the boat.
2 killed by ditto, of those at first wounded.
1 killed by ditto in the wood.
3 killed by the Spaniard.
4 killed, being found dropped here and there of their
    wounds, or killed by Friday in his chase of
    them.
4 escaped in the boat, whereof one wounded, if not
    dead.
—
21 in all.

Those that were in the canoe worked hard to get out
of gun-shot; and though Friday made two or three
shots at them, I did not find that he hit any of them.

Friday would fain have had me take one of their canoes, and pursue them; and, indeed, I was very anxious about their escape, lest carrying the news home to their people they should come back perhaps with two or three hundred of their canoes, and devour us by mere multitude. So I consented to pursue them by sea, and running to one of their canoes I jumped in, and bade Friday follow me. But when I was in the canoe, I was surprised to find another poor creature lie there alive, bound hand and foot, as the Spaniard was, for the slaughter, and almost dead with fear, not knowing what the matter was; for he had not been able to look up over the side of the boat, he was tied so hard, neck and heels, and had been tied so long, that he had really but little life in him.

I immediately cut the twisted flags or rushes, which they had bound him with, and would have helped him up; but he could not stand or speak, but groaned most piteously, believing, it seems, still that he was only unbound in order to be killed.

When Friday came to him, I bade him speak to him, and tell him of his deliverance; and pulling out my bottle, made him give the poor wretch a dram; which, with the news of his being delivered, revived him, and he sat up in the boat. But when Friday came to hear him speak, and look in his face, it would have moved any one to tears to have seen how Friday kissed him, embraced him, hugged him, cried, laughed, hallooed, jumped about, danced, sung; then cried again, wrung his hands, beat his own face and head, and then sung and jumped about again, like a distracted creature. It was a good while before I could make him speak to me, or tell me what was the matter; and when he came a little to himself, he told me that it was his father.

It is not easy for me to express how it moved me to see what ecstasy and filial affection had worked in this poor savage at the sight of his father, and of his being delivered from death; nor, indeed, can I describe half the extravagancies of his affection after this; for he went into the boat, and out of the boat, a great many times. When he went in to him, he would sit down by him, open his breast, and hold his father's head close to his bosom, half-an-hour together, to nourish it; then he took his arms and ankles, which were numbed and stiff with the binding, and chafed and rubbed them with his hands; and I, perceiving what the case was, gave him some rum out of my bottle to rub them with, which did them a great deal of good.

This action put an end to our pursuit of the canoe with the other savages, who were now gotten almost out of sight; and it was happy for us that we did not, for it blew so hard within two hours after, and before they could be gotten a quarter of their way, and continued blowing so hard all night, and that from the north-west, which was against them, that I could not suppose their boat could live, or that they ever reached to their own coast.

But to return to Friday. He was so busy about his father, that I could not find in my heart to take him off for some time; but after I thought he could leave him a little, I called him to me, and he came jumping and laughing, and pleased to the highest extreme. Then I asked him if he had given his father any bread. He shook his head, and said, " None; ugly dog eat all up self." So I gave him a cake of bread out of a little pouch I carried on purpose. I also gave him a dram for himself, but he would not taste it, but carried it to his father. I had in my pocket also two or three bunches of my raisins, so I gave him a handful of them for his father. He had no sooner given his father these raisins, but I saw him come out of the boat and run away, as if he had been bewitched, he ran at such a rate; for he was the swiftest fellow of his foot that ever I saw. I say, he run at such a rate, that he was out of sight as it were, in an instant; and though I called, and hallooed too, after him, it was all one, away he went; and in a quarter of an hour I saw him come back again, though not so fast as he went; and as he came nearer I found his pace was slacker, because he had something in his hand.

When he came up to me, I found he had been quite home for an earthern jug, or pot, to bring his father some fresh water, and that he had got two more cakes or loaves of bread. The bread he gave me, but the water he carried to his father. However as I was very thirsty too, I took a little sup of it. This water revived his father more than all the rum or spirits I had given him, for he was just fainting with thirst.

When his father had drank, I called him to know if there was any water left. He said " Yes "; and I bade him give it to the poor Spaniard, who was in as much want of it as his father; and I sent one of the cakes, that Friday brought, to the Spaniard too, who was indeed very weak, and was reposing himself upon a green place under the shade of a tree; and whose limbs were also very stiff, and very much swelled with the rude bandage he had been tied with. When I saw that upon Friday's coming to him with the water he sat up and drank, and took the bread, and began to eat, I went to him, and gave him a handful of raisins. He looked up in my face with all the tokens of gratitude and thankfulness that could appear in any countenance; but was so weak, notwithstanding he had so exerted himself in the fight, that he could not stand upon his feet. He tried to do it two or three times, but was really not able, his ankles were so swelled and so painful to him; so I bade him sit still, and caused Friday to rub his ankles, and bathe them with rum, as he had done his father's.

I observed the poor affectionate creature, every two minutes, or perhaps less, all the while he was here, turned his head about to see if his father was in the same place and posture as he left him sitting; and at last he found he was not to be seen; at which he started up, and without speaking a word, flew with that swiftness to him, that one could scarce perceive his feet to touch the ground as he went. But when he came, he only found he had laid himself down to ease his limbs; so Friday came back to me presently and I then spoke to the Spaniard to let Friday help him up, if he could, and lead him to the boat, and then he should carry him to our dwelling, where I would take care of him. But Friday, a lusty, strong fellow, took the Spaniard quite up upon his back, and carried him away to the boat, and set him down softly upon the side or gunnel of the canoe, with his feet in the inside of it, and then lifted him quite in, and set him close to his father; and presently stepping out again, launched the boat off, and paddled it along the shore faster than I could walk, though the wind blew pretty hard too. So he brought them both safe into our creek and leaving them in the boat, runs away to fetch the other canoe. As he passed me, I spoke to him, and asked him whither he went. He told me, " Go fetch more boat." So away he went like the wind, for sure never man or horse ran like him; and he had the other canoe in the creek almost as soon as I got to it by land; so he wafted me over, and then went to help our new guests out of the boat, which he did; but they were neither of them able to walk, so that poor Friday knew not what to do.

To remedy this I went to work in my thoughts, and calling to Friday to bid them sit down on the bank while he came to me, I soon made a kind of hand-barrow to lay them on, and Friday and I carried them up both together upon it between us. But when we got them to the outside of our wall, or fortification, we were at a worse loss than before, for it was impossible to get them over, and I was resolved not to break it down. So I set to work again; and Friday and I, in about two hours' time, made a very handsome tent, covered with old sails, and above that with boughs of trees, being in the space without our outward fence, and between that and the grove of young wood which I had planted; and here we made them two beds of such things as I had, viz., of good rice-straw, with blankets laid upon it to lie on, and another to cover them, on each bed.

CHAPTER XVII

THE SOCIAL LIFE

My island was now peopled, and I thought myself very rich in subjects; and it was a merry reflection, which I frequently made, how like a king I looked. First of all, the whole country was my own mere property, so that I had an undoubted right of dominion. Secondly, my people were perfectly subjected, I was

absolute lord and lawgiver; they all owed their lives
to me, and were ready to lay down their lives, if there
had been occasion of it, for me. It was remarkable,
too, we had but three subjects, and they were of three
different religions. My man Friday was a Protestant,
his father was a Pagan and a cannibal, and the Spaniard
was a Papist. However, I allowed liberty of conscience
throughout my dominions. But this is by the way.

As soon as I had secured my two weak rescued
prisoners, and given them shelter and a place to rest
them upon, I began to think of making some provision
for them; and the first thing I did, I ordered Friday
to take a yearling goat, betwixt a kid and a goat, out
of my particular flock, to be killed; when I cut off the
hinder quarter, and chopping it into small pieces,
I set Friday to work to boiling and stewing, and made
them a very good dish, I assure you, of flesh and
broth, having put some barley and rice also into the
broth; and as I cooked it without doors, for I made
no fire within my inner wall, so I carried it all into the
new tent, and having set a table there for them, I sat
down and ate my own dinner also with them, and as
well as I could cheered them, and encouraged them;
Friday being my interpreter, especially to his father,
and, indeed, to the Spaniard too; for the Spaniard
spoke the language of the savages pretty well.

After we had dined, or rather supped, I ordered
Friday to take one of the canoes and go and fetch our
muskets and other firearms, which, for want of time,
we had left upon the place of battle; and the next
day I ordered him to go and bury the dead bodies of
the savages, which lay open to the sun, and would
presently be offensive; and I also ordered him to
bury the horrid remains of their barbarous feast,

which I knew were pretty much, and which I could
not think of doing myself; nay, I could not bear to
see them, if I went that way. All which he punctually
performed, and defaced the very appearance of the
savages being there; so that when I went again I
could scarce know where it was, otherwise than by the
corner of the wood pointing to the place.

I then began to enter into a little conversation with
my two new subjects; and first, I set Friday to enquire
of his father what he thought of the escape of the
savages in that canoe, and whether we might expect
a return of them, with a power too great for us to
resist. His first opinion was, that the savages in the
boat never could live out the storm which blew that
night they went off, but must, of necessity, be drowned,
or driven south to those other shores, where they were
as sure to be devoured as they were to be drowned if
they were cast away. But as to what they would do
if they came safe on shore, he said he knew not; but
it was his opinion that they were so dreadfully frighted
with the manner of their being attacked, the noise, and
the fire, that he believed they would tell their people
they were all killed by thunder and lightning, not by
the hand of man; and that the two which appeared,
viz., Friday and me, were two heavenly spirits, or furies,
come down to destroy them, and not men with weapons.
This, he said, he knew, because he heard them all cry
out so in their language to one another; for it was
impossible to them to conceive that a man could dart
fire, and speak thunder, and kill at a distance without
lifting up the hand, as was done now. And this old
savage was in the right; for, as I understood since by
other hands, the savages never attempted to go over
to the island afterwards. They were so terrified with

the accounts given by those four men (for, it seems, they did escape the sea), that they believed whoever went to that enchanted island would be destroyed with fire from the gods.

This, however, I knew not, and therefore was under continual apprehensions for a good while, and kept always upon my guard, me and all my army; for as we were now four of us, I would have ventured upon a hundred of them, fairly in the open field, at any time.

In a little time, however, no more canoes appearing, the fear of their coming wore off, and I began to take my former thoughts of a voyage to the main into consideration; being likewise assured, by Friday's father, that I might depend upon good usage from their nation, on his account, if I would go.

But my thoughts were a little suspended when I had a serious discourse with the Spaniard, and when I understood that there were sixteen more of his countrymen and Portuguese who, having been cast away, and made their escape to that side, lived there at peace, indeed, with the savages, but were very sore put to it for necessaries, and indeed for life. I asked him all the particulars of their voyage, and found they were a Spanish ship bound from the Rio de la Plata to the Havana, being directed to leave their loading there, which was chiefly hides and silver, and to bring back what European goods they could meet with there; that they had five Portuguese seamen on board, whom they took out of another wreck; that five of their own men were drowned when the first ship was lost, and that these escaped, through infinite dangers and hazards, and arrived, almost starved, on the cannibal coast, where they expected to have been devoured every moment.

He told me they had some arms with them, but they were perfectly useless, for that they had neither powder or ball, the washing of the sea having spoiled all their powder but a little, which they used, at their first landing, to provide themselves some food.

I asked him what he thought would become of them there, and if they had formed no design of making any escape? He said they had many consultations about it; but that having neither vessel, or tools to build one, or provisions of any kind, their councils always ended in tears and despair.

I asked him how he thought they would receive a proposal from me, which might tend towards an escape; and whether, if they were all here, it might not be done? I told him with freedom, I feared mostly their treachery and ill usage of me if I put my life in their hands; for that gratitude was no inherent virtue in the nature of man, nor did men always square their dealings by the obligations they had received, so much as they did by the advantages they expected. I told him it would be very hard that I should be the instrument of their deliverance, and that they should afterwards make me their prisoner in New Spain, where an Englishman was certain to be made a sacrifice, what necessity or what accident soever brought him thither; and that I had rather be delivered up to the savages, and be devoured alive, than fall into the merciless claws of the priests, and be carried into the Inquisition. I added, that otherwise I was persuaded, if they were all here, we might, with so many hands, build a bark large enough to carry us all away, either to the Brazils, southward, or to the islands, or Spanish coast, northward; but that if, in requital, they should, when I had put weapons into

their hands, carry me by force among their own people,
I might be ill used for my kindness to them, and make
my case worse than it was before.

He answered, with a great deal of candour and
ingenuity, that their condition was so miserable, and
they were so sensible of it, that he believed they
would abhor the thought of using any man unkindly
that should contribute to their deliverance; and that,
if I pleased, he would go to them with the old man,
and discourse with them about it, and return again, and
bring me their answer; that he would make conditions
with them upon their solemn oath that they should
be absolutely under my leading, as their commander
and captain; and that they should swear upon the
holy sacraments and the gospel to be true to me, and
to go to such Christian country as that I should agree
to, and no other, and to be directed wholly and absolutely by my orders till they were landed safely in such
country as I intended; and that he would bring a con-
tract from them, under their hands, for that purpose.

Then he told me he would first swear to me himself, that he would never stir from me as long as he
lived till I gave him orders; and that he would take
my side to the last drop of his blood, if there should
happen the least breach of faith among his countrymen.

He told me they were all of them very civil, honest
men, and they were under the greatest distress imaginable, having neither weapons or clothes, or any food,
but at the mercy and discretion of the savages; out
of all hopes of ever returning to their own country;
and that he was sure, if I would undertake their
relief, they would live and die by me.

Upon these assurances I resolved to venture to relieve
them, if possible, and to send the old savage and this

Spaniard over to them to treat. But when we had
gotten all things in a readiness to go, the Spaniard
himself started an objection, which had so much
prudence in it on one hand, and so much sincerity on
the other hand, that I could not but be very well satisfied in it, and by his advice put off the deliverance of
his comrades for at least half a year. The case was thus.

He had been with us now about a month, during
which time I had let him see in what manner I had
provided, with the assistance of Providence, for my
support; and he saw evidently what stock of corn
and rice I had made up; which, as it was more than
sufficient for myself, so it was not sufficient, at least
without good husbandry, for my family, now it was
increased to number four; but much less would it be
sufficient if his countrymen, who were, as he said,
fourteen, still alive, should come over; and least of
all would it be sufficient to victual our vessel, if we
should build one, for a voyage to any of the Christian
colonies of America. So he told me he thought it would
be more advisable to let him and the two others dig
and cultivate some more land, as much as I could
spare seed to sow; and that we should wait another
harvest, that we might have a supply of corn for his
countrymen when they should come; for want might
be a temptation to them to disagree, or not to think
themselves delivered, otherwise than out of one
difficulty into another. " You know," says he, " the
children of Israel, though they rejoiced at first for
their being delivered out of Egypt, yet rebelled even
against God Himself, that delivered them, when they
came to want bread in the wilderness."

His caution was so seasonable, and his advice so
good, that I could not but be very well pleased with

his proposal, as well as I was satisfied with his fidelity. So we fell to digging all four of us, as well as the wooden tools we were furnished with permitted; and in about a month's time, by the end of which it was seed-time, we had gotten as much land cured and trimmed up as we sowed twenty-two bushels of barley on, and sixteen jars of rice; which was, in short, all the seed we had to spare; nor, indeed, did we leave ourselves barley sufficient for our own food for the six months that we had to expect our crop; that is to say, reckoning from the time we set our seed aside for sowing; for it is not to be supposed it is six months in the ground in that country.

Having now society enough, and our number being sufficient to put us out of fear of the savages, if they had come, unless their number had been very great, we went freely all over the island, wherever we found occasion; and as here we had our escape or deliverance upon our thoughts, it was impossible, at least for me, to have the means of it out of mine. To this purpose I marked out several trees which I thought fit for our work, and I set Friday and his father to cutting them down; and then I caused the Spaniard, to whom I imparted my thought on that affair, to oversee and direct their work. I showed them with what indefatigable pains I had hewed a large tree into single planks, and I caused them to do the like, till they had made about a dozen large planks of good oak, near two feet broad, thirty-five feet long, and from two inches to four inches thick. What prodigious labour it took up, any one may imagine.

At the same time, I contrived to increase my little flock of tame goats as much as I could; and to this purpose I made Friday and the Spaniard go out one

day, and myself with Friday the next day, for we
took our turns, and by this means we got above twenty
young kids to breed up with the rest; for whenever
we shot the dam, we saved the kids, and added them
to our flock. But above all, the season for curing the
grapes coming on, I caused such a prodigious quantity
to be hung up in the sun, that I believe, had we been
at Alicant, where the raisins of the sun are cured, we
could have filled sixty or eighty barrels; and these,
with our bread, was a great part of our food, and very
good living too, I assure you; for it is an exceeding
nourishing food.

It was now harvest, and our crop in good order. It
was not the most plentiful increase I had seen in the
island, but, however, it was enough to answer our end;
for from our twenty-two bushels of barley we brought
in and thrashed out above two hundred and twenty
bushels, and the like in proportion of the rice; which
was store enough for our food to the next harvest,
though all the sixteen Spaniards had been on shore
with me; or if we had been ready for a voyage, it
would very plentifully have victualled our ship to
have carried us to any part of the world, that is to
say, of America.

When we had thus housed and secured our magazine
of corn, we fell to work to make more wicker-work, viz.,
great baskets, in which we kept it; and the Spaniard
was very handy and dexterous at this part, and often
blamed me that I did not make some things for defence
of this kind of work; but I saw no need of it.

And now having a full supply of food for all the
guests I expected, I gave the Spaniard leave to go over
to the main, to see what he could do with those he
had left behind him there. I gave him a strict charge

in writing not to bring any man with him who would not first swear, in the presence of himself and of the old savage, that he would no way injure, fight with, or attack the person he should find in the island, who was so kind to send for them in order to their deliverance; but that they would stand by and defend him against all such attempts, and wherever they went would be entirely under and subjected to his commands, and that this should be put in writing, and signed with their hands. How we were to have this done, when I knew they had neither pen or ink, that indeed was a question which we never asked.

Under these instructions, the Spaniard and the old savage, the father of Friday, went away in one of the canoes which they might be said to come in, or rather were brought in, when they came as prisoners to be devoured by the savages.

I gave each of them a musket, with a firelock on it, and about eight charges of powder and ball, charging them to be very good husbands of both, and not to use either of them but upon urgent occasion.

This was a cheerful work, being the first measures used by me, in view of my deliverance, for now twenty-seven years and some days. I gave them provisions of bread and of dried grapes sufficient for themselves for many days, and sufficient for all their countrymen for about eight days' time; and wishing them a good voyage, I saw them go, agreeing with them about a signal they should hang out at their return, by which I should know them again, when they came back, at a distance, before they came on shore.

They went away with a fair gale on the day that the moon was at full, by my account in the month of October; but as for an exact reckoning of days, after

I had once lost it, I could never recover it again; nor had I kept even the number of years so punctually as to be sure that I was right, though as it proved, when I afterwards examined my account, I found I had kept a true reckoning of years.

It was no less than eight days I had waited for them, when a strange and unforeseen accident intervened, of which the like has not perhaps been heard of in history. I was fast asleep in my hutch one morning, when my man Friday came running in to me, and called aloud, " Master, master, they are come, they are come!"

I jumped up, and, regardless of danger, I went out as soon as I could get my clothes on, through my little grove, which, by the way, was by this time grown to be a very thick wood; I say, regardless of danger, I went without my arms, which was not my custom to do; but I was surprised when, turning my eyes to the sea, I presently saw a boat at about a league and half's distance standing in for the shore, with a shoulder-of-mutton sail, as they call it, and the wind blowing pretty fair to bring them in; also I observed presently that they did not come from that side which the shore lay on, but from the southernmost end of the island. Upon this I called Friday in, and bid him lie close for these were not the people we looked for, and that we might not know yet whether they were friends or enemies.

In the next place, I went in to fetch my perspective glass, to see what I could make of them; and having taken the ladder out, I climbed up to the top of the hill, as I used to do when I was apprehensive of any-thing, and to take my view the plainer, without being discovered.

I had scarce set my foot on the hill, when my eye

plainly discovered a ship lying at an achor at about
two leagues and an half's distance from me, south-
south-east, but not above a league and an half from
the shore. By my observation, it appeared plainly
to be an English ship, and the boat appeared to be
an English longboat.

I cannot express the confusion I was in; though
the joy of seeing a ship, and one who I had reason to
believe was manned by my own countrymen, and
consequently friends, was such as I cannot describe.
But yet I had some secret doubts hung about me, I
cannot tell from whence they came, bidding me keep
upon my guard. In the first place, it occurred to me
to consider what business an English ship could have
in that part of the world, since it was not the way to or
from any part of the world where the English had any
traffic; and I knew there had been no storms to drive
them in there as in distress; and that if they were
English really, it was most probable that they were
here upon no good design; and that I had better
continue as I was, than fall into the hands of thieves
and murderers.

CHAPTER XVIII

NEW ARRIVALS

I HAD not kept myself long in this posture, but I saw
the boat draw near the shore, as if they looked for a
creek to thrust in at, for the convenience of landing.
However, as they did not come quite far enough,
they did not see the little inlet where I formerly
landed my rafts; but ran their boat on shore upon the
beach, at about half a mile from me, which was very
happy for me; for otherwise they would have landed

just, as I may say, at my door, and would soon have beaten me out of my castle, and perhaps have plundered me of all I had.

When they were on shore, I was fully satisfied that they were Englishmen, at least most of them; one or two I thought were Dutch, but it did not prove so. There were in all eleven men, whereof three of them I found were unarmed and, as I thought, bound; and when the first four or five of them were jumped on shore, they took those three out of the boat, as prisoners. One of the three I could perceive using the most passionate gestures of entreaty, affliction, and despair, even to a kind of extravagance; and the other two, I could perceive, lifted up their hands sometimes, and appeared concerned indeed, but not to such a degree as the first.

I was perfectly confounded at the sight, and knew not what the meaning of it should be. Friday called out to me in English as well as he could, " O master! you see English mans eat prisoner as well as savage mans." " Why," says I, " Friday, do you think they are a-going to eat them then? " " Yes," says Friday, " they will eat them." " No, no," says I, " Friday, I am afraid they will murder them indeed, but you may be sure they will not eat them."

All this while I had no thought of what the matter really was, but stood trembling with the horror of the sight, expecting every moment when the three prisoners should be killed; nay, once I saw one of the villains lift up his arm with a great cutlass, as the seamen call it, or sword, to strike one of the poor men; and I expected to see him fall every moment, at which all the blood in my body seemed to run chill in my veins.

I wished heartily now for my Spaniard, and the savage that was gone with him; or that I had any

way to have come undiscovered within shot of them,
that I might have rescued the three men, for I saw
no firearms they had among them; but it fell out to
my mind another way.

After I had observed the outrageous usage of the
three men by the insolent seamen, I observed the
fellows run scattering about the land, as if they wanted
to see the country. I observed that the three other
men had liberty to go also where they pleased; but
they sat down all three upon the ground, very pensive,
and looked like men in despair.

This put me in mind of the first time when I came
on shore, and began to look about me; how I gave
myself over for lost; how wildly I looked round me;
what dreadful apprehensions I had; and how I lodged
in the tree all night, for fear of being devoured by
wild beasts.

As I knew nothing that night of the supply I was
to receive by the providential driving of the ship
nearer the land by the storms and tide, by which I
have since been so long nourished and supported;
so these three poor desolate men knew nothing how
certain of deliverance and supply they were, how near
it was to them, and how effectually and really they
were in a condition of safety, at the same time that
they thought themselves lost, and their case desperate.

It was just at the top of high-water when these
people came on shore; and while partly they stood
parleying with the prisoners they brought, and partly
while they rambled about to see what kind of a place
they were in, they had carelessly stayed till the tide
was spent, and the water was ebbed considerably
away, leaving their boat aground.

They had left two men in the boat, who, as I found

afterwards, having drank a little too much brandy, fell asleep. However, one of them waking sooner than the other, and finding the boat too fast aground for him to stir it, hallooed for the rest, who were straggling about, upon which they all soon came to the boat; but it was past all their strength to launch her, the boat being very heavy, and the shore on that side being a soft oozy sand, almost like a quicksand.

In this condition, like true seamen, who are perhaps the least of all mankind given to forethought, they gave it over, and away they strolled about the country again; and I heard one of them say aloud to another, calling them off from the boat, " Why, let her alone, Jack, can't ye? she will float next tide "; by which I was fully confirmed in the main inquiry of what countrymen they were.

All this while I kept myself very close, not once daring to stir out of my castle, any farther than to my place of observation near the top of the hill; and very glad I was to think how well it was fortified. I knew it was no less than ten hours before the boat could be on float again, and by that time it would be dark, and I might be at more liberty to see their motions, and to hear their discourse, if they had any.

In the meantime, I fitted myself up for a battle, as before, though with more caution, knowing I had to do with another kind of enemy than I had at first. I ordered Friday also, whom I had made an excellent marksman with his gun, to load himself with arms. I took myself two fowling-pieces, and I gave him three muskets. My figure, indeed, was very fierce. I had my formidable goat-skin coat on, with the great cap I have mentioned, a naked sword by my side, two pistols in my belt, and a gun upon each shoulder.

It was my design, as I said above, not to have made any attempt till it was dark; but about two o'clock, being the heat of the day, I found that, in short, they were all gone straggling into the woods, and, as I thought, were laid down to sleep. The three poor distressed men, too anxious for their condition to get any sleep, were, however, set down under the shelter of a great tree, at about a quarter of a mile from me, and, as I thought, out of sight of any of the rest.

Upon this I resolved to discover myself to them, and learn something of their condition. Immediately I marched in the figure as above, my man Friday at a good distance behind me, as formidable for his arms as I, but not making quite so staring a spectre-like figure as I did.

I came as near them undiscovered as I could, and then, before any of them saw me, I called aloud to them in Spanish, " What are ye, gentlemen? "

They started up at the noise, but were ten times more confounded when they saw me, and the uncouth figure that I made. They made no answer at all, but I thought I perceived them just going to fly from me, when I spoke to them in English. " Gentlemen," said I, "do not be surprised at me; perhaps you may have a friend near you, when you did not expect it." " He must be sent directly from heaven then," said one of them very gravely to me, and pulling off his hat at the same time to me, " for our condition is past the help of man." " All help is from heaven, sir," said I, " But can you put a stranger in the way how to help you, for you seem to be in some great distress? I saw you when you landed; and when you seemed to make applications to the brutes that came with you, I saw one of them lift up his sword to kill you."

The poor man, with tears running down his face, and trembling, looking like one astonished, returned, " Am I talking to God, or man? Is it a real man, or an angel? " " Be in no fear about that, sir," said I. " If God had sent an angel to relieve you, he would have come better clothed, and armed after another manner than you see me in. Pray lay aside your fears; I am a man, an Englishman and disposed to assist you, you see. I have one servant only; we have arms and ammunition; tell us freely, can we serve you? What is your case? "

" Our case," said he, " sir, is too long to tell you while our murderers are so near; but in short, sir, I was commander of that ship; my men have mutinied against me, they have been hardly prevailed on not to murder me; and at last have set me on shore in this desolate place, with these two men with me, one my mate, the other a passenger, where we expected to perish, believing the place to be uninhabited, and know not yet what to think of it."

" Where are those brutes, your enemies? " said I. " Do you know where they are gone? " " There they lie, sir," said he, pointing to a thicket of trees. " My heart trembles for fear they have seen us, and heard you speak. If they have, they will certainly murder us all."

" Have they any firearms? " said I. He answered, they had only two pieces, and one which they left in the boat. " Well then," said I, " leave the rest to me, I see they are all asleep; it is an easy thing to kill them all; but shall we rather take them prisoners? " He told me there were two desperate villains among them that it was scarce safe to show any mercy to; but if they were secured, he believed all the rest would

H

return to their duty. I asked him which they were. He told me he could not at that distance describe them, but he would obey my orders in anything I would direct. " Well," says I, " let us retreat out of their view or hearing, lest they awake, and we will resolve further." So they willingly went back with me, till the woods covered us from them.

" Look you, sir," said I, " if I venture upon your deliverance, are you willing to make two conditions with me? " He anticipated my proposals, by telling me that both he and the ship, if recovered, should be wholly directed and commanded by me in everything; and if the ship was not recovered, he would live and die with me in what part of the world soever I would send him; and the two other men said the same.

" Well," says I, " my conditions are but two. 1. That while you stay on this island with me, you will not pretend to any authority here; and if I put arms into your hands, you will, upon all occasions, give them up to me, and do no prejudice to me or mine upon this island; and in the meantime, be governed by my orders. 2. That if the ship is, or may be, recovered, you will carry me and my man to England, passage free."

He gave me all the assurances that the invention and faith of man could devise that he would comply with these most reasonable demands; and, besides, would owe his life to me, and acknowledge it upon all occasions, as long as he lived.

" Well then," said I, " here are three muskets for you, with powder and ball; tell me next what you think is proper to be done." He showed all the testimony of his gratitude that he was able, but offered to be wholly guided by me. I told him I thought it was hard venturing anything; but the best method I could think of was to fire upon them at once as they lay; and if any was not killed at the first volley, and offered to submit, we might save them, and so put it wholly upon God's providence to direct the shot.

He said very modestly that he was loth to kill them, if he could help it; but that those two were incorrigible villains, and had been the authors of all the mutiny in the ship, and if they escaped, we should be undone still; for they would go on board and bring the whole ship's company, and destroy us all. " Well then," says I, " necessity legitimates my advice, for it is the only way to save our lives." However, seeing him still cautious of shedding blood, I told him they should go themselves, and manage as they found convenient.

In the middle of this discourse we heard some of them awake, and soon after we saw two of them on their feet. I asked him if either of them were of the men who he had said were the heads of the mutiny. He said, " No." " Well then," said I, " you may let them escape; and Providence seems to have wakened them on purpose to save themselves. Now," says I, " if the rest escape you, it is your fault."

Animated with this, he took the musket I had given him in his hand, and a pistol in his belt, and his two comrades with him, with each man a piece in his hand. The two men who were with him going first made some noise, at which one of the seamen who was awake turned about, and seeing them coming cried out to the rest; but it was too late then, for the moment he cried out they fired; I mean the two men, the captain wisely reserving his own piece. They had so well aimed their shot at the men they knew, that one of them was killed on the spot, and the other very

much wounded; but not being dead, he started up
upon his feet, and called eagerly for help to the other.
But the captain stepping to him, told him 'twas too
late to cry for help, he should call upon God to for-
give his villainy; and with that word knocked him
down with the stock of his musket, so that he never
spoke more. There were three more in the company,
and one of them was also slightly wounded. By this
time I was come; and when they saw their danger,
and that it was in vain to resist, they begged for mercy.
The captain told them he would spare their lives if
they would give any assurance of their abhorrence of
the treachery they had been guilty of, and would swear
to be faithful to him in recovering the ship, and afterwards in carrying her back to Jamaica, from whence
they came. They gave him all the protestations of
their sincerity that could be desired, and he was
willing to believe them, and spare their lives, which
I was not against, only I obliged him to keep them
bound hand and foot while they were upon the island.

While this was doing, I sent Friday with the captain's mate to the boat, with orders to secure her,
and bring away the oars and sail, which they did;
and by-and-by three straggling men, that were (happily for them) parted from the rest, came back upon
hearing the guns fired, and seeing their captain, who
before was their prisoner, now their conqueror, they
submitted to be bound also, and so our victory was
complete.

It now remained that the captain and I should
inquire into one another's circumstances. I began
first, and told him my whole history, which he heard
with an attention even to amazement; and particularly at the wonderful manner of my being furnished

with provisions and ammunition; and, indeed, as my story is a whole collection of wonders, it affected him deeply. But when he reflected from thence upon himself, and how I seemed to have been preserved there on purpose to save his life, the tears ran down his face, and he could not speak a word more.

After this communication was at an end, I carried him and his two men into my apartment, leading them in just where I came out, viz., at the top of the house, where I refreshed them with such provisions as I had, and showed them all the contrivances I had made during my long, long inhabiting that place.

All I showed them, all I said to them, was perfectly amazing; but above all, the captain admired my fortification, and how perfectly I had concealed my retreat with a grove of trees, which, having been now planted near twenty years, and the trees growing much faster than in England, was become a little wood, and so thick, that it was unpassable in any part of it but at that one side where I had reserved my little winding passage into it. I told him this was my castle and my residence, but that I had a seat in the country, as most princes have, whither I could retreat upon occasion, and I would show him that too another time; but at present, our business was to consider how to recover the ship. He agreed with me as to that, but told me he was perfectly at a loss what measures to take, for that there were still six and twenty hands on board, who having entered into a cursed conspiracy, by which they had all forfeited their lives to the law, would be hardened in it now by desperation, and would carry it on, knowing that if they were reduced, they should be brought to the gallows as soon as they came to England, or to any of the English colonies;

and that therefore there would be no attacking them
with so small a number as we were.

I mused for some time upon what he said, and found
it was a very rational conclusion, and that therefore
something was to be resolved on very speedily, as well
to draw the men on board into some snare for their
surprise, as to prevent their landing upon us, and
destroying us. Upon this it presently occurred to me
that in a little while the ship's crew, wondering what
was become of their comrades, and of the boat, would
certainly come on shore in their other boat to see for
them; and that then, perhaps, they might come
armed, and be too strong for us. This he allowed was
rational.

Upon this, I told him the first thing we had to do
was to stave the boat, which lay upon the beach, so
that they might not carry her off; and taking everything out of her, leave her so far useless as not to be
fit to swim. Accordingly we went on board, took the
arms which were left on board out of her, and whatever else we found there, which was a bottle of brandy,
and another of rum, a few biscuit-cakes, a horn of
powder and a great lump of sugar in a piece of canvas
—the sugar was five or six pounds; all which was
very welcome to me, especially the brandy and sugar,
of which I had had none left for many years.

When we had carried all these things on shore (the
oars, mast, sail, and rudder of the boat were carried
away before, as above), we knocked a great hole in
her bottom, that if they had come strong enough to
master us, yet they could not carry off the boat.

Indeed, it was not much in my thoughts that we
could be able to recover the ship; but my view was,
that if they went away without the boat, I did not

much question to make her fit again to carry us away to the Leeward Islands, and call upon our friends the Spaniards in my way; for I had them still in my thoughts.

CHAPTER XIX

THE MUTINEERS

WHILE we were thus preparing our designs, and had first, by main strength, heaved the boat up upon the beach so high that the tide would not fleet her off at high-water mark; and besides, had broke a hole in her bottom too big to be quickly stopped, and were sat down musing what we should do, we heard the ship fire a gun, and saw her make a waft with her ancient as a signal for the boat to come on board. But no boat stirred; and they fired several times, making other signals for the boat.

At last, when all their signals and firings proved fruitless, and they found the boat did not stir, we saw them, by the help of my glasses, hoist another boat out, and row towards the shore; and we found, as they approached, that there was no less than ten men in her, and that they had firearms with them.

As the ship lay almost two leagues from the shore, we had a full view of them as they came, and a plain sight of the men, even of their faces; because the tide having set them a little to the east of the other boat, they rowed up under shore, to come to the same place where the other had landed, and where the boat lay.

By this means, I say, we had a full view of them, and the captain knew the persons and characters of all the men in the boat, of whom he said that there were three very honest fellows, who, he was sure, were led into this conspiracy by the rest, being over-powered and frighted; but that as for the boatswain, who, it seems, was the chief officer among them, and all the rest, they were as outrageous as any of the ship's crew, and were no doubt made desperate in their new enterprise; and terribly apprehensive he was that they would be too powerful for us.

I smiled at him, and told him that men in our circumstances were past the operation of fear; that seeing almost every condition that could be was better than that which we were supposed to be in, we ought to expect that the consequence, whether death or life, would be sure to be a deliverance. I asked him what he thought of the circumstances of my life, and whether a deliverance were not worth venturing for?" "And where, sir," said I, "is your belief of my being preserved here on purpose to save your life, which elevated you a little while ago? For my part," said I, "there seems to be but one thing amiss in all the prospect of it." "What's that?" says he. "Why," says I, "'tis that, as you say, there are three or four honest fellows among them, which should be spared; had they been all of the wicked part of the crew I should have thought God's providence had singled them out to deliver them into your hands; for depend upon it, every man of them that comes ashore are our own, and shall die or live as they behave to us."

As I spoke this with a raised voice and cheerful countenance, I found it greatly encouraged him; so we set vigorously to our business. We had, upon the first appearance of the boat's coming from the ship, considered of separating our prisoners, and had, indeed, secured them effectually.

Two of them, of whom the captain was less assured than ordinary, I sent with Friday and one of the three delivered men to my cave, where they were remote enough, and out of danger of being heard or discovered, or of finding their way out of the woods if they could have delivered themselves. Here they left them bound, but gave them provisions, and promised them, if they continued there quietly, to give them their liberty in a day or two; but that if they attempted their escape, they should be put to death without mercy. They promised faithfully to bear their confinement with patience, and were very thankful that they had such good usage as to have provisions and a light left them; for Friday gave them candles (such as we made ourselves) for their comfort; and they did not know but that he stood sentinel over them at the entrance.

The other prisoners had better usage. Two of them were kept pinioned, indeed, because the captain was not free to trust them; but the other two were taken into my service, upon their captain's recommendation, and upon their solemnly engaging to live and die with us; so with them and the three honest men we were seven men well armed; and I made no doubt we should be able to deal well enough with the ten that were a-coming, considering that the captain had said there were three or four honest men among them also.

As soon as they got to the place where their other boat lay, they ran their boat into the beach, and came all on shore, hauling the boat up after them, which I was glad to see; for I was afraid they would rather have left the boat at an anchor some distance from the shore, with some hands in her to guard her, and so we should not be able to seize the boat.

Being on shore, the first thing they did they ran
*H

all to their other boat; and it was easy to see that
they were under a great surprise to find her stripped,
as above, of all that was in her, and a great hole in
her bottom.

After they had mused a while upon this, they set
up two or three great shouts, hallooing with all their
might, to try if they could make their companions
hear; but all was to no purpose. Then they came
all close in a ring, and fired a volley of their small arms,
which, indeed, we heard, and the echoes made the
woods ring. But it was all one; those in the cave we
were sure could not hear, and those in our keeping,
though they heard it well enough, yet durst give no
answer to them.

They were so astonished at the surprise of this, that,
as they told us afterwards, they resolved to go all on
board again, to their ship, and let them know there
that the men were all murdered, and the longboat
staved. Accordingly, they immediately launched their
boat again, and gat all of them on board.

The captain was terribly amazed, and even confounded at this, believing they would go on board the
ship again, and set sail, giving their comrades for lost,
and so he should still lose the ship, which he was in
hopes we should have recovered; but he was quickly
as much frightened the other way.

They had not been long put off with the boat but
we perceived them all coming on shore again; but
with this new measure in their conduct, which it seems
they consulted together upon, viz., to leave three men
in the boat, and the rest to go on shore, and go up
into the country to look for their fellows.

This was a great disappointment to us, for now we
were at a loss what to do; for our seizing those seven

men on shore would be no advantage if we let the boat escape, because they would then row away to the ship, and then the rest of them would be sure to weigh and set sail, and so our recovering the ship would be lost. However, we had no remedy but to wait and see what the issue of things might present. The seven men came on shore, and the three who remained in the boat put her off to a good distance from the shore, and came to an anchor to wait for them; so that it was impossible for us to come at them in the boat.

Those that came on shore kept close together, marching towards the top of the little hill under which my habitation lay; and we could see them plainly, though they could not perceive us. We could have been very glad they would have come nearer to us, so that we might have fired at them, or that they would have gone farther off, that we might have come abroad.

But when they were come to the brow of the hill, where they could see a great way into the valleys and woods which lay towards the north-east part, and where the island lay lowest, they shouted and hallooed till they were weary; and not caring, it seems, to venture far from the shore, nor far from one another, they sat down together under a tree, to consider of it. Had they thought fit to have gone to sleep there, as the other party of them had done, they had done the job for us; but they were too full of apprehensions of danger to venture to go to sleep, though they could not tell what the danger was they had to fear neither.

The captain made a very just proposal to me upon this consultation of theirs, viz., that perhaps they would all fire a volley again, to endeavour to make their fellows hear, and that we should all sally upon them, just at the juncture when their pieces were all discharged, and they would certainly yield, and we should have them without bloodshed. I liked the proposal, provided it was done while we were near enough to come up to them before they could load their pieces again.

But this event did not happen, and we lay still a long time, very irresolute what course to take. At length I told them there would be nothing to be done, in my opinion, till night; and then, if they did not return to the boat, perhaps we might find a way to get between them and the shore and so might use some stratagem with them in the boat to get them on shore.

We waited a great while, though very impatient for their removing; and were very uneasy when, after long consultations, we saw them start all up, and march down towards the sea. It seems they had such dreadful apprehensions upon them of the danger of the place, that they had resolved to go on board the ship again, give their companions over for lost, and so go on with their intended voyage with the ship.

As soon as I perceived them go towards the shore, I imagined it to be, as it really was, that they had given over their search, and were for going back again; and the captain, as soon as I told him my thoughts, was ready to sink at the apprehensions of it; but I presently thought of a stratagem to fetch them back again, and which answered my end to a tittle.

I ordered Friday and the captain's mate to go over the little creek westward, towards the place where the savages came on shore when Friday was rescued, and as soon as they came to a little rising ground, at about half a mile distance, I bade them halloo as loud as they could, and wait till they found the seamen heard them; that as soon as ever they heard the seamen answer them, they should return it again; and then keeping out of sight, take a round, always answering when the other hallooed, to draw them as far into the island, and among the woods, as possible, and then wheel about again to me by such ways as I directed them.

They were just going into the boat when Friday and the mate hallooed; and they presently heard them, and answering, ran along the shore westward, towards the voice they heard, when they were presently stopped by the creek, where the water being up, they could not get over, and called for the boat to come up and set them over, as, indeed, I expected.

When they had set themselves over, I observed that the boat being gone up a good way into the creek, and, as it were, in a harbour within the land, they took one of the three men out of her to go along with them, and left only two in the boat, having fastened her to the stump of a little tree on the shore.

That was what I wished for; and immediately leaving Friday and the captain's mate to their business, I took the rest with me, and crossing the creek out of their sight, we surprised the two men before they were aware; one of them lying on shore, and the other being in the boat. The fellow on shore was between sleeping and waking, and going to start up. The captain, who was foremost, ran in upon him, and knocked him down, and then called out to him in the boat to yield, or he was a dead man.

There needed very few arguments to persuade a single man to yield when he saw five men upon him, and his comrade knocked down; besides, this was, it seems, one of the three who were not so hearty in the mutiny as the rest of the crew, and therefore was easily persuaded not only to yield, but afterwards to join very sincerely with us.

In the meantime, Friday and the captain's mate so well managed their business with the rest, that they drew them, by hallooing and answering, from one hill to another, and from one wood to another, till they not only heartily tired them, but left them where they were very sure they could not reach back to the boat before it was dark; and, indeed, they were heartily tired themselves also by the time they came back to us.

We had nothing now to do but to watch for them in the dark, and to fall upon them, so as to make sure work with them.

It was several hours after Friday came back to me before they came back to their boat; and we could hear the foremost of them, long before they came quite up, calling to those behind to come along, and could also hear them answer and complain how lame and tired they were, and not able to come any faster; which was very welcome news to us.

At length they came up to the boat; but 'tis impossible to express their confusion when they found the boat fast aground in the creek, the tide ebbed out, and their two men gone. We could hear them calling to one another in a most lamentable manner, telling one another they were gotten into an enchanted island; that either there were inhabitants in it, and they should all be murdered, or else there were devils and spirits in it, and they should all be carried away and devoured.

They hallooed again, and called their two comrades by their names a great many times; but no answer. After some time we could see them, by the little light there was, run about, wringing their hands like men in despair, and that sometimes they would go and sit down in the boat to rest themselves, then come ashore again, and walk about again, and so the same thing over again.

My men would fain have me give them leave to fall upon them at once in the dark; but I was willing to take them at some advantage, so to spare them, and kill as few of them as I could; and especially I was unwilling to hazard the killing any of our own men, knowing the others were very well armed. I resolved to wait, to see if they did not separate; and, therefore, to make sure of them, I drew my ambuscade nearer, and ordered Friday and the captain to creep upon their hands and feet, as close to the ground as they could, that they might not be discovered, and get as near them as they could possibly, before they offered to fire.

They had not been long in that posture but that the boatswain, who was the principal ringleader of the mutiny, and had now shown himself the most dejected and dispirited of all the rest, came walking towards them, with two more of their crew. The captain was so eager, as having this principal rogue so much in his power, that he could hardly have patience to let him come so near as to be sure of him, for they only heard his tongue before; but when they came nearer, the captain and Friday, starting up on their feet, let fly at them.

The boatswain was killed upon the spot; the next man was shot into the body, and fell just by him, though he did not die till an hour or two after; and the third ran for it.

At the noise of the fire I immediately advanced with my whole army, which was now eight men, viz., myself, generalissimo; Friday, my lieutenant-general; the captain and his two men, and the three prisoners of war, whom we had trusted with arms.

We came upon them, indeed, in the dark, so that they could not see our number; and I made the man we had left in the boat, who was now one of us, call to them by name, to try if I could bring them to a parley, and so might perhaps reduce them to terms, which fell out just as we desired; for indeed it was easy to think, as their condition then was, they would be very willing to capitulate. So he calls out as loud as he could to one of them, "Tom Smith! Tom Smith!" Tom Smith answered immediately, "Who's that? Robinson?" For it seems he knew his voice. The other answered, "Ay, ay; for God's sake, Tom Smith, throw down your arms and yield, or you are all dead men this moment."

"Who must we yield to? Where are they?" says Smith again. "Here they are," says he; "here's our captain, and fifty men with him, have been hunting you this two hours; the boatswain is killed, Will Frye is wounded, and I am a prisoner; and if you do not yield, you are all lost."

"Will they give us quarter then," says Tom Smith, "and we will yield?" "I'll go and ask, if you promise to yield," says Robinson. So he asked the captain, and the captain himself then calls out, "You, Smith, you know my voice, if you lay down your arms immediately, and submit, you shall have your lives, all but Will Atkins."

Upon this Will Atkins cried out, "For God's sake, captain, give me quarter; what have I done? They have been all as bad as I"; which by the way, was not true neither; for, it seems, this Will Atkins was the first man that laid hold of the captain when they first mutinied, and used him barbarously, in tying his hands, and giving him injurious language. However, the captain told him he must lay down his arms at discretion, and trust to the governor's mercy; by which he meant me, for they all called me governor.

In a word, they all laid down their arms, and begged their lives; and I sent the man that had parleyed with them and two more, who bound them all; and then my great army of fifty men, which, particularly with those three, were all but eight, came up and seized upon them all, and upon their boat; only that I kept myself and one more out of sight for reasons of state.

Our next work was to repair the boat, and think of seizing the ship; and as for the captain, now he had leisure to parley with them, he expostulated with them upon the villainy of their practices with him, and at length upon the farther wickedness of their design, and how certainly it must bring them to misery and distress in the end, and perhaps to the gallows.

They all appeared very penitent, and begged hard for their lives. As for that, he told them they were none of his prisoners, but the commander of the island; that they thought they had set him on shore in a barren uninhabited island; but it had pleased God so to direct them that the island was inhabited, and that the governor was an Englishman; that he might hang them all there, if he pleased; but as he had given them all quarter, he supposed he would send them to England to be dealt with there as justice required, except Atkins, whom he was commanded by the governor to advise to prepare for death, for that he would be hanged in the morning.

Though this was all a fiction of his own, yet it had

its desired effect. Atkins fell upon his knees, to beg the captain to intercede with the governor for his life; and all the rest begged of him, for God's sake, that they might not be sent to England.

It now occurred to me that the time of our deliverance was come, and that it would be a most easy thing to bring these fellows in to be hearty in getting possession of the ship; so I retired in the dark from them, that they might not see what kind of a governor they had, and called the captain to me. When I called, as at a good distance, one of the men was ordered to speak, again, and say to the captain, "Captain, the commander calls for you." And presently the captain replied, "Tell his excellency I am just a-coming." This more perfectly amused them, and they all believed that the commander was just by with his fifty men.

Upon the captain's coming to me, I told him my project for seizing the ship, which he liked of wonderfully well, and resolved to put it in execution the next morning. But in order to execute it with more art, and secure of success, I told him we must divide the prisoners, and that he should go and take Atkins and two more of the worst of them, and send them pinioned to the cave where the others lay. This was committed to Friday and the two men who came on shore with the captain.

They conveyed them to the cave, as to a prison. And it was, indeed, a dismal place, especially to men in their condition. The others I ordered to my bower, as I called it, of which I have given a full description; and as it was fenced in, and they pinioned, the place was secure enough, considering they were upon their behaviour.

To these in the morning I sent the captain, who was

to enter into a parley with them; in a word, to try them, and tell me whether he thought they might be trusted or no to go on board and surprise the ship. He talked to them of the injury done him, of the condition they were brought to; and that though the governor had given them quarter for their lives as to the present action, yet that if they were sent to England they would all be hanged in chains, to be sure; but that if they would join in so just an attempt as to recover the ship, he would have the governor's engagement for their pardon.

Any one may guess how readily such a proposal would be accepted by men in their condition. They fell down on their knees to the captain, and promised, with the deepest imprecations, that they would be faithful to him to the last drop, and that they should owe their lives to him, and would go with him all over the world; that they would own him for a father to them as long as they lived.

" Well," says the captain, " I must go and tell the governor what you say, and see what I can do to bring him to consent to it." So he brought me an account of the temper he found them in, and that he verily believed they would be faithful.

However, that we might be very secure, I told him he should be back again and choose out five of them, and tell them they might see that he did not want men, that he would take out those five to be his assistants, and that the governor would keep the other two and the three that were sent prisoners to the castle, my cave, as hostages for the fidelity of those five; and that if they proved unfaithful in the execution, the five hostages should be hanged in chains alive upon the shore.

This looked severe, and convinced them that the governor was in earnest. However, they had no way left them but to accept it; and it was now the business of the prisoners, as much as of the captain, to persuade the other five to do their duty.

Our strength was now thus ordered for the expedition. 1. The captain, his mate, and passenger. 2. Then the two prisoners of the first gang, to whom, having their characters from the captain, I had given their liberty, and trusted them with arms. 3. The other two whom I had kept till now in my bower, pinioned, but upon the captain's motion had now released. 4. These five released at last; so that they were twelve all, besides five we kept prisoners in the cave for hostages.

I asked the captain if he was willing to venture with these hands on board the ship; for as for me and my man Friday, I did not think it was proper for us to stir, having seven men left behind, and it was employment enough for us to keep them asunder and supply them with victuals. As to the five in the cave, I resolved to keep them fast; but Friday went in twice a day to them, to supply them with necessaries; and I made the other two carry provisions to a certain distance, where Friday was to take it.

When I showed myself to the two hostages, it was with the captain, who told them I was the person the governor had ordered to look after them, and that it was the governor's pleasure they should not stir anywhere but by my direction; that if they did, they should be fetched into the castle, and be laid in irons; so that as we never suffered them to see me as governor, so I now appeared as another person, and spoke of the governor, the garrison, the castle, and the like, upon all occasions.

The captain now had no difficulty before him but to furnish his two boats, stop the breach of one, and man them. He made his passenger captain of one, with four other men; and himself, and his mate, and five more went in the other; and they contrived their business very well, for they came up to the ship about midnight. As soon as they came within call of the ship, he made Robinson hail them, and tell them they brought off the men and the boat, but that it was a long time before they had found them, and the like, holding them in a chat till they came to the ship's side; when the captain and the mate entering first, with their arms, immediately knocked down the second mate and carpenter with the butt-end of their muskets, being very faithfully seconded by their men. They secured all the rest that were upon the main and quarter decks, and began to fasten the hatches to keep them down who were below; when the other boat and their men entering at the fore-chains, secured the fore-castle of the ship, and the scuttle which went down into the cook-room, making three men they found there prisoners.

When this was done, and all safe upon deck, the captain ordered the mate, with three men, to break into the round-house, where the new rebel captain lay, and having taken the alarm was gotten up, and with two men and a boy had gotten firearms in their hands; and when the mate with a crow split open the door, the new captain and his men fired boldly among them, and wounded the mate with a musket-ball, which broke his arm, and wounded two more of the men, but killed nobody.

The mate calling for help, rushed however into the round-house wounded as he was, and with his pistol shot the new captain through the head, the bullet entering at his mouth and came out again behind one of his ears, so that he never spoke a word; upon which the rest yielded, and the ship was taken effectually, without any more lives lost.

As soon as the ship was thus secured, the captain ordered seven guns to be fired, which was the signal agreed upon with me to give me notice of his success, which you may be sure I was very glad to hear, having sat watching upon the shore for it till near two of the clock in the morning.

Having thus heard the signal plainly, I laid me down; and it having been a day of great fatigue to me, I slept very sound, till I was something surprised with the noise of a gun; and presently starting up, I heard a man call me by the name of " Governor," " Governor," and presently I knew the captain's voice; when climbing up to the top of the hill, there he stood, and pointing to the ship, he embraced me in his arms. " My dear friend and deliverer," says he, " there's your ship, for she is all yours, and so are we, and all that belong to her." I cast my eyes to the ship, and there she rode within little more than half a mile of the shore; for they had weighed her anchor as soon as they were masters of her, and the weather being fair, had brought her to an anchor just against the mouth of the little creek, and the tide being up, the captain had brought the pinnace in near the place where I at first landed my rafts, and so landed just at my door.

I was at first ready to sink down with the surprise; for I saw my deliverance, indeed, visibly put into my hands, all things easy, and a large ship just ready to carry me away whither I pleased to go. At first, for some time, I was not able to answer him one word; but as he had taken me in his arms, I held fast by him, or I should have fallen to the ground.

He perceived the surprise, and immediately pulls a bottle out of his pocket, and gave me a dram of cordial, which he had brought on purpose for me. After I had drank it, I sat down upon the ground; and though it brought me to myself, yet it was a good while before I could speak a word to him.

All this while the poor man was in as great an ecstasy as I, only not under any surprise, as I was; and he said a thousand kind tender things to me, to compose me and bring me to myself. But such was the flood of joy in my breast, that it put all my spirits into confusion. At last it broke out into tears, and in a little while after I recovered my speech.

Then I took my turn, and embraced him as my deliverer, and we rejoiced together. I told him I looked upon him as a man sent from heaven to deliver me, and that the whole transaction seemed to be a chain of wonders; that such things as these were the testimonies we had of a secret hand of Providence governing the world, and evidence that the eyes of an infinite Power could search into the remotest corner of the world, and send help to the miserable whenever He pleased.

CHAPTER XX

THE END OF THE STORY

I FORGOT not to lift up my heart in thankfulness to heaven; and what heart could forbear to bless Him, who had not only in a miraculous manner provided for one in such a wilderness, and in such a desolate condition, but from whom every deliverance must always be acknowledged to proceed?

When we had talked a while, the captain told me he had brought some little refreshment, such as the ship afforded, and such as the wretches that had been so long his masters had not plundered him of. Upon this he called aloud to the boat, and bid his men bring the things ashore that were for the governor; and, indeed, it was a present as if I had been one, not that was to be carried away along with them, but as if I had been to dwell upon the island still, and they were to go without me.

First, he had brought me a case of bottles full of excellent cordial waters, six large bottles of Madeira wine (the bottles held two quarts apiece), two pounds of excellent good tobacco, twelve good pieces of the ship's beef, and six pieces of pork, with a bag of peas, and about a hundredweight of biscuit.

He brought me also a box of sugar, a box of flour, a bag full of lemons, and two bottles of lime-juice, and abundance of other things; but besides these, and what was a thousand times more useful to me, he brought me six clean new shirts, six very good neck-cloths, two pair of gloves, one pair of shoes, a hat, and one pair of stockings, and a very good suit of clothes of his own, which had been worn but very little; in a word, he clothed me from head to foot.

It was a very kind and agreeable present, as any one may imagine, to one in my circumstances; but never was anything in the world of that kind so unpleasant, awkward, and uneasy, as it was to me to wear such clothes at their first putting on.

After these ceremonies passed, and after all his good things were brought into my little apartment, we began to consult what was to be done with the prisoners we had; for it was worth considering whether we might venture to take them away with us or no, especially two of them, whom we knew to be incorrigible and refractory to the last degree; and the captain said he knew they were such rogues, that there was no obliging them; and if he did carry them away, it must be in irons, as malefactors, to be delivered over to justice at the first English colony he could come at; and I found that the captain himself was very anxious about it.

Upon this I told him that, if he desired it, I durst undertake to bring the two men he spoke of to make it their own request that he should leave them upon the island. " I should be very glad of that," says the captain, " with all my heart."

" Well," says I, " I will send for them up, and talk with them for you." So I caused Friday and the two hostages, for they were now discharged, their comrades having performed their promise; I say, I caused them to go to the cave and bring up the five men, pinioned as they were, to the bower, and keep them there till I came.

After some time I came thither, dressed in my new habit; and now I was called governor again. Being all met, and the captain with me, I caused the men to be brought before me, and I told them I had had a full account of their villainous behaviour to the captain, and how they had run away with the ship, and were preparing to commit farther robberies, but that Providence had ensnared them in their own ways, and that they were fallen into the pit which they had digged for others.

I let them know that by my direction the ship had been seized, that she lay now in the road, and they might see, by and by, that their new captain had received the reward of his villainy, for that they might see him hanging at the yard-arm; that as to them, I wanted to know what they had to say why I should not execute them as pirates, taken in the fact, as by my commission they could not doubt I had authority to do.

One of them answered in the name of the rest that they had nothing to say but this, that when they were taken the captain promised them their lives, and they humbly implored my mercy. But I told them I knew not what mercy to show them; for as for myself, I had resolved to quit the island with all my men, and had taken passage with the captain to go for England. And as for the captain, he could not carry them to England other than as prisoners in irons, to be tried for mutiny, and running away with the ship; the consequence of which, they must needs know, would be the gallows; so that I could not tell which was best for them, unless they had a mind to take their fate in the island. If they desired that, I did not care, as I had liberty to leave it. I had some inclination to give them their lives, if they thought they could shift on shore.

They seemed very thankful for it, said they would

much rather venture to stay there than to be carried
to England to be hanged; so I left it on that issue.

However, the captain seemed to make some difficulty of it, as if he durst not leave them there. Upon
this I seemed a little angry with the captain, and told
him that they were my prisoners, not his; and that
seeing I had offered them so much favour, I would
be as good as my word; and that if he did not think
fit to consent to it, I would set them at liberty, as I
found them; and if he did not like it, he might take
them again if he could catch them.

Upon this they appeared very thankful, and I
accordingly set them at liberty, and bade them retire
into the woods to the place whence they came, and
I would leave them some firearms, some ammunition,
and some directions how they should live very well,
if they thought fit.

Upon this I prepared to go on board the ship, but
told the captain that I would stay that night to prepare
my things, and desired him to go on board in the
meantime, and keep all right in the ship, and send the
boat on shore the next day for me; ordering him, in
the meantime, to cause the new captain, who was
killed, to be hanged at the yard-arm, that these men
might see him.

When the captain was gone, I sent for the men up
to me to my apartment, and entered seriously into
discourse with them of their circumstances. I told
them I thought they had made a right choice; that
if the captain carried them away, they would certainly
be hanged. I showed them the new captain hanging
at the yard-arm of the ship, and told them they had
nothing less to expect.

When they all declared their willingness to stay, I

then told them I would let them into the story of my living there, and put them into the way of making it easy to them. Accordingly I gave them the whole history of the place, and of my coming to it, showing them my fortifications, the way I made my bread, planted my corn, cured my grapes; and in a word, all that was necessary to make them easy. I told them the story also of the sixteen Spaniards that were to be expected, for whom I left a letter, and made them promise to treat them in common with themselves.

I left them my firearms, viz., five muskets, three fowling-pieces, and three swords. I had above a barrel and half of powder left; for after the first year or two I used but little, and wasted none. I gave them a description of the way I managed the goats, and directions to milk and fatten them, and to make both butter and cheese.

In a word, I gave them every part of my own story, and I told them I would prevail with the captain to leave them two barrels of gunpowder more, and some garden seeds, which I told them I would have been very glad of. Also I gave them the bag of peas which the captain had brought me to eat, and bade them be sure to sow and increase them.

Having done all this, I left them the next day, and went on board the ship. We prepared immediately to sail, but did not weigh that night. The next morning early two of the five men came swimming to the ship's side, and making a most lamentable complaint of the other three, begged to be taken into the ship for God's sake, for they should be murdered, and begged the captain to take them on board, though he hanged them immediately.

Upon this the captain pretended to have no power

without me; but after some difficulty, and after their solemn promises of amendment, they were taken on board, and were some time after soundly whipped and pickled, after which they proved very honest and quiet fellows.

Some time after this the boat was ordered on shore, the tide being up, with the things promised to the men, to which the captain, at my intercession, caused their chests and clothes to be added, which they took, and were very thankful for. I also encouraged them by telling them that if it lay in my way to send any vessel to take them in, I would not forget them.

When I took leave of this island, I carried on board, for relics, the great goatskin cap I had made, my umbrella, and my parrot; also I forgot not to take the money I formerly mentioned, which had lain by me so long useless that it was grown rusty or tarnished, and could hardly pass for silver till it had been a little rubbed and handled; as also the money I found in the wreck of the Spanish ship.

And thus I left the island, the 19th of December as I found by the ship's account, in the year 1686, after I had been upon it eight and twenty years, two months, and nineteen days, being delivered from this second captivity the same day of the month that I first made my escape in the *barco-longo*, from the Moors of Sallee.

In this vessel, after a long voyage, I arrived in England, the 11th of June, in the year 1687, having been thirty and five years absent.

When I came to England, I was as perfect a stranger to all the world as if I had never been known there. My benefactor and faithful steward, whom I had left in trust with my money, was alive, but had had great misfortunes in the world, was become a widow the

second time, and very low in the world. I made her
easy as to what she owed me, assuring her I would
give her no trouble; but on the contrary, in gratitude
to her former care and faithfulness to me, I relieved
her as my little stock would afford; which, at that
time, would indeed allow me to do but little for her;
but I assured her I would never forget her former
kindness to me, nor did I forget her when I had
sufficient to help her, as shall be observed in its place.

I went down afterwards into Yorkshire; but my
father was dead, and my mother and all the family
extinct, except that I found two sisters, and two of
the children of one of my brothers; and as I had been
long ago given over for dead, there had been no provision made for me; so that, in a word, I found nothing
to relieve or assist me; and that little money I had
would not do much for me as to settling in the world.

I met with one piece of gratitude, indeed, which I
did not expect; and this was, that the master of the
ship whom I had so happily delivered, and by the
same means saved the ship and cargo, having given a
very handsome account to the owners of the manner
how I had saved the lives of the men, and the ship,
they invited me to meet them, and some other merchants concerned, and all together made me a very
handsome compliment upon the subject, and a present
of almost two hundred pounds sterling.

But after making several reflections upon the circumstances of my life, and how little way this would
go towards settling me in the world, I resolved to go
to Lisbon, and see if I might not come by some information of the state of my plantation in the Brazils, and
of what was become of my partner, who I had reason
to suppose had some years now given me over for dead.

COMMENTARY AND QUESTIONS

THE BOOK & THE WRITER

DANIEL DEFOE, born in or about 1660, was the son of James Foe, a butcher; and his grandfather was a yeoman. This is important, for it means that Defoe, in spite of a good education in many languages, including his own, naturally spoke and wrote plain, strong, middle-class English without polish or any sort of pomposity or erudition. He was a middle-class, common-sense Englishman, though a genius of course; and he had a Shakespearean capacity for putting himself into other people's shoes, so to speak; and if he too often wrote of rogues, thieves, and pirates, that was probably in order to sell his books, and one cannot blame him. After all, we see the same thing in our own day in the vogue of crook stories and detective yarns. Defoe even wrote a *History of the Devil*.

The power of his writing lies in its *truth*—the piling up of innumerable apparently trivial details till the reader's mind says: "He *must* have seen it, or he never could have put it all down!" Thus, when he describes the Plague of London one can hardly believe that he is not recounting what he actually remembers—but in point of fact he was a very small child when it happened.

And in his immortal work, *Robinson Crusoe*, he simply *is* the lonely sailor. The book is the best example of the "adventure as told by oneself" which came before the true novel; and Defoe is the literary father of Richardson and Fielding; while in his "Scandal Club" he really hit upon the idea of the *Tatlers* and *Spectators* which soon followed.

I

He made a great deal of money by his writings, and built himself "a very handsome house" in London. He was "a middle-sized spare man of a brown complexion, and dark brown hair, but wearing a wig; a hooked nose, a sharp chin, grey eyes, and a large mole near his mouth. Such was the description published when the author was "wanted" to stand in the pillory—which he did three times for his political writings. For he wrote about everything. Before he began his novels he had written more than two hundred treatises, pamphlets, and booklets on all sorts of subjects, all with a knowledge of other people's business such as no one else has ever approached—not even Shakespeare.

He had a very wonderful way, too, of making difficult and complicated subjects quite understandable—just as certain great English scientists have at the present day. That was partly because he was extremely clear-headed himself—so clear-headed that in some respects he was centuries ahead of his time. But it was due quite as much to the fact that he was used to expressing himself in ordinary straightforward English without any frills or flourishes. He thought clearly, and as he thought, he wrote. The grand scholars affected to despise him; but the great English public is wiser than the scholars, and *Robinson Crusoe* remains, and is likely to remain, one of the best-loved and most widely read books in the language. And that brings us to another point.

The book as we have it here stops short a little before the end of the First Part. There is still that bit at the end, and the whole of Part II to come; but while every educated person in the country has read Part I as it is here, not one person in twenty thousand has ever read the rest. Now how is that? Well, the reason is not very far to seek. In the first part Robinson Crusoe is a unique and lonely figure, "monarch of all he surveys," centre of one of the most romantic and convincing stories in the world. Up to the time of his return to England, as recounted at the end of this volume, he keeps this glamour, as a lone, romantic, and most memorable man. But after that, and all through Part II, he is just a man of the world, one among many. He drops on to a lower plane altogether; and, in spite of his adventures, we lose interest in him and his doings. And so quite rightly, unless we are great readers, we make the break where the editor of this volume has made it, and leave Robinson Crusoe in his grandeur.

One is loath to leave Man Friday, however. In Part II he is shot with arrows and killed by his own people while addressing them from the deck of the ship. But there is one jolly and typical scene before that which it would be a pity to miss; and so I add it here:

Man Friday and the Bear

"My man Friday had delivered our guide, and when we came up to him he was helping him off from his horse; for the man was both hurt and frighted, and indeed the last more than the first; when, on the sudden, we spied the bear come out of the wood, and a vast monstrous one it was, the biggest by far that ever I saw. We were all a little surprised when we saw him; but when Friday saw him, it was easy to see joy and courage in the fellow's countenance. 'O! O! O!' says Friday, three times pointing to him. 'O master! you give me te leave; me shakee te hand with him; me make you good laugh.''

"I was surprised to see the fellow so pleased. 'You fool you,' says I, 'he will eat you up.' 'Eatee me up!

eatee me up!' says Friday, twice over again; 'me eatee
him up; me make you good laugh; you all stay here, me
show you good laugh.' So down he sits, and gets his
boots off in a moment, and put on a pair of pumps, as
we call the flat shoes they wear, and which he had in
his pocket, gives my other servant his horse, and with
his gun away he flew, swift like the wind.

"The bear was walking softly on, and offered to
meddle with nobody till Friday, coming pretty near,
calls to him, as if the bear could understand him,
'Hark ye, hark ye,' says Friday, 'me speakee wit you.'
We followed at a distance; for now being come down on
the Gascoign side of the mountains, we were entered a
vast great forest, where the country was plain and
pretty open, though many trees in it scattered here
and there.

"Friday, who had, as we say, the heels of the bear,
came up with him quickly, and takes up a great stone
and throws at him, and hit him just on the head, but
did him no more harm than if he had thrown it against
a wall. But it answered Friday's end, for the rogue was
so void of fear, that he did it purely to make the bear
follow him, and show us some laugh, as he called it.

"As soon as the bear felt the stone, and saw him, he
turns about, and comes after him, taking devilish long
strides, and shuffling along at a strange rate, so as would
have put a horse to a middling gallop. Away runs
Friday, and takes his course as if he run towards us for
help; so we all resolved to fire at once upon the bear,
and deliver my man; though I was angry at him heartily
for bringing the bear back upon us, when he was going
about his own business another way; and especially I
was angry, that he had turned the bear upon us, and
then run away; and I called out, 'You dog,' said I, 'is

this your making us laugh?   Come away, and take your
horse, that we may shoot the creature.'   He hears me,
and cries out, 'No shoot, no shoot; stand still, you get
much laugh.'   And as the nimble creature run two feet
for the beast's one, he turned on a sudden, on one side
of us, and seeing a great oak tree fit for his purpose, he
beckoned to us to follow; and doubling his pace, he gets
nimbly up the tree, laying his gun down upon the ground,
at about five or six yards from the bottom of the tree.

"The bear soon came to the tree, and we followed at
a distance.   The first thing he did, he stopped at the
gun, smelt to it, but let it lie, and up he scrambles into
the tree, climbing like a cat, though so monstrously
heavy.   I was amazed at the folly, as I thought it, of
my man, and could not for my life see anything to
laugh at yet, till seeing the bear get up the tree, we all
rode nearer to him.

"When we came to the tree, there was Friday got out
to the small end of a large limb of the tree, and the bear
got about half way to him.   As soon as the bear got
out to that part where the limb of the tree was weaker,
'Ha!' says he to us, 'now you see me teachee the bear
dance.'   So he falls a-jumping and shaking the bough,
at which the bear began to totter, but stood still, and
began to look behind him, to see how he should get
back.   Then, indeed, we did laugh heartily.   But
Friday had not done with him by a great deal.   When he
sees him stand still, he calls out to him again, as if he
had supposed the bear could speak English, 'What, you
no come farther? pray you come farther'; so he left
jumping and shaking the tree; and the bear, just as if
he had understood what he said, did come a little
farther; then he fell a-jumping again, and the bear
stopped again.

"We thought now was a good time to knock him on the head, and I called to Friday to stand still, and we would shoot the bear; but he cried out earnestly, 'O pray! O pray! no shoot, me shoot by and then'; he would have said by and by. However, to shorten the story, Friday danced so much, and the bear stood so ticklish, that we had laughing enough indeed, but still could not imagine what the fellow would do: for first we thought he depended upon shaking the bear off; and we found the bear was too cunning for that too; for he would not go out far enough to be thrown down, but clings fast with his great broad claws and feet, so that we could not imagine what would be the end of it, and where the jest would be at last.

"But Friday put us out of doubt quickly; for seeing the bear cling fast to the bough, and that he would not be persuaded to come any farther, 'Well, well,' says Friday, 'you no come farther, me go, me go; you no come to me, me go come to you'; and upon this he goes out to the smallest end of the bough, where it would bend with his weight, and gently lets himself down by it, sliding down the bough till he came near enough to jump down on his feet, and away he ran to his gun, takes it up, and stands still.

"'Well,' said I to him, 'Friday, what will you do now? Why don't you shoot him?' 'No shoot,' says Friday, 'no yet; me shoot now, me no kill; me stay, give you one more laugh.' And, indeed, so he did, as you will see presently; for when the bear sees his enemy gone, he comes back from the bough where he stood, but did it mighty leisurely, looking behind him every step, and coming backward till he got into the body of the tree; then with the same hinder end foremost he comes down the tree, grasping it with his claws, and moving one foot at a time, very leisurely. At this juncture, and just before he could set his hind feet upon the ground, Friday stepped up close to him, clapped the muzzle of his piece into his ear, and shot him dead as a stone.

"Then the rogue turned about to see if we did not laugh; and when he saw we were pleased by our looks, he falls a-laughing himself very loud. 'So we kill bear in my country,' says Friday. 'So you kill them?' says I; 'why, you have no guns.' 'No,' says he, 'no gun, but shoot great much long arrow.'"

THE ORIGINAL ROBINSON CRUSOE

THE charm of *Robinson Crusoe* lies, to a great extent, in its detail. One either reads the story carefully or not at all; but as soon as interest has been aroused, each statement or description must be pondered over and checked, as far as possible. Then comes the inevitable question: "How far was Daniel Defoe relying upon fact, how far using his wonderful powers of imagination?" And, in searching for an answer to this double question, we encounter the name of Alexander Selkirk, who is generally regarded as the "prototype" of Robinson Crusoe.

He was a Scottish sailor, a native of Largo, Fifeshire, and was born in 1676. In May 1703 he joined Captain Dampier in a privateering expedition to the South Seas, acting as sailing master of the galley *Cinque Ports*, which, in September, put in at Juan Fernandez Island, west of Valparaiso. After a dispute with his captain Selkirk was put ashore at his own request with a few necessaries, and he lived on the island for four years and four months. He was taken off by Captain Woodes

Rogers of the *Duke* privateer and returned to London in 1711. He afterwards went to sea again and died in 1721 as master's mate of H.M.S. *Weymouth*. The story of his adventure was published in several books [1] before the appearance of *Robinson Crusoe* in 1719, and the author had met Selkirk at Bristol and heard his story from his own mouth. Moreover, Selkirk afterwards said that he had handed over his papers to Defoe, who kept to the main outline of Selkirk's story, but makes his island more tropical, while he invented the story of the cannibals' visits. In 1713 Richard Steele, the essayist and associate of Addison, wrote a short essay on the adventurer and his story, which appeared in the *Englishman*. In this paper we read that "his portion was a sea-chest, his wearing clothes and bedding, a firelock, a pound of gunpowder, a large quantity of bullets, a flint and steel, a few pounds of tobacco, a hatchet, a knife, a kettle, a Bible and other books of devotion; together with pieces that concerned navigation, and his mathematical instruments."

"When I first saw him," Steele continues, "I thought, if I had not been let into his character and story, I could have discerned that he had been much separated from company, from his aspect and gestures; there was a strong but cheerful seriousness in his looks, and a certain disregard to the ordinary things about him, as if he had been sunk in thought. When the ship which brought him off the island came in, he received them with the greatest indifference with relation to the prospect of going off with them, but with great satisfaction in an opportunity to help and refresh them.

---

[1] *Cruising Voyage Round the World* (1712), by Woodes Rogers. *Voyage in the South Sea and Round the World* (1712), by Edward Cooke.

"This plain man's story is a memorable example that he is happiest who confines his wants to natural necessities, and he that goes further in his desires increases his wants in proportion to his acquisitions; or, to use his own expression, 'I am now worth eight hundred pounds, but shall never be so happy as when I was not worth a farthing.'"

A LETTER FROM CHARLES LAMB

THOSE of you who are no longer juniors will like to know more about a book than just the story it tells. You will be interested to know what great men thought about it—especially men who were themselves distinguished writers. Now Charles Lamb was a great writer, and had a very great love for what is called *style*. He studied style in other men, and his own style is "just like himself," as we say. It should interest you—those of you who are no longer juniors—to hear what he thought about Defoe's style. So here is a letter from Charles Lamb to a friend; and the subject of the letter is *Robinson Crusoe*:

"E. I. H. 16th Dec. 1822.

"Dear Wilson,

"*Lightning* I was going to call you. You must have thought me negligent in not answering your letter sooner. But I have a habit of never writing letters but at the office; 'tis so much time cribbed out of the Company: and I am just got out of the thick of a tea-sale, in which most of the entry of notes, deposits, etc. usually falls to my share.

"I have nothing of De Foe's but two or three novels and the *Plague History*. I can give you no information about him. As a slight general character of what I remember of them, (for I have not looked into them latterly,) I would say that in the appearance of *truth*, in all the incidents and conversations that occur in them, they exceed any works of fiction I am acquainted with. It is perfect illusion. The *author* never appears in these self-narratives, (for so they ought to be called, or rather autobiographies,) but the *narrator* chains us down to an implicit belief in every thing he says. There is all the minute detail of a log-book in it. Dates are painfully pressed upon the memory. Facts are repeated over and over in varying phrases, till you cannot choose but believe them. It is like reading evidence given in a court of justice. So anxious the story-teller seems that the truth should be clearly comprehended, that when he has told us a matter of fact or a motive, in a line or two farther down he *repeats* it, with his favourite figure of speech, 'I say,' so and so, though he had made it abundantly plain before. This is in imitation of the common people's way of speaking, or rather of the way in which they are addressed by a master or mistress who wishes to impress something upon their memories, and has a wonderful effect upon matter-of-fact readers. Indeed it is to such principally that he writes. His style is everywhere beautiful, but plain and *homely Robinson Crusoe* is delightful to all ranks and classes but it is easy to see that it is written in phraseology peculiarly adapted to the lower conditions of readers; hence it is an especial favourite with seafaring men, poor boys, servant-maids, etc. His novels are capital kitchen-reading, while they are worthy, from their deep interest, to find a shelf in the libraries of the wealthiest and the most learned. His passion for *matter-of-fact narrative* sometimes betrayed him into a long relation of common incidents, which might happen to any man, and have no interest but the intense appearance of truth in them, to commend them.   The whole latter half or two-thirds of *Colonel Jack* is of this description. The beginning of *Colonel Jack* is the most affecting natural picture of a young thief that was ever drawn. His losing the stolen money in the hollow of a tree, and finding it again when he was in despair, and then being in equal distress at not knowing how to dispose of it, and several similar touches in the early history of the Colonel, evince a deep knowledge of human nature; and putting out of question the superior *romantic* interest of the latter, in my mind very much exceed Crusoe. *Roxana* (first edition) is the next in interest, though he left out the best part of it in subsequent editions from a foolish hypercriticism of his friend Southerne.   But *Moll Flanders*, the *Account of the Plague*, etc. are all of one family, and have the same stamp of character. Believe me, with friendly recollections, *Brother*, (as I used to call you,)

"Yours,

"C. LAMB."

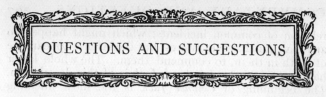

QUESTIONS AND SUGGESTIONS

1. How did the Crusoes get their queer name, and why was the hero of the book called Robinson? Where did they live, and from what port did he start on his first voyage?

2. What great men started life by running away to sea?

3. You should compare this chapter about the voyage and the storm with the chapter at the beginning of *Gulliver's Travels*.

4. Make a list of as many things as you can remember, collected by Robinson Crusoe from the wreck and taken ashore on his raft.

5. What did Crusoe see from the top of the hill? (Notice that this is a very clever contrivance on the part of Defoe to *tell the reader* what the island was like.)

6. "O drug! What art thou good for? Thou art not worth to me, no, not the taking off of the ground." What is this about?

7. Explain how Crusoe kept his calendar.

8. Give an account of Crusoe's carpentering.

9. Give some examples from the first five chapters of Defoe's wonderful capacity for making everything sound absolutely real and true.

10. Describe all Crusoe's pets.

11. What was Crusoe's "terrible dream" about? Do you remember any other dreams in literature?

268

12. What was the effect of the earthquake?

13. Have you ever built a hut? If so, describe it, and explain how you built it, with a picture or diagram.

14. How do you make baskets? If you do not know, look it up.

15. What was the first word spoken on the island "by any mouth but my own," as Crusoe puts it?

16. "What odd, misshapen, ugly things I made." Explain this.

17. Why did Crusoe give up the idea of digging a trench or canal up to his dug-out boat?

18. Draw a picture of Crusoe in full rig, not forgetting the "mustachios."

19. How did he catch the goats, and how did he keep them safe when he had caught them?

20. "I think I was never more vain of my own performance, or more joyful for anything I found out than for my being able to make——" What? And why was he so pleased?

21. Read the first paragraph of Chapter XI—about the Footprint, and write some of it out as nearly as you can in the same words. It is a very famous passage.

22. What was the horrid spectacle which confounded and amazed him later on?

23. Describe Crusoe's cave. Have you ever been in a great cave, such as the caves at Cheddar, or Kent's Cavern near Torquay?

24. How is gunpowder made? Look it out.

25. Tell the incident of the dog on the wreck. Why do you suppose he mentions it?

26. Make a fresh list of things recovered from the wreck "in the twenty-third year of residence in the island."

27. Tell in your own words the story of the rescue of Man Friday.

28. How did Crusoe cure Friday of eating man's flesh?

29. Make up a conversation (as in Chapter XV) about the gun, and gunpowder.

30. "But I wronged the poor honest creature very much." Explain this.

31. Man Friday "stood like one astonished and amazed" when he saw how a boat was sailed. How do you sail a boat? And what is meant by "tacking?"

32. Describe the meeting of Friday with his father.

33. What did Crusoe learn from his talk with the Spaniard?

34. "Master, master, they are come, they are come!" Explain this fully.

35. Draw a sketch of Crusoe as he appeared when he met the English captain.

36. Look out the Leeward Islands.

37. "I immediately advanced with my whole army." Of whom did this "army" consist?

38. Find a picture of a merchant ship of the late seventeenth century. What is meant by "the fore-chains" and the "fore-castle" (p. 245)?

39. Whom did Robinson Crusoe leave behind in the island? What happened to the parrot?

40. Were any of his family still alive in Yorkshire?

MADE AT THE
TEMPLE PRESS
LETCHWORTH

GREAT BRITAIN